DEATH
IN THE
SUNSHINE

ALSO BY THE AUTHOR

WRITING AS STEPH BROADRIBB:

Deep Down Dead

Deep Blue Trouble

Deep Dirty Truth

Deep Dark Night

WRITING AS STEPHANIE MARLAND:

My Little Eye

You Die Next

DEATH IN THE SUNSHINE

STEPH BROADRIBB

THOMAS & MERCER

Text copyright © 2022 by Steph Broadribb
All rights reserved.

Published by Thomas & Mercer, Seattle

www.apub.com

Amazon, the Amazon logo, and Thomas & Mercer are trademarks of Amazon.com, Inc., or its affiliates.

ISBN-13: 9781542029803
ISBN-10: 1542029805

Cover design by @blacksheep-uk.com

Printed in the United States of America

To Andy – for everything

1

MOIRA

Just before sunrise is Moira's favourite time. Dawn is when the day has most promise; it's still a blank slate – a *tabula rasa*. It gives her another opportunity to try and forget what happened and focus on making something new. Again.

Closing the gate to the backyard, she checks the coast is clear and steps out on to the white gravel path. She's happy no one's around. She doesn't like to be watched; prefers to blend into the background, hidden in plain sight, but it's proving much harder here on The Homestead than she'd imagined.

She follows the circular walking track as it snakes around the perimeter of the Ocean Mist district towards Manatee Recreation Park. There's a chill to the air and it's a twenty-minute walk. Zipping up her hoodie, Moira ups her pace. She'll try to do the walk in eighteen minutes today. She always likes to have a goal.

As she walks, Moira hums to herself. The sun is starting to rise and the path ahead is free of people for as far as she can see. Good. It isn't that she dislikes people exactly, but since moving to The Homestead retirement community a month ago she's come to realise just how much the people here like to talk. It's a relief to start the day not having to be cordial with anyone. She's never been very good at being cordial.

Everyone here in this purpose-built community for people over fifty-five years old is just so damn friendly. There's no anonymity like you have in a big city. She hopes she'll get used to it, because at this time of day, with the sun starting to burn the dew from the grass, and the silence broken only by the morning call of the birds, the place is so peaceful. And she really needs some peace.

She checks her watch: it's 6.49 a.m. She's on track; in the groove she's got into since moving – rise at 6 a.m., have a protein shake, head to the park for a swim as the sun finishes coming up, then back to the house to walk the dogs. It's the end of week four and she's got the timings down pat. If she's free and clear of the pool by eight thirty she should have the place to herself and avoid any chance of small talk.

It's a good motivator. The gravel crunches beneath her trainers as she powers up an incline. Before moving here she'd always thought of Florida as flat, but she was wrong. This part of central Florida is pretty undulating and that's fine; she's glad of the added cardio workout.

Slowing her pace as she reaches the top of the ridge, Moira takes a sip from her water bottle and looks at the view. On her left are the backyards of the uniformly cream stucco houses that border the path; lawns of the coarse Florida grass that's much better in the heat than its more delicate British counterpart; screened-in stone patios, huge gas-powered grills; and the occasional plunge pool or hot tub. All of them neat and ordered, and manicured to within an inch of their lives as stipulated in the rules of residency.

She keeps walking and takes another sip. To her right she can see straight across the open grasslands of Misty Plains all the way to the distant line of trees that stand sentry along the border between Ocean Mist district and the as yet unconstructed and unnamed district eleven. Moira doesn't know how many acres lie between her and the trees, but it has to be a hell of a lot. Until just over a month ago she'd only ever lived and worked in London. The wide, open space here still seems alien.

But even though it's alien, she's glad of it. The space is one of the main reasons she picked this place to retire. She's had enough of urban, enough of London, enough of the ever-increasing bureaucracy and paperwork that being an undercover detective had come to involve. She wanted a total change and that's what The Homestead sells itself on – a new home for a new chapter of your life. Moira grimaces. She needs that fresh start. Given everything that happened earlier this year, leaving was the right thing, and the safest thing, to do.

She just hadn't anticipated it would be so damn hard.

Moira checks her watch again and increases her pace. She doesn't have time to mess about if she's going to stay on track. Striding along the path she crosses the ridge and starts the descent down to the park. Every time her mind wanders back to her old team, and the last case they'd worked, she forces herself to move faster. But the memories keep coming. In her mind's eye she sees the group of them getting ready for the takedown on the last job – Riley, Pang, Kress and McCord. The memory freeze-frames on McCord; he's smiling, his fist bumping hers before they get into the vehicle to ride out.

She bites her lip. Forces down the wave of emotion. Clenching her fists, she lets her nails pinch into her palms, hoping the pain will be a distraction.

She can't think about McCord right now. She just can't.

Instead she focuses on the white archway entrance of Manatee Recreation Park and strides towards it. She knows she shouldn't block her emotions this way; was told enough times by the police doc that she needed to face things, but it's just too hard. If she's honest, she feels kind of shell-shocked, like it hasn't sunk in.

She feels like that about the retirement too.

It seems as if in one misjudged split second, everything she loved and had worked for turned to dust. It happened so fast. She used to say she was good with change, but now she knows that isn't true.

Moira shakes her head to rid herself of the memories. Stopping under the archway, she checks her watch. She's made the walk in seventeen minutes, fifty-three seconds. It should feel like a small triumph – a good start to chalk up on the *tabula rasa* – but she doesn't feel anything but empty.

Live in the moment, she tells herself, repeating the bullshit psychobabble the police doc said to her when she'd asked for their advice on retirement. *Be the change.*

She takes a deep breath. Says out loud, 'Okay then.'

Walking under the archway into the park, she follows the stone pathway past the pickleball courts and the bocce area, and heads past the splash-zone fun pools and hot tubs to the largest lap pool. Everything's quiet. There's no one else here, just as she'd hoped.

Focus on the positive, on every win no matter how small. That's what the police doc had said. Maybe she should stop being so damn cynical and give it a try. Push herself more to feel something. She supposes it couldn't hurt.

Moira forces a smile. 'This. Is. Going. To. Be a good day.'

She feels an idiot saying it out loud.

The police doc said that she shouldn't expect to be okay right away. *Stay present*, they'd said, *don't beat yourself up if things aren't perfect.*

Yeah right. She shakes her head again. One thing she's sure as dammit learned in her fifty-eight years is that nothing is ever perfect.

She keeps walking. Up ahead there's a blue jay sitting on the gate to the last pickleball court. Smiling at him, Moira tries again. 'This is going to be a *good* day.'

It's easier second time around; almost feels like it could be true.

Taking it as a small win, she pushes open the white gate beside the high hedge that screens the pool and fixes the latch behind her. She follows the path around the end of the hedge. The pool comes into view.

'Oh Jesus.' Her breath catches in her throat.

Heart pounding, she rushes forward. At the last minute she sees the blood splattered across the stone patio, and just manages to stop before she treads in it.

She takes a breath, feeling her training kicking in and her brain click into work mode. As if on autopilot, she tugs the phone from the pocket of her hoodie and dials. As the call connects she scans the scene, taking in all the details.

'911. State your emergency.' The female voice sounds tinny and distant.

'There's been a death at Manatee Recreation Park, Ocean Mist district, at The Homestead. The body is in one of the swimming pools and it looks like—'

'Wait, what? A death *in a pool* at The Homestead?'

'Yes, that's what I said.' Moira doesn't know why the despatcher isn't listening properly – that's their job, after all. Despatchers are trained to stay on-script; work through their questions and stay calm. This one has deviated off-script from the start and sounds rattled. Moira frowns. It's not professional. She needs them to do their job. 'The victim is a young woman. There's evidence this was a violent death. At first look I'd say that the victim was—'

'Homicide? At the seniors' retirement community?' There's shock in the despatcher's voice. 'But that's never—'

'You need to get first responders out to me now,' says Moira. 'I need police and medical. Can you do that?'

'Yes, I . . . for sure.' The girl on the emergency line sounds like she's found some of her composure again; there's just the slight hint of a tremble in her voice now. Moira hears the sound of typing, then the girl says, 'Okay, I've despatched medics and police to you at Manatee Park. Their ETA is twelve minutes.'

'Good.' Moira checks the time, and works out when the blue lights will arrive. She scans the pool area, and then looks out across the lawn. There's no sign of anyone or anything else here. She looks back towards the woman in the pool as she speaks. 'Before you ask me, I don't think I'm in danger. I'd say whatever happened took place a number of hours ago. I'm happy to stay here and wait for the first responders to arrive.'

'Don't hang up. Please stay on the line.' The 911 despatcher sounds flustered again. 'Can you tell me your name, ma'am?'

'Moira Flynn, I'm a resident here.'

'And the person you called about, are you sure they're—'

'She definitely looks dead, and it doesn't look like an accident.' Moira steps around the blood and closer to the edge of the pool. The young woman is floating on her back in the middle of the water. Her eyes are open, and her long black hair has fanned around her head like a dark halo. There's blood smeared over her chest and across the top of her pale yellow dress, but that isn't the weirdest thing.

The weirdest thing is she's surrounded by thousands of floating dollar bills.

2

PHILIP

Philip always gets a rush from attending a crime scene, and today's no exception. His first sight of the blue lights at the end of the street brings with it the familiar adrenaline kick, and right away he's feeling more alert and on his game. He's ready.

Getting as close to the roadblock as he can, he manoeuvres the Toyota into a gap at the kerb and switches off the engine. He takes a moment to study the scene. Outside the entrance to the Manatee Recreation Park there are two patrol cars, an ambulance and a meat wagon. The wagon's rear end is flush to the archway entrance of the park. Philip's been a detective in the Thames Valley for over thirty-five years. Wherever you are in the world, a turnout like this means one thing: a dead body.

Getting out of the Toyota, he smooths imagined creases from the front of his navy polo shirt and strides past the patrol cars. A group of rubberneckers have formed at the end of the cordon closest to the park. He counts five people; all grey-haired and older – obviously residents. He recognises a couple from the golf club. Sees one of the ladies is sitting in the latest top-of-the-range mobility cart, a Platinum Swiftster. These aren't your usual rubberneckers.

The tall moustached guy from the golf club raises his hand and beckons Philip to come join them. Philip doesn't have time for small talk, though. He gives the man a nod and wave, but keeps walking. He can't be distracted. Has to stay focused on the scene.

Ducking under the yellow crime-scene tape, he hurries towards the park entrance. He clocks the CSIs working just inside the archway and the meat handlers wheeling an empty gurney away along the stone path between the pickleball courts.

Definitely one stiff, he thinks. *Minimum.*

'Sir, you need to stop right there.'

Turning, Philip sees a uniformed cop climbing out of the furthest patrol car. He stops and lets the cop catch him up. The lad looks like a real young gun – mirrored shades, deep tan and the kind of authoritarian tone boys lacking in confidence put on to overcompensate.

Philip gestures towards the park. 'So what have we got?'

The cop stops beside him. 'Sir—'

'It's a homicide, yes?' prompts Philip. It's a long shot – until recently, the crime rate on The Homestead has been virtually zero – but with the cops, medics and a meat wagon it's obvious something serious has gone down.

The cop frowns and ignores the question. He steps closer, too close really. He's taller than Philip at around six foot, but looks barely out of college. 'I'm going to have to ask you to move back, sir. No unauthorised personnel allowed beyond this point.'

Philip doesn't appreciate the youngster's tone. He's a DCI; uniforms should do as *he* says. 'I understand, officer, I'm law enforcement too.'

The cop frowns again. 'You got a badge?'

'Well, no, not here in the US, but I'm—'

'Then I can't let you any closer.'

Philip clenches his fists. 'Now look here, I'm . . .' He stops and puts telling this cocky kid just who he's dealing with on hold, because there's a woman emerging from the back of the ambulance and he recognises her. He's good like that. Never forgets a face or a name. And Moira is a memorable kind of woman; tall and athletic with her black hair cropped into a pixie cut and a face that looks far younger than anyone else's here at The Homestead. She's a new resident. His wife, Lizzie, told him that before she introduced them the other day when they'd met in Publix doing the weekly shop. Moira and Lizzie had met at yoga a few weeks before. He doesn't know why Moira's in the ambulance, but he's damn sure he's going to find out.

Drawing himself up to his full height so he's almost eye to eye with the officer, Philip points towards the ambulance. 'Look son, you need to let me through. I'm here to support my friend.'

The young cop follows his gaze. Frowns again. Says nothing.

Philip senses the youngster is feeling uncertain. He needs to exploit that. 'Moira,' he calls, waving towards the ambulance.

She looks over but there's no sign in her expression that she recognises him.

Damn it, thinks Philip. *Come on, remember.*

There's a silver space blanket around her shoulders and a stressed-looking paramedic seems to be trying to coax her back into the ambulance. Maybe she's injured or concussed or something. Philip raises his hand and waves again. 'Moira. You okay?'

She frowns, and starts to turn away.

Philip can't have that. He needs her to buck up and pay attention. He shouts her name louder. Repeats it a few times.

The young cop shifts his weight from foot to foot. 'Sir, really, you need to—'

'Moira, it's Philip, I'm coming to help you.' Philip can't let this boy turn him away. He needs to be on the inside. He won't tolerate being held outside like some random member of Joe public. He just can't allow that to happen. He waves more frantically. 'Moira!'

She turns again. She's frowning now, and Philip thinks she's going to ignore him again, but then she raises a hand. It's not a proper wave but it's good enough.

'You see,' Philip says to the cop. 'She's in shock, hardly recognised me. I have to go to her.'

The kid looks conflicted, dithering. He looks over towards the patrol cars but there's no sign of his colleagues.

The boy's out of his depth, thinks Philip. He almost feels sorry for him. Almost but not quite.

When they both turn back towards the ambulance Moira's disappeared but even though he can't see her, Philip can hear her well enough. The voices coming from inside the ambulance – one male and American, one female and British – are loud and rising in volume.

'You hear that, officer?' Philip says, in his most earnest voice. 'I can help.'

The youngster rubs his brow, glances once more back towards the patrol cars, then says, 'Okay then, but don't go into the park. Stay with your friend, okay?'

'Will do,' says Philip. He feels like punching the air in triumph as he strides away from the cop towards the ambulance. He's back in the thick of things, and rightfully so. He never should have had to retire.

3

MOIRA

She hates everything about hospitals – the smell, the over-starched sheets, and the intrusion. But most of all, she hates the lack of control being a patient brings, and so she'll be damned if she's letting these paramedics take her to Lake County General. Moira looks around for her water bottle. She wants out of the ambulance now, but doesn't want to leave the bottle behind.

The paramedic in charge has barely drawn breath he's arguing his case so hard, and his taller, sturdier colleague keeps nodding along in agreement. Both are refusing to take no for an answer, which leaves the three of them at loggerheads because she sure as hell isn't going to change her mind.

The lead paramedic, red-haired and red-faced, gestures towards a trolley made up as a bed. 'Please, take a seat.'

'I'm fine.' Moira stays standing. She reaches out, putting her hand on the wall of the ambulance to steady herself, waiting for the spinning in her head to stop. When it does, she glances around for her water bottle again and spots it over on one of the bench seats.

As she moves towards it, the red-haired paramedic steps into her path. 'As I explained, ma'am, we need to do a more thorough exploration of—'

'No.' Moira hugs the silver space blanket closer and folds her arms. 'You can't take me against my will and I've told you I'm not going.'

The sturdier paramedic clears his throat. 'Your blood pressure is elevated and you should really be—'

'Everything all right here?' asks a male voice with a British accent.

Moira turns towards the back of the ambulance and sees Lizzie Sweetman's balding, portly husband peering in through the open doors. *Damn*. He's the last thing she needs. All that waving and shouting a few minutes ago was totally unnecessary. She'd hoped feigning confusion about who he was would put him off, but it seems not. She gives him a curt nod. Doesn't want to engage. Hopes he'll get the message this time. 'It will be.'

She sees the paramedics look at Philip. The sturdier one raises an eyebrow. They're probably trying to work out if he's an ally or foe. Moira decides not to give him the chance to be either.

Pulling the space blanket from around her shoulders, she pushes past the paramedic and throws the blanket on to the bench seat. Grabbing her water bottle she turns towards the doors.

The sturdier paramedic blocks her exit. 'Ma'am, I really need you to—'

'Look, I appreciate you're just doing your job, but like I said, I'm fine.' She pushes past him and climbs down from the ambulance. Once on the ground she turns back to face the pair. 'There's no point you taking me to hospital.'

The red-haired one shakes his head. 'As I said before, ma'am, I think there's reason to—'

'Maybe you should get checked out.' Philip steps closer to Moira and puts a hand on her shoulder. 'It can't hurt.'

Moira shrugs away his hand. 'I don't need to, and I don't want to, so no.' Her tone is assertive, bordering on angry. Why can't

12

he get the message and go? Why is he here anyway? She glares at Philip. 'I saw a dead body. I'm not injured.'

Philip takes a step backwards. 'Just calm down a—'

'Okay, ma'am, I'm not arguing any longer.' The paramedic taps something on the screen of his tablet. 'I'm putting in my call notes you declined transportation to the hospital.'

'You do that,' Moira snaps. Then she feels a bit sorry for him. She knows he's just trying to do his job, but there are people out there who need his skills and a hospital bed far more than she does. And she feels okay. Well, kind of okay. A bit dizzy, and slightly nauseous; otherwise fine. She gives him a small smile. 'And thank you.'

As the paramedics get ready to leave, Moira picks up her sports bag from beside the ambulance and pushes her water bottle into the side pocket. As she straightens up she feels more light-headed. Philip's saying something to her, but his voice seems muffled, as if she's listening underwater. She doesn't want to chat. She looks at Philip. 'See you around.'

As she says the words she knows they're not true. She needs to avoid seeing Philip and his wife Lizzie. She can't afford to get involved with them; it's too risky.

Philip starts to reply but she turns away and walks around the ambulance, heading over to the police cars. Movement helps to clear her head. It's a blood-sugar thing, the dizziness, she's sure of it. She's had spells like this before, and it's different to the panic attacks. She knows she can handle this; she just needs to get home and eat something.

Reaching the police cars, she raps on the window of the nearest vehicle, startling the officer wearing mirrored shades inside, and gives him a wave. 'I'm leaving now, okay?'

The young cop opens the door and jumps out. Looks flustered. 'You're not going to hospital?'

She shakes her head, blinking as her vision goes hazy. Puts a hand out on to the car to steady herself. 'I'm going home.'

'Well, okay then. The lead detective did say it's okay for you to leave. He's got your details and will follow up if there's something more.' The cop takes a card from the pocket of his shirt and hands it to Moira. 'If you think of anything, you can reach him on this number.'

Moira takes the card and reads the name: *Detective James R Golding – Robbery Homicide Division*. She purses her lips. When he'd first arrived Detective Golding had asked her a few cursory questions, but nothing of any depth. He'd seemed distracted, and mentioned several times he was nearing the end of a night shift. From his performance so far Moira is unimpressed. Still, she doesn't say that; she just says, 'Thanks.'

'No problem, ma'am, you have yourself a good day.'

She gives a little shake of her head at the standard platitude that's so out of place given they're inside the crime-scene cordon of a murder. 'I'll try to do that.'

The cop climbs back into his vehicle and Moira knows it's time to go. She hesitates, and glances back towards the park. It feels strange going when she has so many questions. She wants to know who the woman is and why there was all that money floating in the water.

She's still thinking about it when Philip stops beside her. He's looking at her in a kindly fashion like she's a lost child or an injured puppy. It really grates on her.

Reaching out, he pats her shoulder. 'You've had a shock, it's not right that you walk home alone. Let me drive you?'

Moira glares at him and takes a couple of steps back so he can't touch her. She doesn't need to be treated like some fragile flower. She's seen a lot of crime scenes in her career, many far worse than this one, so she has no need for company. Dead bodies don't shock her, not any more, and the last thing she can stomach right now is a load of small talk and nonsense. She'd much rather be alone.

Philip seems to sense her hesitation and changes tack. 'Come back to our place, see Lizzie, have some tea.' Lowering his voice, his tone becomes more conspiratorial. 'And tell us everything you saw here at the crime scene.'

Moira holds his gaze. She's only met Philip once and if she was just going on what she's observed of him, she'd say he's harmless even if far too tactile for her liking, but she knows better than to get involved. It's a shame because she liked his wife, Lizzie, when they met at yoga. Thought she could be a friend. But when they'd had coffee a couple of weeks later and Lizzie had told her both she and Philip were ex-police, that put a different spin on things. She's come all this way to escape the force and everything that happened. She can't blow it by being friends with these people.

What was it that the police doc said? *When you start a new life, you have to make an effort to meet new people – push outside of your comfort zone.* But there's pushing outside your comfort zone and then there's being a total idiot. She can't risk it. She just can't.

'Lizzie would love to see you,' Philip continues. 'She said you've not made the last few yoga classes?'

She hasn't, and she isn't planning on going back. Easier just to be a no-show and fade quietly out of Lizzie's life rather than having to talk about it. Because from what she knows about Lizzie and Philip so far, she'd say they were talkers, and so at some point they'll want to talk about the jobs they did, and the colleagues they worked with, and then they'll ask her all about herself. And she won't want to speak about it, and that will be a problem. Because if there's one thing she knows about law-enforcement types, it's that they love a puzzle. For all she knows they could still be in touch with people in the force. They might mention her to them. Start asking questions. She shudders. That would ruin everything. It just can't happen.

Moira shakes her head. Her vision swims. The light-headedness has returned. Her voice sounds weaker, further away somehow. 'I need to get back.'

'Are you okay?' Philip's frowning. There's concern in his eyes. 'You're looking really pale.'

She shakes her head again, but it makes the dizziness worse. 'I'm . . . I . . .'

Then she's falling.

Philip grabs her. Holds her upright. 'You okay? Stay with me. Look at me.'

She looks at him. He's blurry, his features hazy. Her legs feel weak, as if they can't support her weight any more. She leans into him, even though she doesn't want his help.

'You really mustn't be walking anywhere,' says Philip. He glances back towards the ambulance. 'You should go back and let them take you to hospital.'

'No.' She tries to pull away from Philip. Staggers like a booze-soaked drunk after a twenty-four-hour happy hour. Reluctantly she lets him support her again.

'Well, okay then. But let me drive you. Come back to mine, see Lizzie, have some sweet tea, please. It'll help with the shock. Make you feel better.'

It's not shock. Moira knows that. She doesn't shock easy; never has. This is different. Another way her traitorous body has found to betray her. She doesn't want to go with him, but if he lets go of her she fears she'll drop down on to the tarmac. Suppressing a sigh, she nods instead. Against her better judgement she says, 'Okay.'

Philip gestures up the street. 'My car's just over here.'

They set off slow and steady. Philip keeps a strong grip on her, supporting under her elbow, holding her upright. They duck under the yellow crime-scene tape of the outer cordon and he escorts her towards his car.

Moira concentrates on putting one foot in front of the other. Her legs still feel wobbly. The dizziness is still there. She wants to tell him she's fine, she'll make her own way home and have tea there, thanks very much, but she's not sure she'll make it. She curses under her breath. Hating the feeling of being dependent, especially on this man who she wants to avoid.

'What's that?' Philip says.

'Nothing.' Her voice sounds strange, weaker than normal. It's beyond annoying.

Philip frowns, but doesn't press her. 'Almost there now.'

As they walk, he starts chattering away.

'There's never been a murder at The Homestead before,' he says, barely drawing breath. 'It's going to be the talk of the community.'

They'd better not all try to talk to me about it, thinks Moira.

She hears a rattling sound behind her, and glances over her shoulder towards the park. Beyond the small group of grey-haired rubberneckers gathered at the cordon near the park gates she sees the coroner's people are wheeling a gurney with a zipped-up body bag on it along the path between the pickleball courts. Moira bites her lip as she remembers the last person she'd seen taken away in a body bag. She sees his face in her mind's eye. Swallows hard. Blinking the image away before the grief and the anger can overwhelm her.

'Here we are,' Philip says, stopping beside a gleaming black Toyota.

As he opens the passenger door for her, Moira takes one last look towards the park and feels a pang of . . . something. She remembers how it felt when she saw the body, and how she switched from retired lady of leisure, Moira Flynn, back into her old, original skin. It'd felt like she was on autopilot – confident, professional,

17

and knowing exactly what to do and what to say – and it had felt good. So good. Like she was useful again. Like there was a point to her. Like she still had purpose.

'Shall I help you?' Philip asks.

'No, I'm fine,' she says.

As Philip moves around to the driver's side, Moira goes to turn back towards the park one last time. It's then that she sees someone is watching. On the other side of the street, half-crouched behind one of the parked cars – a silver VW Beetle – is a young, wiry-looking guy with short blond hair and black-framed glasses. He's staring right at her.

He's wearing a navy hoodie and has a chunky maroon and gold knitted scarf around his neck even though the day is warming up and the temperature must be pushing 25°C.

Moira meets his gaze. He doesn't look away. Instead the weird intensity to his expression grows stronger. Then he raises his mobile phone towards her and she hears the click as he takes a photo.

'What the hell are you doing?' Rather than strong her voice sounds shaky, timid. Moira hates it. She takes a step towards the guy, but her vision swims again and she feels another wave of nausea take her.

'Moira!' Philip jumps out of the driver's seat and rushes around the Toyota. Grasping her arm, he just manages to stop her from falling. 'Please, let me help you.'

'Did you see him?' she asks.

Philip shakes his head. Frowns. 'See who?'

Moira turns back towards the parked VW on the opposite side of the road, but there's no one there: not standing or crouching. 'I . . . I thought I . . .' She shakes her head. Wonders if she's seeing things. 'It doesn't matter.'

Slowly, with Philip's support, she gets into the car. The nausea is still there and she swallows hard, then lowers herself down on to the passenger seat. As she fastens the seat belt, the police doc's voice repeats inside her head: *You need time to heal, and you need to do that in a safe place away from violence. Otherwise nothing will ever change.*

You're retired, she tells herself. You are not the person you used to be. Investigating isn't your job, and that's not your crime scene. You have a different life now. You have to walk the hell away.

4

LIZZIE

Standing in front of her easel, paintbrush in hand, Lizzie squints at the photo clipped to the top of her canvas. The light on the screened-in patio is always perfect at this time of the morning, but today it isn't helping. Capturing the likeness of Dolly, the ageing spaniel of their neighbour two doors down, is proving a challenge. The dog's slightly crossed eyes are tricky to get right.

She shakes her head and puts her brush into the turps pot. There's nothing more to be done about the eyes right now; she's out of time. Philip and Moira will be here any moment. It must be almost five minutes since Philip messaged. There's been a spate of burglaries over the past few weeks. From what Philip said, it seems Moira is the latest victim.

If she's honest she's surprised Moira's coming here. Lizzie had liked her immediately when they'd met, laughing about the awkwardness of downward dog together, and the unfeasibly stretchy yoga teacher who must be at least ten years older than them. They'd gone out for coffee a couple of weeks ago, promised to do the same after the next yoga class, and then . . . nothing. Moira hadn't been back to class, and hadn't given Lizzie her address or her mobile number. Then they'd bumped into each other in Publix and Lizzie had got the distinct impression Moira was desperate to escape from them as soon as she could. It'd been weird.

Lizzie's still packing away her paints when she hears Philip's key in the door. Popping into the bathroom, she washes a paint smudge from her cheek then hurries out into the hallway. Philip and Moira are already inside. Philip's putting his coat into the hallway closet. Moira's standing, arms crossed, and looking uncomfortable.

Lizzie switches into host mode; it's a role she enjoys. 'Moira, welcome.'

'Been slaughtering a rainbow?' says Philip, eyeing her paint-splattered dungarees. He plants a kiss on Lizzie's cheek as he drops his keys into the bowl on the dresser.

'Something like that.' Lizzie wipes her still-damp hands on her dungarees and turns to Moira. 'Sorry I'm a bit of a mess. I tend to lose track of time when I'm painting.'

Moira looks unsure. 'I don't want to intrude.'

'You're not intruding at all. Now, would you like tea, coffee, maybe something stronger?' Lizzie glances at her husband then back to Moira. Usually bold and confident, now Moira looks pale and subdued, and Philip seems to be supporting her under the elbow. 'Are you doing okay?'

'She had a bit of a funny turn,' says Philip. 'Needs some sweet tea and a couple of biscuits to sort her out.'

'I'd prefer coffee if that's okay.'

'Of course.' Lizzie smiles as she appraises Moira again. Her eyes look oddly unfocused and her voice has a tremble to it, nothing like it's been before. 'I think you need a sit-down.' She gestures through to the kitchen and the stools on the other side of the island. 'Come, sit. And tell me what happened.'

Philip helps Moira to a seat at the island and then sits down opposite her. Lizzie collects three white mugs from the cabinet and sets them down on the white granite countertop. Taking the flask from the hot plate on the coffee maker, she pours each of them a strong coffee and adds three lumps of sugar to the mug for Moira. She sets the coffees down in front of Moira, Philip and the spare stool beside him, then takes a packet of shortbread out of the cupboard and tips them on to a plate. She puts the plate in front of Moira.

As Lizzie climbs up on to the nearest stool, Moira picks up a biscuit. She nibbles the corner off, then sets the rest down on the counter beside her coffee mug. Lizzie hopes Philip doesn't notice. He hates crumbs.

Philip's tapping away one-fingered at his phone, his lips pursed in concentration. He glances at her as she sits down. 'I'm messaging Rick, we need to call a meeting of the community watch – see if any of the patrols saw anything last night.'

'Good idea,' says Lizzie. The community watch is Philip's new obsession – his way of doing something good for the neighbourhood. Lizzie knows how important it is to him. He's always needed a purpose or to be leading a crusade of some sort, and since handing over the captaincy of the Tall Grass Golf Club earlier in the year she knows he's been feeling rather adrift. Ideally she'd prefer his crusades to be non-law-enforcement related, but as crime goes she reasons that burglaries are towards the less violent end. She looks across at Moira. 'Philip said something about a crime. Were you burgled?'

Moira shakes her head. 'There was a dead body in the lap pool this morning.'

Lizzie inhales hard. Feels her chest tighten. There's never been a murder on The Homestead. Until about a month ago there'd never really been any kind of crime. It's one of the reasons they've chosen to live here; they've both seen enough in their careers to last several lifetimes. They chose The Homestead to forget about all that. Lizzie

22

frowns. Tries not to show Moira that the news has unsettled her. 'Really? That's . . . unexpected.'

Moira takes another nibble of shortbread. 'I thought so too.'

Lizzie glances at her husband but he's still typing, all his attention on his phone screen. It's just as well because the crumbs are spreading out from the half-eaten shortbread in front of Moira. Lizzie tries not to look at them. 'Philip said you were in an ambulance. Did you get hurt?'

'No, nothing like that, the paramedics were making a fuss about things, saying I should go to the hospital, but there was no need.'

Lizzie says nothing for a moment. She's seen the way Moira's nostrils flared when she asked if she was hurt, and the way she broke eye contact when she mentioned the paramedics. Lizzie's pretty sure Moira's hiding something. Leaning across the counter, she lowers her voice. 'You sure you're okay?'

'I'm fine, really. I just started feeling really light-headed. I get low blood sugar sometimes.' Moira pauses, and takes another bite of shortbread. 'This is helping though, thank you.'

Lizzie doesn't say anything. She's not convinced.

Moira gives her a forced-looking smile. 'Look, you don't need to worry about me. I don't scare easily.'

Lizzie wonders what Moira used to do for a job. If she's not shocked by a dead body maybe she was a nurse or paramedic, or a doctor; something where death was part of the job. As a CSI Lizzie saw the aftermath of every kind of crime. To see that stuff every day, and stick at the job until retirement, takes a certain type of person. 'Yes, of course. Still, it must have been a shock? Crime scenes are pretty grim.'

'True. It was strange leaving, though. I felt like I should stay and help out or something, because I found her.'

Lizzie nods like she understands, but really she doesn't. She likes retirement. This is her time to relax and enjoy the simple pleasures. She's had enough of dead bodies and bodily fluids to last a lifetime, and Philip really can't be around that kind of thing any more. That's why she likes The Homestead – it's like a permanent holiday; a place where only good things happen. She doesn't want to be reminded of all the dreadful things people do to one another. She thinks she's earned that.

'So tell us what you saw, Moira,' says Philip, putting his phone on to the counter and picking up his coffee. 'How did you find the body? Was there any sign of the killer? Did you notice anything out of place in the park?'

Lizzie keeps her gaze on her husband. She's seen that animated expression before, so many times, and every time he's worked a big case. Cases like that always consumed him. He'd work non-stop, obsessed like a bloodhound on a scent, and he loved it. Lived for it. Right up until the moment when a heart attack and sky-rocketing blood pressure forced him to give it all up.

She bites her lip. Now the expression's back, and Lizzie knows the obsession won't be far behind. She inhales, and gives a barely audible sigh.

Her relaxing retirement has been shattered. Her only move now is to try and limit the damage, and hope their peaceful life here won't be forced to come to an end.

5

MOIRA

Moira doesn't want to be here and she sure as hell doesn't want to talk about the murder. The more they discuss it, the more likely she is to slip up and for them to realise she has a past in law enforcement. She doesn't want that.

'So, tell us, what was it like?' Philip's tone is more urgent, bossier this time. He's looking at her all super-eager, like a cat watching a cornered mouse. 'I want all the details.'

She doesn't like his tone. If she were feeling better she'd tell him to get lost and then she'd leave, but she isn't feeling better. She's still feeling odd – a bit light-headed, and slightly detached. She doesn't feel well enough to walk home yet, which means she's stuck here for the time being, and it's easier to go along with him and answer his questions than resist. She needs to be careful though. 'There was no sign of the killer, but I think there were things out of place in the pool.'

'How exactly?' asks Philip, leaning closer. His eyes are bright, and his phone buzzing on the counter seems forgotten. His whole focus is on her now.

Lizzie on the other hand seems distracted, frowning as she twists her mug back and forth on the white granite.

Moira hesitates. She thinks about the scene – the blood on the victim's chest, the floating dollars and the bag sunk to the bottom of the pool – not a death by natural causes, or an accidental death, but a violent and suspicious death, and the sort of puzzle that gets inside your head. She's worked cases like this before in her old life, and she knows the danger of them; the need to *know* what happened can become a kind of mania.

She is supposed to be avoiding that mania. She's left that world. Shed her old life like an outgrown skin and now she's someone new. She thinks back to the police doc's last words to her. How she emphasised again that Moira must stay away from violence and danger, her words a warning: *You need to take the time to heal.*

Moira looks from Philip to Lizzie. She can't tell them any of this; they mustn't know her secret. They'd been in law enforcement, so every moment she's here is a risk. And the more she speaks about what she saw, the deeper they'll pull her into their world. She needs to leave. Right now.

Gripping the countertop, she slides her feet to the ground. Her legs feel weak, like they won't support her weight. She tries to stand but her knees give way and she sits back on to the stool with a bump. This is hopeless. She's trapped here.

'You okay?' asks Lizzie. She pushes the plate of shortbread towards Moira. 'Have another.'

'Thanks.' Moira hates how weak she sounds. 'I'm not feeling great, to be honest.'

'Best to stay here a while, and let us take care of you,' says Philip. 'And tell us all about what you saw. A problem shared is a problem halved and all that. Telling us about it will help you feel better. And don't worry about telling us all the details – I know it's hard for you as a civilian, but we worked in law enforcement so we can handle it.'

Moira's sure that it won't make her feel better, but she's in no position to resist. She takes a sip of her coffee, and grimaces at the overload of sugar. Philip's so keen he's virtually salivating. He nods encouragingly. She fights the urge to tell him that she's more than capable of handling the details of a crime scene. That she's worked enough of them.

She opens her mouth to reply.

The back door flies open. It bangs against the wall, causing the glasses in the display cabinet beside the door to rattle.

Moira flinches, and twists round towards the noise. 'What the . . . ?'

A barrel-chested guy the size of a mountain strides into the kitchen. His white hair, deep tan and huge arms make him look like Popeye's older, more muscular brother. When he speaks his voice is gravel deep, the accent Bostonian rather than Floridian.

'I've called the troops to action. Meeting's in half an hour.'

'Excellent,' says Philip, gesturing towards her. 'Moira here found the body, she's going to talk us through what she saw.'

'Sounds good,' says the man mountain. Pouring himself a mug of coffee, he moves across the kitchen to the space next to Moira at the island and leans his hip against the counter.

Philip gestures towards the empty stool. 'Take a seat.'

'I'm okay standing,' says the big guy. He looks at Moira. 'You go right ahead.'

Moira frowns. Who the hell is this guy? With him towering over her, the kitchen that had seemed so big and spacious moments ago now seems more like a hobbit house. 'And you are?'

'I'm Rick, ma'am.' Putting his coffee down, he stretches out his hand in greeting. 'Rick Denver.'

Moira shakes his hand. It's at least double the size of hers. He's got a firm grip and a cool, dry palm. 'I'm Moira.'

'Great accent,' Rick says, grinning. 'I guess you're another transplant from England like these guys?'

He says the word England as if it has three syllables – En-ger-land. And his smile makes him look less imposing, more goofy, but Moira isn't prepared to drop her guard. 'I am.'

'You live here?' He holds her eye contact.

She gives a curt nod. 'Moved in last month.'

'Cool.' Rick glances from Moira to the others. 'So the crime scene, what did you see?'

Moira hesitates. She didn't like the idea of telling Lizzie and Philip, and now there's this Rick guy she's even less keen.

'Go ahead,' says Philip, nodding encouragingly. 'Rick's ex-DEA. He's law enforcement, just like me and Lizzie.'

Like me too, thinks Moira, but she says nothing because, shit, this is all she needs – yet another person from law enforcement.

'It's okay,' says Philip. 'Continue. You're perfectly safe with us.'

Biting back the urge to tell him she's been a cop herself and doesn't need his patronising assurances, Moira looks at Rick instead. 'That true about you being ex-DEA?'

'Sure is. Did forty-one years. Real long-timer.'

Moira stares at him. She has to be guarded to protect herself. It's easy enough, having almost become a habit after years of working undercover, where it's a force of necessity to make the right moves and stay alive. But she also needs to fit in and not arouse suspicion, so she takes a breath and forces a smile. 'Well, like I said, there were some things out of place at the pool that didn't make sense.'

Lizzie stops rotating the bottom of her mug against the counter. 'How?'

'Well, when I spoke to the detective he seemed to be working on the idea it was a mugging, but that seemed odd to me.' Moira tries to inject more doubt into her voice, as if she's talking about something she's not an expert in. 'I mean, if it was a mugging, why did the killer leave all the money and the—'

'Wait.' Philip puts his hand out to stop her. 'What money? How much? Where—?'

'Tell us from the beginning,' Rick says, cutting over Philip. 'Describe how you found the scene.'

'Okay.' There's something solid and honest-looking about this new guy, Rick. He seems interested, but he's not pushy like Philip. It makes her feel more inclined to talk. Moira closes her eyes and concentrates on the memory. 'So I let myself into the pool through the latch gate. It was closed when I arrived, it always is at that time, so I opened it and walked towards the lap pool. The floodlights are motion-activated. As soon as they switched on I saw her. She was floating, on her back, and although I couldn't yet see her face I knew she was dead.' Moira opens her eyes. Looks at Rick. 'It was strange that I could tell, even from that distance. I guess it's something about how still she was?'

Rick's expression is serious. 'Yep. Could be.'

Philip leans closer across the countertop. 'What did you do next?'

'I hurried to the pool's edge. The woman was floating in the middle. She was young, twenties at most, and had long black hair that had fanned out around her head in the water. She was wearing a yellow dress and as I got closer I could see there was blood on her chest and over the top of the dress.'

'Did you recognise her?' Lizzie says.

Moira shakes her head. 'No.'

'And the money?' Philip asks.

'It was in the pool with her. Floating on the surface, like an oil slick made of dollars. There must have been thousands of bills.'

Lizzie clasps her hands together. 'If it was a mugging, it makes no sense that the killer would leave all the money in the pool.'

Moira meets her gaze. 'Exactly. Unless they weren't after the money.'

Rick frowns. 'You saw something else?'

'There was a black bag on the bottom of the pool.'

'Like a handbag?' Lizzie asks.

Moira shakes her head. 'I couldn't see it properly because of all the dollars on the surface, but it was a rucksack, I think. It was just sitting on the bottom which struck me as weird – there must have been something really heavy inside.'

'You think that's what they were after?' Philip asks.

'I don't know. Maybe.'

Lizzie tilts her head, frowning. 'Then why didn't they take it?'

'Could be they couldn't swim,' says Moira. 'The lap pool is deep all the way along – no shallow end.'

'Maybe the perpetrator was interrupted?' suggests Philip.

'If it wasn't a mugging, and they weren't after the cash, could be they *did* take what they wanted.' Rick runs his hand across his jaw. 'We just don't know what that was.'

Lizzie shakes her head. 'But who leaves that much cash behind, even if it wasn't their main motivation? If it was just floating there . . .'

'Well, isn't that the million-dollar question?' Rick looks from Lizzie to Moira. 'Were you there when the crime-scene team pulled the bag from the pool?'

Moira nods. 'Yeah, but I was too far away. I tried to move closer but the cops stopped me. I didn't get a clear look.'

'But?' Philip prompts.

'But nothing.' Moira frowns at him. 'Like I said, I couldn't get close enough. As they fished the bag out the detective, Golding his name was, came over and asked me a few questions, and after that the paramedics insisted on me going back to the ambulance. You know the rest.'

'I'm guessing you didn't think too much of the detective?' says Rick.

She gives him a small smile. 'That obvious, huh?'

Rick smiles back, the laughter lines deepening around his eyes. 'Kind of.'

'He was distracted, you know, and coming off a night shift. It didn't seem like he wanted to be there or had much time for it.' She exhales hard. 'I thought the woman in the pool, whoever she was, deserved better.'

Rick is looking sympathetic. Lizzie's gaze is on Philip, who's frowning.

Moira wonders whether to come clean and tell them what she did.

Philip shakes his head. Looks earnest. 'Every victim deserves justice.'

Rick and Lizzie nod agreement. Moira makes her decision.

'They do. That's why I kept the pictures.' Pulling her phone from the pocket of her hoodie, she unlocks the screen and goes to her photos. 'I know it might seem creepy, but I just . . .' She shrugs.

Holding her phone towards the group, she scrolls through the pictures she took at the crime scene before the cops arrived. The first few are the wide view of the pool and the patio. Then come the close-ups, stark and uncompromising in the early morning sun-light – the young woman in the pool, crimson smeared across her chest and yellow dress; the trail of blood and the splatter on the stone edging; the dollar bills floating on the water; the black bag submerged beneath the surface.

None of them speaks for a moment, then Rick asks, 'You tell this Detective Golding you got these?'

'No. I was going to delete them.' She meets Rick's gaze. 'Then, when he seemed so distracted, I couldn't bring myself to do it. I felt involved because I found her. Almost like I should do something to help myself, you know? Like I was somehow responsible.'

Philip nods. Rick as well.

'It's understandable,' says Lizzie, a sympathetic expression on her face. 'Finding someone dead is a big deal.'

'Yes, yes,' says Philip, patting Moira on the arm. 'It's bad even when you're a trained professional and used to crime scenes, but for a civilian like yourself it must be especially hard.'

'It's not just that.' Moira doesn't let herself rise to Philip's patronising comment. Instead she taps the screen, enlarging the young woman's face – her eyes open yet unseeing. Gripping the phone tighter, Moira looks back at the three retired law enforcers. The tremble is back in her voice when she speaks and it's not entirely due to the light-headedness. 'The way the detective – Golding – seemed so unbothered really riled me. This poor young woman died last night. *Someone* should care about what happened to her.'

6

RICK

As he pulls off Sea Spray Boulevard into the parking lot of the Roadhouse, Rick feels his Apple watch vibrate again. Glancing down, he sees there's another message from Sandi – the manager of the Roadhouse – asking where they are. It's the third she's sent in the last ten minutes and this one's a whole lot less polite than the first. Word is, things are getting rowdy in the back room. Rowdy by The Homestead's standards anyways.

'Problem?' says Philip.

'The guys wondering where we're at is all.'

Rick parks round back and they hurry towards the building. He can hear rock music through the open windows and the noise of chatter over the top of it. No shouting, no breaking furniture – nothing that constitutes rowdy in any place but this.

Reaching the entrance, they go inside. The Roadhouse is barely ten years old, but built to look like it's been standing for a couple of hundred more. Rustic weatherboard, exposed brick walls, dark wood furniture and low lighting make Rick feel like he's going straight from day to night. It's designed to look rough around the edges but, as this is The Homestead, the smell of polish is stronger than the beer, and chewing tobacco and smokes are banned. Still, even though he quit near on five years ago, Rick feels the urge for a smoke every time he sets foot in the place.

They pass through the main bar area, past pool tables and a couple of one-armed bandits, and down the hallway towards the back room where the community watch always meets. The noise of chatter grows louder the closer they get.

They're a few metres away when the door to the back room opens and Sandi – a bottle-blonde in her late fifties, with a generous figure and a stern tone that keeps even the drunkest resident in line – bustles out into the hallway.

She frowns when she sees them. 'Where've you been?'

'Got tied up walking through the crime scene,' says Philip. 'Sorry we're late.'

She puts her hands on her hips and cocks her head to the side. 'The crime scene, huh?' She looks from Philip to Rick. 'You ask me to open up early just for you, then you boys get real tardy on me.'

She's annoyed, he can tell that, but there's a teasing tone to her words as well. Sandi and him, they had a few dates about twelve months back, but nothing more than that. She's good company, but he hadn't been ready for romance. Even though it's five years since her passing, he's stayed hung up on his late wife, Alisha.

He touches the fingers of his right hand to his forehead. 'Sorry, ma'am. Won't happen again.'

'Just see that it doesn't,' says Sandi with a wink. She gestures through the doorway. 'As you're here now, you'd better get to business.'

As he follows Philip through into the back room, Rick thinks about the reason for their tardiness. He's never late, hates it in himself and others, yet this morning it hadn't seemed to matter. He couldn't just split and run without dropping the new Brit, Moira, at her place on the way over here, so she could let her dogs out for a run in the yard. Especially when she was still feeling under the weather. It was weird. As she was getting out the jeep he'd had a hankering to stay with her. He shook his head. Didn't know what that was about. She was an attractive woman, for sure, although kind of tight-assed that way the English oftentimes are. But the way she'd talked about justice, and caring about what happened to the victim, had sucker-punched him right in the gut. All that sincerity and passion she had going on had him charmed, and that didn't happen often. He shook his head. Who was he kidding? It pretty much never happened; the last woman who'd charmed him had been Alisha.

Philip nudges him with his elbow. 'They haven't even noticed we're here yet. We need to call this to order.'

'For sure.'

'And get this damn music turned down.'

The community watch are gathered around the long table towards the back of the room. Rick does a quick head count; all twenty-nine volunteer patrollers are here. Stepping across the room to the private bar, he opens the shutter and leans over the counter. Finding what he's looking for by feel, he flicks the switch and stifles the rock music. The patrollers stop their chatter and turn to see what's happening.

'Sorry we're late, guys,' says Rick, moving towards the table. 'But let's get to it.'

Philip takes a seat at the head of the table. Rick pulls a chair out and sits at the corner of the table, a little ways back. All eyes are on them now.

Philip clears his throat and makes a performance of taking his notes from his jacket pocket. Rick wishes he'd get a move on.

'This better be important,' mutters Rory Kempler to his wife, Melly, taking an exaggerated look at his watch. 'I was meant to be teeing off five minutes ago.'

Philip frowns at Rory and makes eye contact with each of the group before he speaks. His tone is dead serious. 'This meeting is about a homicide.'

There's a moment of silence, then the patrollers all start talking at once.

Bert turns to Philip. He's frowning, his eyes concerned beneath bushy salt-and-pepper eyebrows. 'Where'd it happen?'

'Here, in Ocean Mist?' asks Melly, pushing her pink sun visor higher on to her head. The years of Botox mean her expression is always one of surprise, but there's worry in her voice now.

'I saw cops over at Manatee Park this morning when I was out power walking,' says Hank, smoothing his polo shirt down over his flat stomach. 'Must have been there.'

The patrollers talk over each other. The volume and anxiety levels are rising.

Stepping up to the table, Rick thumps his fist against the solid wooden surface twice. 'Quieten down.'

The chatter stops. Everyone is looking at Rick and Philip.

Philip clears his throat again. 'A woman lost her life last night, here, in our neighbourhood. She was found this morning in Manatee Recreation Park.'

'How did it happen?' asks Donald. He looks pale beside all the others, but then he always does. Rick's never seen someone living in Florida be so untanned, but then he knows Donald's one of those computer nerds. What was it he'd said at the first watch meeting? Oh, yeah, he'd spent his working life with one of the big tech companies. *Figures*, thinks Rick. From the look of him, Donald still spends most of his time inside with his computers.

Melly looks from Donald to Philip. 'Do you know who did it?'

Philip shakes his head. 'At this time—'

'Who died? Oh my God, was it Maeve?' Dorothy puts her hands to her face. 'She didn't call me back last night, she said she would but she never did and I didn't think to try her again after I'd finished watching my programmes. Did the killer get her? I'll never forgive myself if she—'

'The cops are establishing the facts now,' Philip continues. 'But the victim was a young woman, too young to be a resident here. There's no ID right now, but—'

Hank pushes his glasses back up to the bridge of his nose. 'Why don't they know who she is? How did she get here?'

'Every entrance is gated, there should be a record,' says Donald, running a hand across his chin. 'They'll get her name from that.'

'But people won't feel safe in their homes,' says Dorothy. Her eyes are tearing up behind her glasses. 'It's bad enough with the burglaries, but murder? Who would do such a thing? Our little neighbourhood used to feel so safe but now—'

'It's outsiders coming in, has to be.' Rory's clenching his fists and his face is getting red. 'They're coming into our community and terrorising our residents . . .'

'Yeah, this all started same time as the construction over in district eleven,' says Donald. 'We had no crime before then, but those workers came in and suddenly it's like we're crime central.'

Rick watches the group. He can tell from the voices of those closest to him, and the body language of those further away, that the tension is rising. He glances at Philip. Knows that Philip's style is to let them talk themselves out, then once they're done, focus on taking action – it's the tactic he used after the first few burglaries – but he needs to step in sooner today. Take control.

'Yeah, first the burglaries, now homicide,' agrees Clint. 'My grandkids visit on the weekends. It's no good if this place isn't safe for them.'

'For sure,' says Rick. 'We need to help the cops solve this. That's why we called the meeting.'

There's uncertainty on the patrollers' faces now. Fear too.

'How can we do that?' asks Dorothy. She's petite and must be pushing eighty years old, but Rick can tell there's a steely core to her. With her white hair pulled into a tight bun and her pink twinset and pearls, she reminds him of the stern maths teacher he had in seventh grade.

'We've been patrolling the streets at night for weeks now, ma'am, and we were out there last night. Between us, we know things the cops don't. We need to make that intelligence available for them.'

Dorothy nods. There are murmurs of agreement from around the group.

'So how are we going to do that?' Donald says.

'Firstly, I need your weekly logs a day early – we'll drop by you all this afternoon and collect them, so please have them ready,' says Philip. 'And secondly, I need you all to look at a photo. It's not pleasant, but it could help the police ID the victim.'

'You want us to look at a picture of the dead girl?' asks Dorothy, her expression real serious.

Philip looks solemn. 'That I do.'

There's silence. Rick's not sure what way the group will go on this. It's always hard to say with civilians. Over the years he's gotten used to crime-scene pictures and dead bodies up close. Didn't like it, but that was part of the job. Things didn't always go right. People didn't always make good choices. It was a bad day if someone ended up dead, but in the world of narcotics it was something you just had to deal with. Rick looks at Dorothy. 'Can you do that?'

Dorothy holds his gaze for a long moment, then nods. 'I want this murdering asshole caught,' she says firmly. She looks at Philip. 'Okay, let's see this photo.'

7

MOIRA

Silence.

With the dogs out in the garden the house feels strangely empty. It reminds her of how her London apartment had felt towards the end – empty and soulless. As if the joy had been sucked right out of the space, just as it had been out of her. Up until that last job her work had been the love of her life, but what happened with McCord changed that, and afterwards things felt different, wrong.

PTSD, that's what the police doc had said. They told her that with cognitive behaviour therapy and her personalised coping strategies it'd get better with time. That the nightmares would lessen, and she'd keep the panic attacks under control. They must have believed it too, because they'd kept her on paid sick leave and the doc met her once a week to help her work through her shit. And it did help, a bit. But, as she could only ever bring herself to tell them half the story, she supposed she could only ever get half better. And as you can't have a panic attack in the middle of an undercover operation, her offering to take early retirement seemed the best option for everyone; the safest option. Because the very last thing she'd choose to do was to endanger her colleagues. Again.

And now she's here.

She gulps down the last of her orange juice and puts the glass in the sink. The nausea and light-headedness are gone now, and her legs feel less wobbly. It must have been low blood sugar causing them, as she'd thought. It certainly wasn't a panic attack.

Walking across the kitchen to the back door, she steps out into the garden to see what the dogs are up to. Wolfie, the small fluffy mixed-breed terrier, is chasing Marigold, the leggy juvenile Labrador, around the bushes. Pip, the elderly sausage dog, is lying on his back in his favourite dirt patch, sunning himself. When he sees her looking at him, he raises his front legs, encouraging her to tickle his tummy.

'Okay, then,' she says, smiling, and does as he asks.

She'd visited the local shelter the week she moved in, hoping to get one dog, and instead she'd found three. As she strokes Pip, Wolfie hurtles across the lawn to her, looking for attention. Moira sits down on the grass and strokes him too. Marigold brings her a tennis ball and she throws it for her, laughing as the gangly adolescent fetches it and then delightedly capers around the garden with the ball in her mouth, chased by Wolfie. Dogs are so much less demanding than humans.

'You guys crack me up.'

Moira feels her mobile vibrate in the pocket of her jeans. Pulling it out, she reads the message:

> Philip and Rick are due back from community watch soon. Will you come over so we can discuss whatever they find out? Lizzie.

I don't know, thinks Moira.

She doesn't want to. Being around Lizzie and Philip, and now this Rick guy, is too risky. They're all ex-law enforcement. They'll all have contacts back in the forces and departments they worked in. And that means they each have the ability to check her out – to discover her secret. She can't let that happen. Her whole reason

40

for moving here was to get away from crime and law enforcement and lies.

She taps out an answer.

Sorry. Not feeling great. M.

Another lie but what's the alternative?

Lizzie's reply comes back within a few seconds.

If you don't want to walk or drive I can ask Philip to pick you up.

Won't help. I'm still dizzy, Moira replies.

Lizzie replies almost immediately.

You need some proper food, and it's not right you're on your own. I'll make us a meal.

Damn. This is getting awkward. The more she refuses, the more she's going to make Lizzie curious. And the more curious she gets, the more likely she'll be to mention Moira's name to an old colleague and ask them to run a check and find out about her and her old life. And that will be a problem.

She stares at Lizzie's last message. Not sure how to answer.

Another reply pops up on the screen.

We could really do with your help.

Moira frowns. Help with what? Finding out more about the case, or the victim? Canvassing the neighbourhood to see if other residents saw anything? They should be leaving that to the cops.

Although, if she's honest with herself, she can feel the lure of working the case, and puzzling out the mysteries of the crime scene, tugging at her consciousness. Maybe it's because it's the first crime she's seen since she retired. Or because the victim is so young, or Detective Golding seemed so preoccupied and uninterested. Or maybe it's due to more selfish reasons. Because in those moments of finding the body and calling 911 she felt like her old self, her real self; the self with purpose and a point to her. She'd felt like someone who was useful, and it's been a long time since she felt that way.

It's been over two hundred and fifty days since her first panic attack, and twenty-two days since her last, the day before she picked the dogs up. She wasn't triggered when she found the body this morning or when her anger at the detective's indifference threatened to boil over; surely that has to be a good sign. But then the dizziness and the light-headedness were weird, and she's been feeling sick for most of the day. Even if she feels okay right now, there's no way of knowing how long it'll last.

She shakes her head. Getting more involved in the case and with Lizzie would be pure foolishness – and the panic attacks, when they come, give no warning. One moment she's feeling fine, the next she's overwhelmed and unable to breathe. And what if the dizziness she's been feeling and the light-headed nausea are somehow connected? She thinks they're linked to her blood-sugar levels, but what if they're not? If either of these things happens again when she's with Lizzie, Philip or Rick, how will she explain it? She can't. And that will only make them more curious about her. And that could put everything in jeopardy.

Marigold drops the ball in her lap.

'Good girl,' says Moira, stroking the puppy's silken head. Picking up the ball, she throws it over the flower bed to the far side of the lawn. Marigold chases after it with Wolfie yapping in hot pursuit.

She wishes she could stay here. Hide out with her dogs. Lead the simple life that she'd hoped for when she'd moved to The Homestead. Anonymous. Incognito. Undisturbed.

Wolfie starts barking. Looking over to him, Moira sees he's staring into the hedge that shields the garden from the street. Marigold copies him. Her bark is deeper and louder than the older terrier. Moira shakes her head. 'What are you guys barking at?'

Beside her, Pip sits up; suddenly alert. His hackles are raised.

Wolfie barks louder and launches head first into the hedge. It's dense and leafy, and Moira knows there's a wire mesh fence on the other side, so Wolfie can't get out on to the road, but still her heart thumps in her chest a little faster.

She's never seen the dogs act this way. What the hell is on the other side of the hedge?

Jumping up, she hurries across to Wolfie and Marigold. The hedge isn't high – barely four foot – so it's easy to see over, and she can't see anything obvious to upset the dogs. But Wolfie's growling, still focused on the other side. Marigold is standing alongside him with her head cocked. Pip's hackles remain raised.

'What is it?' says Moira. 'What did you see?'

Then she hears an engine start up a little way along the street. Turning towards the noise she peers further over the hedge and sees a vehicle pull away from the kerb and accelerate fast.

Her breath catches in her throat.

It's a silver VW Beetle: the car that had been parked on the road near Manatee Recreation Park. The one the young blond guy who'd taken her photo had been hiding behind.

Her heart beats faster.

What's he doing on the road outside her house? He's not a neighbour. Did the dogs barking and Wolfie being so fixated on a specific spot on the other side of the hedge mean the guy has been loitering on the pavement outside her home?

Was he watching her, again?

Moira shivers. She's always lived alone, and has never felt bothered by the solitude. But seeing the wiry blond guy near the park and now outside her home is weird. He could be connected to the murder. Hell, he could be the actual murderer. Or he could be something, somebody, far, far worse.

He could be looking for *her*.

Moira feels nauseous. Suddenly she's dizzy again.

What if her old life has found her here? She's made a career out of being tough and staying resilient. But her toughness has crumbled over the past year. The idea of being discovered makes her feel weirdly vulnerable. And she hates the feeling.

Her phone buzzes in her pocket. She looks at the screen, glad of the distraction. It's another message from Lizzie:

Please say you'll come over. I could do with your support.

There's a lot of ways to read the message, and meaning is always so hard to determine from a typed note, but the wording strikes Moira as odd. Why would Lizzie need her support? Surely with Philip and Rick they can manage anything that comes from the meeting of the neighbourhood patrollers? They don't even know that she's ex-law enforcement; as far as they're concerned she's just a civilian.

Leaning down, Moira tickles Pip behind his greying ears and takes some comfort as the sausage dog licks her hand. His hackles are down now, and Wolfie and Marigold have gone back to chasing around the lawn with the ball. Moving here, starting this new life was meant to be her *tabula rasa. Do something different,* the police doc had said. *Leave this life, and what's happened, behind and start a new chapter.*

I tried, thinks Moira, but this morning there was a dead body on her *tabula rasa.* Her blank slate is now splattered with water and blood, and sprinkled with dollars. She needs to find a way to clean it off.

Maybe her finding the victim was a test – part of her recovery. Or maybe it's just Sod's law. She's tried to distance herself from Lizzie and Philip. Worked hard to protect her secret and avoid making connections with people who could compromise that. But a young woman died. Can she really walk away when Lizzie, Philip and Rick are trying to find information to help the cops solve the murder?

She knows she needs to stop fooling herself. Maybe if she does this she'll be able to scrub the blood from her blank slate and start again. Perhaps helping them is a way for her to atone for what happened; a way she can work towards redemption. Or maybe she's about to learn that nowhere is far enough when you're running from your past.

She's not sure. But she needs to make a decision.

Waking the phone screen, she taps a message back to Lizzie and presses send before she can rethink it. It's only one meal, after all. And she can't hide from them forever.

Sometimes doing the right thing means you have to step into the danger zone.

8

PHILIP

Taking his phone from his trouser pocket, Philip presses the photo icon and selects the picture Moira had messaged to him. It's a close-up of the young woman's face cropped from one of the crime-scene pictures she had taken. The blood isn't visible, but from the vacant, staring eyes it is obvious she's dead.

He looks at Dorothy. 'You ready?'

'Just give it me already,' she says, holding her hand out for the phone.

He passes it to her. Watches her pale beneath her tan as she looks at the image.

Dorothy shakes her head. Turning the phone over so it's face down, she slides it back across the table to him. 'Sorry, I don't think I've seen her before. And definitely not while I've been on patrol.'

Philip takes the phone, then reaches out and gives Dorothy's hand a pat. 'Appreciate you looking.'

She gives him a sad smile. Fiddles with the clasp of her pearls. 'No problem.'

'Who else is going to look?' He scans the group, but no one will meet his gaze. It reminds him how difficult dealing with the public can be – they always want a perpetrator caught fast, and get hooked on those true-crime podcasts and whatever, but faced with the real thing most still prefer to turn a blind eye. It's not good enough. He needs the patrollers to step up.

Since the second break-in, when he and Rick had set up the community watch, they'd split the Ocean Mist district into four quadrants and deployed single-person patrols to each quadrant every night. He glances down at the picture on his phone. If this young woman was seen by anyone, chances are it'll be one of his volunteer patrollers. But still no one's giving him eye contact. There's just a lot of awkward shuffling on seats and Melly whispering something he can't hear to Rory. He needs to tell them what's what; make them engage on this. He clears his throat again. Holds the phone towards Rory, Melly and Donald – the people sitting closest to him. 'Who's going to—?'

'I just don't think I can.' Melly's shaking her head, leaning away from Philip and the phone towards Rory. Rory shakes his head and looks at his watch. 'It's too horrible to have to look at—'

'Oh come on, goddammit,' snaps Dorothy. She points her finger at Rory and Melly. 'Shame on you if you won't even glance at the poor girl.'

Melly stares from Dorothy to Philip, open-mouthed.

'And don't be staring at him like that, missy, catching flies in that chatterbox mouth of yours, that isn't gonna save no one. And, Rory, you take a look at the damn photo, else it seems to me you're putting more importance on a round of golf than a human life,' says Dorothy. Her voice is getting louder, angrier. She points at Donald. 'And shame on you, Donald, if you don't take a look at the picture.'

Donald flinches. His cheeks flush and he turns to Philip, gesturing for the phone. 'Yes, ma'am.'

Philip passes it to him. As Donald catches sight of the screen Philip sees what looks like a flicker of recognition in his eyes, but Donald doesn't speak. Does he know something? Philip wonders.

He wants to question Donald, but Dorothy's getting to her feet now, smacking her palms on to the table.

She points at each of the patrollers. Her voice is louder with every word. 'And shame on every one of you if you don't look. We're all real long in the tooth here, and we've all been around the block and seen bad things that we'd rather unsee, but a girl died here and maybe we know something that'll help catch the asshole who came to our home and killed her.' She gestures towards the phone that Donald's holding. 'So get a look at the photo and see if the someone who knows something is you.'

There are nods now.

Rory tries to take the phone from Donald, but he won't give it up. 'Hey, man, that's not cool to hog the—'

'Philip?' Donald ignores Rory, keeps looking at Philip. 'I've seen her before.'

Philip feels adrenaline pulse through him. Finally they could be getting somewhere. 'When?'

'Must have been a couple of nights back.' Donald rubs the bridge of his nose. Closes his eyes as he's trying to remember. 'Pretty sure it was over on Seahorse Drive. It was late, sometime after midnight, I remember because I'd had my twelve o'clock espresso and was feeling sharp so . . .'

'Yes, yes,' says Philip. *Get to the point, man.* 'What was she doing?'

'There was this beat-up station wagon parked up at the kerb, with the windows all steamy, and I thought, "Hello, what's going on in there?" So I slowed down some to take a look-see. Anyways, next thing I know, the passenger door flies open and a girl' – he points to the picture on the phone – '*this* girl, comes stumbling out.'

Philip glances at Rick. Sees his own excitement mirrored in his friend's expression.

'Anyways, there was shouting from inside the car, a male voice,' continues Donald. 'But I didn't get a good look at the guy, because the girl had gone back over and was yelling at him through the open passenger window.'

'You hear what was being said?'

'I had my windows up, so not much. I didn't want to get in the middle of whatever beef they had going on. Only clear thing I heard was the guy saying, "*Don't you walk away from me.*"'

'Then what?'

'Then nothing.' Donald shrugs. 'Way she was dressed it was obvious she wasn't a burglar. I thought she was most likely . . .' He pauses and glances at Dorothy and the other ladies. Looks embarrassed. 'I thought she was a *professional*, you know what I mean? So I drove on.'

Dorothy frowns. 'You don't need to speak in hushed tones around me. You might be one of the young ones around here, but I was young once and I'm not easily spooked. A man getting some sugar from a prostitute, well that's hardly the first time I've heard something like that.'

Philip smiles. He likes Dorothy; she's got grit.

Donald shifts in his seat. 'Yes, ma'am, and, well, I thought that if they were in their car rather than their house maybe they were trying to keep it a secret from—'

'Their wife,' says Dorothy, raising her eyebrows. 'How very discreet of you.'

Rick leans across the table towards Donald. 'You get the colour and plate of this station wagon?'

'It was a light colour, hard to tell exactly in the dark, but I'd say beige. I noted down the plate, let me check my book.'

As Donald flicks through his notepad, Clint at the other end of the table raises his hand.

'You got something to say, Clint?' says Rick.

Clint takes his Dodgers baseball cap off and sets it on the table. Rubs his forehead. 'I was patrolling quadrant three last night and I seen an old beige station wagon with a Bulls sticker, it was parked up over at the head of the Wild Ridge Trail.'

Rick catches Philip's gaze. Philip gives him a small nod. They're both feeling it. This could be a solid lead on the girl, maybe also on the killer.

'What time?' asks Philip.

'I saw it on a couple of my rounds. Must have been around one o'clock the first time, then again at about two. I'll check my book when I get home and confirm.'

'You see who was inside?' says Rick.

Clint shakes his head. 'No, sir, the vehicle was empty, both times.'

Interesting, thinks Philip. Two sightings of the beige station wagon within the week, and one that puts last night's murder victim with the driver. The head of Wild Ridge Trail isn't far from Manatee Park. The guy could easily have parked there, taken the trail part way and then looped back to the park and killed the young woman.

'I got the plate here,' says Donald.

'Shoot,' says Rick.

'6JB7892 on a Maryland plate.'

'Is that right?' says Rick. He looks at Philip, his expression dead serious.

Philip gets what Rick's thinking. That their potential murder suspect isn't a resident, but someone who shouldn't be able to access their neighbourhood and their homes easily – someone who should have been tracked from the moment they entered through one of the security-manned gatehouses and flagged if they overstayed.

An outsider.

9

MOIRA

As Lizzie opens the door, Moira's struck by how different their homes are. She'd been too dizzy and nauseous to notice earlier, but now the contrast is striking. Not so much on the outside; they both own the same mid-range model – a Country Classic – one of the eight variations of home you can buy in the Ocean Mist district of The Homestead. But inside the feel is totally different. Whereas her own space is still cluttered with half-unpacked boxes and make-do furniture, Lizzie and Philip's place is classically stylish and spotless.

Lizzie is like that too, thinks Moira. She admires her easy elegance: the flowing green maxi dress she's now wearing, and the way her long white-blonde hair is twisted into a bun held in place with a paintbrush.

'Come in, come in,' says Lizzie, beckoning her inside. 'Were your dogs okay? I hope they didn't mind you'd been away longer than usual? My daughter, Elsa, the middle one, she's got this cute little cockerpoo but it gets really stressed if she goes out for more than an hour or so and barks the place down.'

'They're fine, thanks,' says Moira, turning back to glance along the street one last time. The anxiety is still there, twisting an ever-tighter knot in her stomach, the question repeating in her mind over and over: *Am I being followed?*

She holds her breath. Checks twice to be sure. Then, satisfied there's no sign of the silver Beetle or the wiry blond guy from earlier, she steps into the hallway.

Lizzie closes the door behind her and Moira's anxiety morphs into something else. She feels suddenly claustrophobic, like she's just been caged. Because as Lizzie turns back towards her, Moira sees that although her dress looks carefree, there's something else going on in Lizzie's body language – there's tension in her shoulders, rigidity in her jaw, and her hands are clasped together in front of her stomach as if trying to protect herself. The smile she's giving Moira doesn't seem to reach all the way to her eyes.

'Are Philip and Rick back yet?' asks Moira, trying to keep her tone light when in truth she feels anything but. She glances towards the window; sees no sign of the silver Beetle or the blond guy. Swallows hard as the knot in her stomach tightens. She can hear a radio playing somewhere in an upstairs room, but other than that the house seems silent.

'No, not yet.' Lizzie shakes her head. 'I'm not sure when they'll be back. Let's go through to the kitchen.'

Moira follows Lizzie towards the kitchen. She's on her guard, already anxious from the guy watching her; now Lizzie acting strange is making it worse. It feels like this could be some kind of trap. Does Lizzie know something? Has she asked an ex-colleague about her already? Is the real reason she's been asked here to confront Moira about the truth of who she is?

I should attempt small talk, Moira thinks, *to try and make the situation feel more normal.* She looks at the photos on the hallway walls. Tries to concentrate. They're family group shots of Lizzie, Philip and four children – three girls and one boy – at various ages; holiday snaps in front of a caravan, inside a tent, on the steps of a Cotswold stone house, at Disneyland. There are graduation photos too for three of the children, and wedding pictures for two. 'Do your kids still live in the UK?'

'Three of them do,' says Lizzie. 'Jennifer, our youngest, travels a lot for work. She's in Australia at the moment. They come out here and visit when they can, but it's not the same as having them down the road.'

Moira hears a tinge of sadness in Lizzie's voice mixed with a slight tremble, and sees that she's twisting the rings on her wedding finger around – a trio of diamonds on the engagement ring, a plain gold band, and a third diamond-studded band. So much for her attempt at small talk – all she's succeeded in doing is upping the angst level. She silently curses her blunder and makes a mental note to stick to the weather. There have to be fewer pitfalls in that conversation, surely.

They reach the kitchen.

'Let's get some coffee and then we can sit outside, the weather's glorious.' Lizzie's smile is over-bright, her eyes shiny. Blinking, she cocks her head to the side. 'And how about something to eat, a sandwich, to tide you over until the boys get back and I make us all a meal?'

'Just coffee, thanks.' Moira tries to keep the suspicion from her voice. Lizzie's messages made it sound like Philip and Rick were due home any moment, and that's why she needed Moira to come here. 'You said you needed my help, but if the guys aren't back yet then . . .'

'I wanted you to come over early so we could talk.' Lizzie's expression is serious.

Moira braces herself. 'Okay.'

'But let's get the coffee first.'

As Lizzie makes the coffee, it feels to Moira like every second lasts an hour. She wants to know what's bugging Lizzie, and what she knows. She hates the suspense. Needs to think about mitigation and containment. She needs to find out if Lizzie knows her secret, and if she's going to tell other people. She has to know whether things are going to get so out of control she'll have no choice but to move again.

Still, she tries to act casual. Leaning against the island unit, she looks around. She hadn't really taken in her surroundings when she was here earlier, and now she's struck by how neat and ordered everything is. The white countertops are clear of clutter with just the coffee maker, toaster and a jug with spatulas beside the hob. The island unit has a spotted china bowl with apples and bananas at one end, and on the window sill behind the sink a vase of flowers – vivid purples, pinks and greens – is giving a splash of colour against the white cabinets, countertops and flooring. The whole thing is a far cry from her own scattergun approach to decor. She doesn't even own a fruit bowl.

As the coffee brews, Lizzie unlocks the sliding door to the sun-room – an outside space screened by permanent rigid bug mesh. Then she turns to Moira and beckons her outside. 'Have a seat, I'll be with you in a minute.'

Moira does as she says, stepping out on to the patio and taking the seat at the outdoor table that gives her the best vantage point across the garden. She scans the space – there's no sign of the blond guy in the garden or on the street immediately alongside it. Moira takes a deep breath. She feels slightly calmer out here where she can see her options for an easy exit. The outside is as stylish as the inside: white wicker garden furniture with generously padded seat cushions, the spotlessly clean plunge pool and hot tub and the neatly manicured lawn. Bright Moroccan-style lamps in turquoise, orange and purple give vivid splashes of jewel-like colour against the white furniture and natural greens. There's a side gate at the end of the path that runs down the side of the house, and another on the far side of the screened-in patio; two exits that could get her free and clear fast if needs be.

Moira thinks of the rampaging plants in the unruly borders of her own garden, and the lawn that's almost long enough to break the residents' association rules, and resolves to take them in hand. She looks up as Lizzie approaches. Tries to get her onside with a compliment. 'Your garden is lovely, the house is too.'

Lizzie smiles but it looks tight and forced. 'Thanks. Nothing to do with me though, Philip's the house-proud one. He loves doing all the home-design stuff. Likes everything to be perfect.'

'That's cool,' says Moira, trying to keep the surprise from her voice. She'd never have pegged Philip as the designer of the couple. He seems far too stuffy and traditional to have created this outside space.

Lizzie hands Moira a mug of coffee, then puts some cookies on a plate on to the table and pushes them in front of her. 'They're oatmeal and raisin – the best cookies ever. If you won't have a sandwich, at least eat some of these.'

Moira doesn't feel hungry but, given how tense Lizzie looks, she takes a cookie to show willing. 'Thanks, this is great.'

Lizzie sits down on to the chair opposite. She looks at Moira and frowns. 'So how are you feeling? I know you said you were okay, but it must have been a shock to find the body.'

Moira isn't sure how to respond so she says nothing. Maybe Lizzie is saying this as a test – she's found out what she used to do for a living, and what happened in London, and she wants to see if Moira will mention it. *I'm not falling for that*, thinks Moira. She takes a sip of her coffee.

'It's unsettled me, if I'm honest,' says Lizzie, filling the silence. 'I know I should be hardened to this stuff from the years doing my job, but a murder happening right here in my neighbourhood . . .'

She shakes her head. Fiddles with the rings on her wedding finger again. 'It makes me feel really uneasy.'

'That's understandable,' says Moira, cautiously. 'But I'm new here, and not long out of the job.'

Lizzie bites her lower lip and holds Moira's gaze for a long moment.

That's when Moira realises she's messed up. *Shit.* Why did she mention her job? *This is it*, she thinks. *This is the moment Lizzie tells me that she knows what I used to be and what happened, why I left, and who I really am.*

But Lizzie says nothing. She just sits, holding eye contact and tracing her finger up and down the handle of her mug.

Moira's heart rate accelerates. She can't stand waiting. If what Lizzie is about to reveal is going to shatter her blank slate, she'd rather get it over with so she can get on with picking up the pieces and trying to glue them back together. 'You said you wanted to talk?'

'Yes.' Lizzie slams her mug down on to the table with a bang that makes both of them flinch. She clasps her hands together in a death grip. 'I do.'

'So . . . what's the matter?' says Moira, trying to keep the anxiety from her voice.

'Look, there's no easy way to say this.' Lizzie looks away across the patio towards the pool. 'But what you did . . . it was . . .'

Moira waits for Lizzie to continue. It feels as if her heart is going to punch its way out of her chest. She grips on to the arm of the wicker chair. Swallows hard.

'What you did to me.' Lizzie shakes her head. Hugs herself. 'It was really . . . it really . . .' She glares at Moira. 'It was really out of order.'

Moira's confused. Doesn't get what Lizzie's talking about. Lizzie wasn't in London. She didn't even work for the MET. How could she have been affected by what happened with McCord? She tries to keep her tone level. 'What I did? I don't understand—'

'How dare you.' Lizzie raises her voice. Points her finger at Moira in a stabbing motion. 'Don't you sit there acting all innocent and like you don't know.'

'But I—'

'You ghosted me, Moira, that's what they call it, isn't it? When someone acts all friendly and then disappears?' Lizzie's voice keeps rising in volume and pitch. Her cheeks flush. 'You came to a few yoga classes, acted like we were pals. We had coffee, and I thought we'd got on well and might become good friends.' Lizzie shakes her head. The pink flush across her cheeks deepens and her eyes start looking watery, then she tilts her chin up and Moira can see there's anger behind the tears. 'But then you just disappeared.'

'I didn't mean—'

Lizzie waves her hands. 'No, don't you do that. You played me like a fool. The least you can do is own up to it. That one time when we bumped into each other in the grocery store, you virtually ran away. I felt like a complete idiot. I realised you didn't want to see me, for whatever reason, and it made me feel like crap.'

As Lizzie draws breath, Moira sees her chance to get a word in. 'I'm sorry that you—'

'But I'm not finished yet,' snaps Lizzie, holding her hand up to silence Moira. 'After all this, today you show up on my doorstep with my husband like you're best pals and . . .' She looks into Moira's eyes. Narrows her gaze. 'I want you to tell me exactly what's going on between the two of you.'

Moira takes a breath. It's good news, she tells herself. Lizzie doesn't know her secret; this isn't about her job, or London, or McCord. It's not about the *problem*. But even though she's relieved that Lizzie isn't about to expose her for what she really is, she feels bad. She hadn't expected Lizzie to be feeling like this. They'd only met a couple of times. They hadn't been friends; were barely acquaintances. She'd never imagined her not staying in touch would hurt Lizzie. 'You think me and Philip might have a thing?'

'You tell me.' It's clear from Lizzie's expression that she does think that.

Moira shakes her head. 'No. Absolutely no way. I don't do married men. In fact these days I don't want to do anyone. I'm happy on my own.'

'Really?' Lizzie's tone makes it clear she doesn't believe her.

'Look, Philip saw me when I was in the ambulance outside the crime scene and came to see if I was okay. I didn't have a car with me so he offered me a lift, then when he realised I was feeling rather peculiar he said to come back here.'

Lizzie shakes her head. 'Yeah, right, I saw the way you were all over each other—'

'That's ridiculous. He was propping me up by my arm because I was dizzy. There wasn't anything going on.'

'I'm being ridiculous?' Lizzie's voice is louder again. She stabs her finger at Moira's face. 'You're messing around with my husband and *I'm* the one being ridiculous?'

Moira jumps to her feet. Ignores the nausea that comes from the sudden movement. 'I'm not doing this. I've told you, nothing's going on. If you won't believe me, then that's up to you, but I'm not staying here to be insulted.'

'So if there's nothing going on between you, why did you suddenly drop me?'

'I . . . I'm just . . .' Shaking her head, Moira turns and rushes along the stone path towards the gate at the front of the garden. She can't stay here. There's no reasoning with Lizzie, and it's not like she can tell her the truth anyway.

Grabbing the gate, she yanks it open and hurries out on to the pavement, letting the gate slam behind her. That's when she sees him.

Her mouth goes dry. Her heart rate accelerates. 'What the . . . ?'

The blond man is already sprinting away from her, his maroon and gold striped scarf flapping as he runs.

'Hey,' yells Moira. 'You get back here.'

He glances over his shoulder but keeps running. Moira sets off after him.

She sees the silver Beetle is parked at the side of the street a little way ahead, and knows that's where he's heading. She has to stop him. She needs to know who he is and why he's following her.

Moira sprints faster, but she's too late. He reaches the silver Beetle and jumps inside. As she draws level with the car Moira hears the engine roar into life.

She bangs her fist on the driver's side window. 'Who the hell are you?'

The blond guy turns towards her. His eyes are wide, fearful.

'What do you want from me?' Moira yells, banging on the glass again. She pulls at the door handle, trying to open the door, but it's locked from the inside. 'Tell me what you want. Tell me why you're following me. Tell me who you are.'

The guy stamps on the gas and the Beetle lurches forward.

Moira manages to smack her palm against the window once more before the car is out of reach. She runs after it, but it's a losing game and she knows it. In seconds the car is gone and Moira's left standing in the middle of the street.

There's no doubt in her mind now. Whoever the blond guy is, he's definitely following her. The question is, why?

10

MOIRA

Moira swears under her breath. It's infuriating. Concerning too. She's seen the blond guy three times now, and every time he's got away.

'Who was that?'

Moira turns and is surprised to see Lizzie standing a couple of feet behind her. Moira shakes her head. 'I don't know, but I saw him near the entrance to Manatee Park earlier, and then he was hanging around outside my house before I came here.'

'So he's following you?' Lizzie says, frowning.

'Yeah, I think so,' says Moira.

Lizzie bites her lip. Looks conflicted. Then gestures towards the house. 'You'd better come back inside.'

Moira stays put and says nothing. She doesn't want another argument.

'Look, who knows who that guy is? He could be connected to the murder,' says Lizzie. When Moira still doesn't move, Lizzie shrugs. 'Okay, fine, suit yourself.'

Moira watches Lizzie start walking back towards the house. Thinks of how upset Lizzie was just a few minutes earlier. Knows she could just walk away, but it'd be better – kinder – to try to fix things. 'Okay, Lizzie, wait up.'

They go back through the garden gate and along the path-way to the patio. As they reach the table and chairs, Lizzie turns to Moira. 'You should call that detective and tell him that man's stalking you.'

Moira's been thinking the same thing. 'I will, but first . . . Look, I know you don't believe me, but before today the only time I'd met Philip was in the supermarket when I saw you both together.' Moira shakes her head. 'He isn't the reason I didn't go back to yoga to meet up with you as planned.'

Lizzie frowns. 'Why, then?'

Moira sits down. She knows she needs to give Lizzie enough to convince her she's telling the truth, but not so much that she reveals too much about herself. Lizzie and Philip might be nice enough, but they're still dangerous. She can't drop her guard about her life before, but what's happened since she arrived here at The Homestead is safe ground. 'If I'm honest, I was having a bit of a tough time, settling in. This place is lovely but it's pretty full-on. I hadn't realised it would be like that when I moved here. I found things rather overwhelming so I guess I retreated a bit. I couldn't face showing up and doing a class. I needed a bit of time to be on my own, to get my bearings and adjust to this place.'

'And do you think you're adjusted now?'

'I was getting there.'

'Until you found the body this morning?'

'Yes.'

'So that's why you were reluctant to come back round when I texted earlier?'

What's one more lie, thinks Moira. 'Yes, that's why.'

Lizzie's silent for a moment. Thinking. Then she nods. 'I get it – the need to take a bit of time to get settled in. Life out here is very different to being in the UK. It can be a bit of a shock, especially if you'd not visited much before you moved. I've spoken to

61

a few other Brits out here who've gone through feeling that, so I guess I do understand.'

'Thanks,' says Moira.

They sit for a moment in silence. The awkwardness remains, but at least the shouting has stopped. Moira isn't convinced Lizzie truly believes her about Philip, but it's a start. Still, Moira knows the risks are just as high. She can't cut Lizzie out of her life. If she does, she might ignite the suspicions about her and Philip, and there's a chance that'll encourage Lizzie to try and find out more about her, and Moira doesn't want that. She'll have to keep Lizzie and Philip close. That way, maybe they won't get curious. Right now, it seems the best play open to her.

Lizzie clears her throat. 'You know, I wanted to live here because of the zero crime rate. But with the burglaries and now a murder it feels like we're not safe any more.'

'Sure.' Moira doesn't want to challenge Lizzie straight after the conversation they've just had – it feels like she needs to build their relationship up more before that – but she thinks Lizzie's fooling herself. Nowhere is safe and a world with zero crime is a fantasy nirvana. Humans are hardwired to hurt each other.

Lizzie sighs. 'I really wanted a rest from it all. The job was so all-consuming – all the pressure, and the long hours. Before he retired Philip seemed to have been suffering from fatigue for years, and I'm pretty sure the job was making it worse, although he refused to see that.' She pauses, and seems to be looking to Moira for assurance, or understanding, or something.

Moira nods, but there's something about the way Lizzie winced as she talked about Philip having a blind spot on the impact the job was having on his health that makes her think there's more to the story than Lizzie's letting on. 'And you were happy to leave your job when he retired?'

'I know I'm a bit younger, and had been a CSI for less time but, if I'm honest, I'd had enough.' Lizzie shakes her head. 'You see enough bad things, soon it's hard to see the good in people. I didn't want that to happen to me.'

'What made you choose Florida?'

Lizzie smiles. 'Philip's always loved Disney. Funny I know, such a serious job and yet you take him to the parks and he's like a little kid. We used to bring the children here every few years when they were growing up – it has such happy memories for us.'

'I get that,' says Moira. She'd learnt the hard way that if your work is all death and destruction you need a release – something that pulls you out of the carnage you see every day and into a more light-hearted place. She thinks of McCord, and the last conversation they'd had. Swallows down the emotions that immediately flare within her – pain, anger, sadness. She knows better than anyone that you need respite to stop you getting sucked into the darkness permanently.

'When they told Philip he couldn't go back to work after the heart attack, it hit him hard. They gave him the big send-off – retirement party, commemorative gifts, the works, but that almost made it worse.' Lizzie starts fiddling with her rings again. 'It was like he was grieving for the job. So I booked a big holiday for us – we came to Florida as a family and stayed at Disney, my eldest daughter's little girls loved it. When the others flew home, Philip and I went on a mini-cruise around the Caribbean islands. Afterwards we stayed for a week at a lovely spa resort not far from here. We saw a flyer at the concierge desk for a wine-tasting event here on The Homestead, and decided to go along. When we came here we fell in love with the place.'

Moira's surprised Lizzie's revealing this stuff to her after their argument, but maybe the strong reaction from Lizzie about her not following up on their friendship was because she somehow, even in this place surrounded by people, feels a bit lonely. Maybe she saw Moira as a friend to talk to about how she's feeling, and that's why it hit her so hard. Moira understands loneliness, she's felt it herself often enough, and it isn't like she has many people back in London who'll be missing her. 'How did your kids take the move?'

Lizzie's eyes well up and she blinks rapidly. 'They understood, but not seeing our family is the hardest thing, especially when Covid started and people weren't allowed to travel. The UK seemed a really long way away then. But they come and visit when they can, and we've gone back to see them a few times, so it's been manageable. And it's been worth it, to live here – away from crime, with all the golf Philip can play, and the crafts and activities on our doorstep. It's like a permanent holiday – or at least it was . . .' Lizzie chokes up. She looks down at her coffee. Takes a sip. 'I just really hope the community-watch patrollers have something to help the cops find whoever did this. Then things can go back to the way they were.'

'I guess once the guys are back we'll find out,' says Moira, gently. Lizzie's being naive if she thinks this won't change the neighbourhood. Murder changes everything; it always does. But the way Lizzie is looking at her – that mixture of hope and desperation – makes her hold her tongue. Sometimes you need a little hope to get you through.

Collecting up their mugs, Lizzie pushes her chair back and stands. 'I'll get us some refills while we wait.'

Sitting alone, Moira listens to Lizzie humming to herself as she pours more coffee. She's relieved Lizzie seems more relaxed and the awkwardness between them is lessening now she's got her concerns off her chest, but there's something that doesn't quite ring true. Lizzie's naivety about the murder seems strange in a person who's worked crime scenes before, and there's something about the way she looked when she was talking about Philip's retirement; it was as if just thinking about that time made her feel anxious again. There's something else going on with Lizzie and Philip, Moira's sure of it. She just isn't sure what.

But if there's one thing she learnt from her job undercover, it's that people aren't always what they seem. And Moira knows that better than most.

She certainly isn't.

11

PHILIP

As Rick pulls out of the Roadhouse parking lot on to Sea Spray Boulevard, Philip dials the police precinct and asks for Detective Golding. The tedious, tinny hold music blares through the phone speaker for almost five minutes before the call handler comes back on the line to say she's connecting him.

It rings nine times before a gruff voice answers. 'This is Golding.'

'Detective Golding, this is Philip Sweetman from Ocean Mist. I'm calling about the murder.'

'Ocean Mist?' Golding sounds bored rather than eager.

'It's a district of The Homestead retirement community. You caught a suspected homicide here this morning – a young woman found in one of our swimming pools.'

'Ah yeah, the compound for seniors. You work there?'

'I'm a resident.'

'You live there?' Golding's tone changes from bored to patronising. 'Well, sure, go ahead. I'm listening.'

Philip bristles. He glances at Rick who raises an eyebrow. This isn't how he'd expect a detective in the early stage of an investigation to treat someone offering information – interest, yes; suspicion, perhaps; but not the condescending indifference that's clear in

Golding's voice. Philip ploughs on anyway. 'I've asked around the neighbourhood and have a sighting of the victim arguing with an unidentified male in a beige station wagon earlier this week. In fact, two people mentioned seeing an unfamiliar beige station wagon with a Chicago Bulls bumper sticker around the Wild Ridge Trail head, and that's not far from Manatee Recreation Park.'

'How'd you know the person driving this vehicle was with the victim – you know her?'

'I've never met her, but a friend of mine found the body this morning and described the victim. I wanted to—'

'Your friend is this . . .' There's the sound of papers being shuffled. 'Moira Flynn?'

'Yes, that's correct.'

'All right, so how can I help you?' Golding's tone makes it clear he'd rather do anything but.

'You can help me by listening to what I have to say.' Philip tightens his grip on the phone. It's like Golding doesn't even want the information. Like he's doing Philip a favour by being on the call. 'Shall I tell you the plate of the vehicle?'

'Sure, go ahead.'

'It's from Maryland – 6JB7892.'

'And you saw all of those numbers real clear?'

Philip frowns. 'What are you implying?'

'Well, sir, eyesight is a funny thing, as you get older . . .'

'My eyesight, and that of the person who saw the victim and the car are perfectly fine.'

'So you didn't see the victim for yourself?'

'No, like I said, I asked around the neighbourhood to see if—'

'Sir, investigating is my job, not yours.'

Philip clenches his free fist. 'And what will *you* be doing about it?'

'There's no need to raise your voice. We're following some leads, got a few theories.' Golding's tone is the sort you'd use with a young and not very smart child. 'It's likely a mugging gone wrong, that's an angle we're working.'

Philip glances at Rick, who frowns. He turns into Rip Curl Drive, easing off the gas as he approaches Philip's house.

'Seems unlikely,' says Philip to Golding. 'Why would a mugger leave all the money?'

Golding's tone hardens. 'I'm not at liberty to discuss the details of the case any further. What's all this to you anyways?'

'I'm a concerned citizen and resident of Ocean Mist community. I want to do my public duty. I can come to the precinct now if that helps? Anything I can do to—'

'Look pal, the plate's interesting for sure, but I'm over time on the clock here. I've just finished up the paperwork, and I'm heading out. I'll be back on shift tonight, and I'll be sure to look into this then.'

'You're not going to check the plate until tonight? Don't you know that the first hours are when the case can be—'

'This is my investigation. I'll conduct it however I decide. With all due respect, Mr . . . erm . . . Sweetman, you need to stay out of police business and get back to your golf or pickleball or whatever it is you retired seniors do up there to pass the time in . . . Ocean Mist.'

Rick shakes his head and mouths, 'Don't engage.'

But Philip's had enough of Golding's tone. Anger flares in his chest. How dare the man write him off because of his age? He can't let it pass. Has to call it out. Can't stop himself. 'Shame on you, Detective Golding. I've called you to help and you're hardly even listening. What sort of a detective are you? I was a DCI in the UK. I know what proper police work is and I'm not seeing any of it from you. Men like you don't deserve to carry a badge. You're a disgrace to law—'

The phone goes dead. The connection severed.

Philip looks at Rick. 'The bastard hung up on me.'

Rick shakes his head again. 'I warned you, man.'

'Well, it's not bloody good enough. He's burying the case, and I don't understand why.' Philip throws open the jeep's door and climbs out, slamming it behind him. He meets Rick's gaze. 'I'm not going to let him get away with it.'

12

MOIRA

Lizzie comes back from the kitchen with more coffee. As she sets the mugs down on the table she says to Moira, 'Sorry about earlier, and to accuse you of—'

'It's totally fine,' says Moira. She gives her a reassuring smile, and it seems to work. There's still some tension between them, but it's less than earlier. Moira's not convinced Lizzie really trusts her, but she can live with that. As she watches Lizzie sit down opposite her, she wonders how Lizzie ever coped working as a CSI. She seems too fragile, too emotional and easily worried, to have worked crime scenes for years.

Lizzie takes a sip of coffee before meeting Moira's gaze. 'Anyway, enough about me. What made you decide to come and live here?'

Shit. I don't want to talk about this, thinks Moira. If she's going to build trust, she has to reveal something of herself, but it's not like she can tell Lizzie the real truth. She's stalling by taking a mouthful of coffee when she hears noise – footsteps and raised voices.

'What's that?' she asks.

'Sounds like Philip,' says Lizzie. 'I wonder if—'

Next moment they hear the click of the back gate being unbolted, and Rick and Philip come through the garden and let themselves into the sunroom.

Philip, red-faced and obviously mad as hell, brandishes his phone at them. 'You're not going to bloody well believe this.'

Lizzie looks worried. 'Honey, what's the—'

'The bastard's burying the case,' rants Philip as he takes a seat next to Lizzie. 'I called Golding with the intel we found and he treated me like some old doddering fool, like I'm a washed-up has-been, some old guy who's lost his marbles. He was so disrespectful. Utterly condescending, I—'

'He was an asshole,' says Rick. 'Didn't really listen. Just wanted Philip off the phone as soon as.'

Lizzie purses her lips. There's concern in her eyes.

Moira isn't surprised about Golding. 'That's the impression I got this morning – seemed like one of those guys who's just going through the motions until he can clock off.'

'Yep, one of those for sure.' Rick goes into the kitchen and pours two mugs of coffee. Returning, he takes a seat next to Moira and pushes one of the mugs towards Philip.

Philip ignores the coffee. He smacks his palm down on to the table making all the mugs wobble. 'It's not bloody good enough. Golding should have listened to me. I'm an experienced senior officer, a DCI for God's sake, with good information, useful stuff for his investigation, and he treated me like I'm a . . . like a—'

'Honey, take a breath.' Lizzie puts her hand on Philip's arm, lowers her voice. 'Remember what the doctor told you.'

Philip shakes his head vigorously. 'No, I don't have time. A woman died here, on my watch, and I need to make sure—'

'It wasn't your watch. You're not DCI of Ocean Mist.' Lizzie's voice is tougher now, no-nonsense.

Philip looks at Lizzie. Takes a breath. Says nothing.

Aside from the birdsong, everything is silent. Moira swallows hard as she watches the stand-off between Philip and Lizzie. Gone is the mild-mannered, anxious Lizzie of a few minutes ago. In her

71

place is a strong, assertive Lizzie – a less emotional version of the Lizzie who shouted at her earlier. This version of her Moira can easily see working a crime scene.

Rick catches Moira's gaze. His look is rueful – seeming to say they're both caught in the eye of the storm, and there's no easy way out until Lizzie and Philip have resolved this for themselves. Moira knows he's right. She's thinking the same.

'You're retired. You're not responsible for *this*,' repeats Lizzie. Her voice is still assertive but her expression is softer now, more understanding. Her fingers stroke his arm.

Philip still doesn't reply. As he reaches out to lift the coffee mug in front of him, Moira sees his hands are trembling.

She scans his face. There's conflict in Philip's expression. She's not sure what's going on here, but she guesses that as an ex-DCI, Philip's finding it hard to be a bystander in this murder – to not be the one in charge and instead be forced on to the sidelines.

Moira understands that. She also knows what it's like to feel responsible for something bad, something fatal. Her last operation starts to play out in her mind's eye and her breath catches in her throat. Feeling her heart rate accelerate, she clasps her fingers around her coffee mug tighter. Shakes her head to get rid of the memory. She can't think about that now, here. She can't think about what happened with McCord.

When she glances up she realises Rick is looking at her, frowning. She wonders what her expression looked like as the memory of McCord started playing. Nothing good, she imagines. And whatever it was, it seems Rick noticed. She gives him a little shrug, trying to make light of it. Turns her attention to Philip.

Philip's shoulders have slumped. He's still red-faced and sweat is beading across his forehead. He reaches into his pocket for a tissue and mops his brow. 'I know you're right, Lizzie, you're always right . . .'

'I just wanted you to stop raging. I couldn't bear for you to have another—'

'I understand that,' says Philip. He exhales hard. 'It's just I do feel like I should be taking charge here. Someone needs to make sure the case is run properly.'

Lizzie looks sad, disappointed. She twists her rings around her wedding finger.

Philip puts his hand over hers. 'I know you wanted us to have a quieter life in retirement, but this murder happened right on our doorstep. I can't just let it go.'

'You really need to,' Lizzie says. 'You shouldn't get involved.'

Philip sighs. He looks from Lizzie to Moira and Rick. 'I don't trust this Golding bloke. He just doesn't seem to care about this case.'

Moira puts her mug down on the table. 'I had the same feeling. And I think your experience with him just now has proved the point.'

'Yup,' says Rick. 'Like I said, he's an asshole.'

'The victim deserves better,' says Moira.

'Exactly,' says Philip.

Lizzie rotates her rings faster around her finger. 'But we can't force the cops here to run their investigation how we want them to.'

Rick runs his hand across his jaw. Shakes his head. 'I sure hate the thought that whoever killed that young woman could get away with it because the assigned detective half-asses the investigation.'

There are nods from the others. There's a new feeling in the group. Moira can hear it in their voices and see it in their expressions.

Lizzie frowns. 'So what are you saying?'

It's Philip who answers. His tone firm and determined. 'We're going to make sure things are done right. We'll investigate the murder ourselves.'

13

MOIRA

Moira can tell from Lizzie's body language that she doesn't agree. Her shoulders are raised and tense, and she's fiddling with her rings again. Moira shifts forward in her seat, leaning towards Lizzie. 'Are you okay?'

Lizzie shakes her head hard. 'It's wrong, saying we'll investigate. We shouldn't be doing it. We're retired.' She looks at Philip. 'We need to stay out of it.'

Philip takes her hand. 'We have to do this. I can't let this Detective Golding run some half-cocked investigation that goes nowhere.' He glances from Lizzie to Rick. 'We took an oath when we signed up in law enforcement. That doesn't end just because we retired.'

'It does,' says Lizzie. 'That's the whole point of retirement.'

Philip shakes his head. 'I can't stand by and do nothing.'

Lizzie watches him for a moment, frowning. 'But after what—'

'I *have* to do this.' His voice is loaded with emotion. He's stroking her hand. Eyes fixed on hers.

Moira feels awkward. Like she's intruding on a moment that should be private between Lizzie and Philip. Glancing at Rick, she sees his eyes are downcast, and guesses that he's feeling the same way too.

'I need you with me on this,' says Philip, his voice gentle. 'We all do.'

A few seconds pass before Lizzie speaks. 'Okay. I don't think this is the right thing to do, but I'll help you.' She looks across at Moira and Rick. 'I'll help all of you.'

Moira feels uneasy. She hasn't agreed to investigate the murder with them, and they haven't thought to ask her. She's also concerned about Lizzie's reaction. Is she worried that Philip investigating could cause him another heart attack or is there something else going on? Their body language is tense and with the intense stares and long silences there's something unspoken happening here. It bothers Moira that she doesn't know what it is. You need to be able to trust the people in your life, or at least predict their actions and reactions.

Moira almost laughs out loud at the thought. Who is she kidding? After what happened with McCord she should have learnt you can never trust or predict what people do. No matter how well you think you know them, they're always capable of screwing you over.

Rick breaks the uneasy silence by clearing his throat. He leans forward, elbows on the table. 'So what's our first move?'

'We need to take stock of everything we know so far,' says Philip. Getting up, he disappears into the kitchen. Moira hears drawers being opened and closed.

Philip returns with a marker pen. He pulls the sliding patio door partially across behind him and looks at the group. 'So what do we know?'

Moira clears her throat. Knows she can't sound too much like she knows what she's doing. Tries to inject a note of uncertainty into her voice. 'She was in her twenties most likely, white, about five foot five and slim build. The cops didn't find an ID when I was there. I made the 911 call at 7.14 am, so I found her maybe a minute earlier.'

'Okay, so we've got a Jane Doe,' says Philip. He looks at Moira. 'On the force, that's what we call a female who hasn't yet been identified.'

Moira bites her lip. Doesn't reply in case she says something she regrets.

Oblivious, Philip writes 'Jane Doe' on the glass of the patio doors, creating a make-do murder board. He puts today's date and the time Moira found the body beside it. 'What else?'

Moira glances at Lizzie. There's an earnest expression on her face, but she seems unbothered by her husband defacing their patio door. Moira looks back to Philip. 'The money. When I found her in the pool she was surrounded by what looked like thousands of dollars. And there was a black bag, possibly a rucksack, on the bottom of the pool – so whatever was in there was heavy.'

'Good,' says Philip, making bullet points of what she's told him beneath the name 'Jane Doe'. 'Anything else?'

Rick nods. 'We know she was seen alive earlier in the week, arguing with the driver of a beige station wagon. The vehicle had a Maryland plate, number 6JB7892, and a Chicago Bulls bumper sticker.'

'Yes,' says Philip, drawing a line from 'Jane Doe' to a question mark and the words 'Driver Beige Station Wagon'. He bullet points the information about the sightings. 'We know Donald and Clint both saw the vehicle on different occasions within the last week.'

'Yep, that's right,' says Rick. 'At the watch meeting earlier, Donald said he'd seen the vehicle early in the week on Seahorse Drive. He witnessed the argument with a woman he thinks was our vic, but he didn't get a look at the person inside. Clint said he saw the vehicle last night on his patrols. From memory he thought it was there at one o'clock and also around two, but he was going to double-check his log notes. Both times the vehicle was parked up at the head of the Wild Ridge Trail.'

Philip scribbles the points below the 'Driver Beige Station Wagon' heading.

'The start of the Wild Ridge Trail isn't far from Manatee Park,' says Moira. She glances at Lizzie who seems to be staring over her shoulder, into space. Tilting her head, she focuses on Lizzie until she notices and gives a little nod. Moira looks back at Philip. 'The driver could have used the trail to get around the back into the park to avoid being seen by any street CCTV cameras.'

'We need to know where the cameras are,' says Rick. 'Surely there are some inside the park?'

'There must be.' Lizzie's nodding. It's the first time she's got involved in the discussion about the murder. At first her voice is hesitant, but it grows in strength as she warms to her theme. 'And we need to get exact confirmation of the times Clint and Donald saw the vehicle.'

'We do,' says Philip. He runs his hand over his bald pate, smoothing an imaginary strand of hair back into place. 'We need everything our patrols have seen over the past few weeks. Someone else might have seen something but not remembered it.'

'Agreed,' says Rick. 'I'll get the logs off the patrollers.'

'And we need to get a look at the gate register – a Maryland plate means the driver is most likely an outsider. Anyone coming into the neighbourhood has to sign in at the gate. There should be a record of them arriving and leaving.'

'Good thinking. And we need to get the details on whoever drives the station wagon too,' says Philip. He takes a couple of steps sideways and starts a new list. Writes 'Action Log' at the top, then numbers the actions – first is the community-watch logs, second is the gate register, third is checking the driver ID of the station wagon, fourth is trying to access the CCTV. Turning back towards the group, he asks, 'What else?'

'We need to know who the man following Moira is,' says Lizzie.

Damn. Moira turns to look at Lizzie. She hadn't wanted to bring up the blond guy; she was going to handle that herself. 'It might not be connected.'

'What guy?' asks Rick, frowning. 'Is someone stalking you? That's a real problem, we should—'

'I don't know for sure,' says Moira. 'He was near Manatee Park this morning, parked across the street from Philip, and as I was getting into Philip's car he took a picture of me. Then, when I was out in the garden with the dogs, he was watching me, and—'

'He was here too. Outside the gate on to the street,' says Lizzie. 'Moira chased him but he jumped into a silver Beetle and drove away.'

Rick looks thoughtful. 'Sounds like you've got a stalker to me.'

'And if he was outside the crime scene this morning, he could be connected to the murder. He could have seen something,' says Philip, making a note on the glass.

'Or be the killer,' says Lizzie.

Moira holds up her hands. 'Or he could be nothing to do with it. He could be following me for some other reason.'

'Like what?' asks Lizzie.

Moira shrugs. Tells another lie: 'I don't know.'

Rick shakes his head. 'Well, that doesn't make it any less concerning.'

True, thinks Moira. But she doesn't want to dwell on it. Instead she tries to distract them. 'Where are the cops with the investigation?'

Philip shakes his head. 'Bloody nowhere.'

'Golding said they're working a few angles,' says Rick. 'Seems the one they're running with is that it was a mugging gone wrong.'

Moira rubs her forehead. She's trying to limit her input – doesn't want them to think she's anything more than a concerned citizen playing amateur sleuth – but it's hard to hold back. 'That makes no sense. If it was, why did the mugger leave the money and whatever was in the bag?'

'I said before to Philip, maybe they can't swim?' says Lizzie. She looks from the murder board to Moira. 'Can you message me those pictures you took at the crime scene, so I can look at them on my iPad?'

'Sure.' Taking out her phone, Moira selects all the crime-scene photos and sends them to Lizzie. 'Should be with you now.'

As Philip writes 'non-swimmer?' as a query on the patio door make-do murder board, Lizzie hurries into the kitchen and collects an iPad from a docking station on one of the counters. She taps on the screen as she walks back to the patio. 'Got them.'

Sitting down again, Lizzie focuses on the iPad screen, flicking through the pictures.

Moira looks back at Rick and Philip. 'Manatee Park seems a weird place for a mugging. It shuts at, what, ten in the evening? No one goes there after that. If two or more people met up there last night it had to be prearranged rather than by chance.'

'Yeah.' Rick's nodding. 'So she knew her killer?'

'I'd say so,' says Moira. She glances at Lizzie, but she doesn't look up. Instead she stays silent, studying the pictures. It's good she's getting involved now, but Moira still wonders what the stand-off between her and Philip was about.

'It's sloppy,' says Philip, jotting 'killer known to victim' on to the patio door. 'I reckon they're only thinking of the mugging angle because of the money.'

'Could be,' says Rick. 'But it raises the question why was she carrying that much cash anyways? Everything here is on account.'

'She's too young to be a resident, so she wouldn't have an account,' Moira says. 'Maybe she worked around here somewhere.'

'True,' says Rick. 'Or could be it's connected to the burglaries?'

'Maybe, but there's no way to tell right now,' says Philip. 'No one's reported that much cash going missing.'

Philip adds 'burglary connection?' to the query list on the patio door.

'From what Donald and Clint said, we know she'd been in Ocean Mist before,' says Rick. 'And we know she was meeting up with at least one other person here.'

Moira frowns. She doesn't think the mugging angle has any legs. All that cash, and a spate of burglaries over the past month, seem too coincidental to be unrelated. 'Could be their meetings took place on the same nights as the burglaries, that'd be something.'

'It sure would,' says Rick. 'We can check back through the patrol logs for more sightings of this woman and the station wagon. Folks might have forgotten if it was a few weeks back and—'

'We need to know who owns that vehicle too,' says Philip, tapping the end of the marker pen against the glass beside action three on the murder-board action list. 'That's got to be a priority, and if they're—'

'Shit, this is all wrong,' says Lizzie. There's concern in her voice and a troubled expression on her face.

'What is?' asks Moira, leaning across the table and trying to see what Lizzie is looking at.

'These photos.' Lizzie taps her finger on the iPad screen, enlarging the close-up picture of the young woman in the pool. 'This crime scene, it makes absolutely no sense.'

14

LIZZIE

'It makes no sense,' Lizzie says again, louder this time. Her voice is more urgent. Her tone is assertive, work-like; it's one she's not used since retirement and it feels alien inside her own mouth. But if Philip is determined they have to investigate this murder then she needs the others to take notice. This is important.

Moira's already giving her attention. Now Philip and Rick stop talking and look at her.

'What is it? Tell me,' says Philip.

In his expression, Lizzie sees that look she's not seen from him in a long time – professional respect and the need for her input. She used to get such a kick out of them working together – brainstorming ideas, analysing evidence, tracking investigation pathways. But now, ever since he was forced into retirement, it's the last thing she's wanted. Still, she does as he asks.

'From what I can see, I think this woman was shot. There's not much damage, so they probably used something low calibre, but by zooming in I can get a look at the blood pattern and the rough shape of the wound. It doesn't look consistent with stabbing.'

Philip frowns. 'So why's that—'

'If you're going to mug someone, you don't usually shoot them before you grab the money, do you?' says Moira. 'Especially if they might fall into a swimming pool and you can't swim.'

'True that,' says Rick. 'You'd get a hold of the money, the bag, and then fire to stop them fighting back.'

'Exactly, but that's not the story this scene is telling,' says Lizzie. Moira leans forward. 'What is it showing you?'

'Well, you mentioned the blood trail a minute ago, leading along the path?' Lizzie flicks through the pictures on the iPad to find the photo of the blood splatter on the patio stones. 'This shows that the victim didn't die immediately but was able to move towards the pool after she was shot.'

'Couldn't the killer have pushed or thrown her into the pool, rather than her going that way herself?' Moira asks.

Lizzie bites her lip as she considers the question. 'It's possible, but unlikely.' She gestures to the blood trail on the stones. 'See the drip pattern here, it's consistent from point A – here by the edge of the stone – to point B – at the pool edge – which tells me nothing, or no one, was inhibiting the splatter as she moved. If someone had pushed her, I'd expect some deviation. And if they'd carried or dragged her, the pattern wouldn't have been so uniform – it's hard not to interrupt flow, especially from a chest wound, if you're manhandling a full-size adult.'

'But if she was dying, why did she willingly go in the pool?' asks Moira. 'Surely she'd know that'd be risky?'

'If she knew her killer, could be she knew they couldn't swim and she thought she'd be safe in the water,' says Rick.

'Possibly,' says Lizzie. 'Although the bullet entry is in her chest, and that makes you think heart, it could have missed. With a small-calibre weapon the damage would have been bad but limited. It's possible the wound wasn't fatal, although of course she wouldn't necessarily have known that, and neither might the killer.

As I said, it looks like a low-calibre gun and, although it's hard to be sure from just a picture, I'd say the shot wounded her badly, but didn't kill her.'

'So she might have thought she was dying,' says Moira. 'And got in the pool to stop her attacker getting the bag and the money, if she thought they wouldn't follow her in?'

'Sure, could be,' says Rick. 'But why didn't the attacker stop her, and why didn't they grab the cash?'

Lizzie nods. 'Indeed.'

'Which brings us back to the killer potentially not being able to swim,' says Philip, underlining the words 'non-swimmer' that he's already noted on the list of killer characteristics on the patio door. Taking a couple of steps back, he writes 'Cause of death?' on the glass beneath the heading 'Jane Doe' and then looks back at Lizzie. 'If the bullet didn't kill her, then what did?'

Lizzie holds Philip's gaze for a moment, thinking. She sighs. 'She probably passed out from the pain or the blood loss and drowned.'

Moira frowns. 'But there wasn't much blood on the patio . . .'

'No, there wasn't, but if she entered the water fast after getting shot, most of the blood would have drained out into the pool and been absorbed by the chemicals in there.'

The group is silent for a moment as they stare at the make-do murder board.

Lizzie takes a sip of her now-cold coffee. In the quiet she hears the birds singing and the whine of a distant lawnmower. The sun is at full rise now, the heat is pushing an unseasonal 30°C, but none of that is in the front of her mind. She looks down at the iPad and the close-up of the dead woman on-screen. If you'd asked her half an hour ago how she felt about conducting an off-the-books murder investigation she'd have said she wanted to do anything but, and that she desperately wanted to stop Philip getting involved. But she had tried to stop it. Tried to reason and warn Philip not to do this, as best she could with the others here anyway, and it had made no difference. It's like he doesn't remember what happened; how he was made to retire. It's like he's forgotten why it was that he couldn't be a DCI any more.

She doesn't want them to do this investigation, but if Philip's doing it she needs to be with him, watching him; making sure nothing goes bad. She knows that Detective Golding's indifference and disrespect mean that Philip won't let this go now. And what's that saying? *If you can't beat 'em, join 'em.*

And now she's got involved, the anomalies in the crime scene, and the way they contradict the police's assumptions, have drawn her in. She wants to know the truth of what happened to this woman. Needs to crack the case. She thinks about what she told Moira earlier – about how she'd been ready to leave her job as a CSI and retire with Philip. About how she'd had enough of death. It was true, in part at least; she had been impacted by death. But it was one death in particular that made her want to leave – a death, a wrong, that can't ever be righted.

She looks at the crime-scene picture: the young woman, floating among thousands of dollar bills. Years have passed since Philip retired. Maybe she hasn't fully forgiven him, but she's learned to live with that. And things are different now; better, good even. Maybe it's time for her to use her skills again.

'So what's our next move?' asks Moira.

Lizzie looks up from the iPad and meets her gaze. 'I need to visit the crime scene.'

15

MOIRA

They watch the entrance to Manatee Recreation Park. Their vantage point is one of the benches outside Karlie's – a lemonade and frozen yoghurt hut a little way down the street from the park. They've been here for ages and Moira's starting to wonder if they'll get to see the crime scene today. She looks at her watch, then catches Lizzie's eye. 'It's gone half five.'

Lizzie glances along the street to the police cordon. There are still people milling around in the park. None are showing any sign of leaving. 'We've got an hour or so before the sun goes down. Let's give it a little longer.'

'Okay,' says Moira.

It's still hot out, and humid. Moira scans the area around them again, looking for the athletic blond man. There's no sign of him. Instead she watches as the older woman on the bench opposite feeds her little dog frozen yoghurt. He's a cute, fluffy kind of dog. Moira smiles as she watches him chasing the now-empty paper cup around, trying to get every last taste from it. She wishes she had some frozen yoghurt.

The dog's owner – a round-faced seventy-something lady with a mane of grey-flecked brown curls – looks up and notices her watching. She smiles back at Moira. 'He just loves the yoghurt here.'

'I can see that,' says Moira. 'Lucky pup.'

'He's worth it.' The woman ruffles the fur on her little dog's head, then glances towards the park entrance and police cordon. Her smile drops. 'Jeez it's just awful isn't it? I come here every day so that Teddy here can have his yoghurt and to think that someone died just inside the park there, I . . .' She clutches her hand to her chest. 'It just doesn't bear thinking about.'

Moira nods. Philip said earlier that word travels fast in a community like this. It'd be useful to know what's being said. 'Do you know what happened?'

'I heard it was some kind of accident. My friend, Imani, told me that's what they'd said when she'd called the security hut around lunchtime to ask why the police were cordoning off the park.' She leans closer towards Moira, and lowers her voice. 'But then this afternoon, Donna, who lives a little ways along my street, said she'd heard from someone at the golf club that it was a murder, that the victim was all cut up and . . . and I just . . .' The woman blinks rapidly. Dabs at her eyes with a tissue. 'It's all so terrible. Things like that, they just don't happen here.'

The woman's obviously shaken. Moira knows the truth won't help. 'Whatever happened, I'm sure the police have it under control.'

'Do you think? I sure hope so. I just don't know how I'll sleep tonight.' The woman picks up Teddy the dog and hugs him to her. 'I'm a light sleeper usually and every noise makes me wake up, and now this . . .' She grimaces, hugging Teddy closer. 'How do we know any of us are safe? If it wasn't an accident, for all we know the murderer could be watching us. What do I do if . . .'

'Just make sure you double-lock your doors tonight,' says Lizzie. 'And have your cell phone next to your bed. If you're worried about anything, call security or alert the community-watch patrol.'

The lady's eyes widen. 'So you do think it was murder and not an accident?'

Lizzie glances at Moira.

'We don't know,' says Moira. 'But if we let the police do their job, I'm sure they'll find the answer.'

The woman shakes her head. 'It just doesn't seem right something like that happening here. This is a safe place – a happy place. Someone dying in the park – it's not right at all.'

Moira says nothing. The woman really seems to believe the hype of The Homestead marketing – that it's a perfect neighbourhood and that somehow it's immune to crime. It's a naive view, but then maybe it's not an uncommon belief here. After all, earlier Lizzie had said something fairly similar – as if saying bad things never happen could somehow make it true. Moira knows better though. Bad things happen everywhere. Everywhere there are people, anyway.

Putting Teddy back on the ground, the woman gathers up the frozen-yoghurt carton and puts it in the trash. She turns back to Moira and Lizzie and gives them a little wave, then glances towards the park. 'Stay safe.'

'You too,' says Moira.

They're alone on the benches now. Moira watches as the server inside Karlie's yoghurt hut rolls down the serving hatch. Afternoon is giving way to evening. She looks over at Lizzie. Raises an eyebrow.

'Let's give it ten more minutes,' says Lizzie.

'Okay.'

Finally, just before the ten minutes is up, as the sun is starting to sink lower in the sky and Moira's beginning to think that they won't get the chance to get into the park today, the cops and CSIs start to pack up. Moira and Lizzie stay seated as the CSIs load their gear into the van. Only when they've fired up the engine and headed out do they start to move.

Lizzie knocks back the last of her drink. They've been nursing takeaway cups of fresh lemonade for well over an hour and the dregs must be warm because she grimaces when she swallows. Moira decides to give hers a miss. Taking Lizzie's cup, she fits it inside hers and puts them both in the bin.

She glances back towards the park. A single strand of yellow police tape remains across the entrance, but there's no one standing sentry. She looks at Lizzie. 'Looks like they're all gone. You want to risk it?'

Lizzie gets to her feet. 'Let's do it.'

They cross the street, duck under the loose yellow tape and walk casually through the white wooden archway at the entrance to the park. It seems a lifetime ago that she was last here, but it was only this morning. Less than twelve hours have passed, and yet everything has changed. This morning she was struggling with how to assimilate into her new life and occupy herself meaningfully in retirement. Now she's working on an off-book investigation with a bunch of people she'd be wiser to steer clear of.

They follow the path along past the bocce area and towards the pickleball courts. The birds are singing in the tree canopy above them, and for a moment it seems unreal that something so awful as a murder has happened in this place. Moira shakes her head and tells herself she knows better. Bad things happen everywhere, and the prettiness of nature is not a shield from the dreadful things humans do to each other.

'It's strange here when it's so quiet,' says Lizzie, looking at the empty pickleball courts. 'I've only ever been here in the middle of the day when everything's in use.'

'It's quiet in the mornings. I like it, it's like the calm before the storm.' Moira thinks about what she found that morning. Frowning, she glances around, checking they're alone and the blond guy isn't lurking somewhere. She looks back at Lizzie. 'Maybe the silence feels eerier now.'

They come to an intersection in the path and take a right towards the pool area along the tree-lined walkway. There's some shade beneath the trees, but although the heat of the sun is fading, the humidity seems just as strong. Moira wipes the sweat from her forehead and thinks maybe Philip and Rick got the better job – visiting the community-watch members to collect their patrol logs. At least they'll be in their air-conditioned cars for most of the time.

They come to the white gate that leads to the pool. Moira slows her pace, noting the two lines of yellow crime-scene tape fixed in a cross from gatepost to gatepost. She looks over the gate and knows that around the corner, currently hidden from view by the hedge, is the pool.

Lizzie catches up with her. 'Oh, it's still sealed.'

Moira nods but she can't speak. Her breath has caught in her throat. She stops walking. The image of crime-scene tape crossed over another door flits across her mind's eye. That tape was blue and white with the words 'POLICE LINE DO NOT CROSS' printed along it, and it was blocking off the entrance of a high-end penthouse apartment. It was two days after the raid, and Moira returning there was a last-ditch attempt to make sense of what had happened; to try and fathom how everything went to shit. She remembers unpinning the tape and entering the apartment; coughing as the smell, sour and rotten as death, hit the back of her throat as she stepped across the threshold; the bloodstains on the blond wood floor – two stains in the open living space, the larger splattered across the marble kitchen countertop and pooled on the floor beneath; the shards of glass from the shattered safety screen littering the balcony.

Blinking, she tries to rid herself of the image. She swallows hard as she feels the dreaded fluttering start up in her chest. This is how they begin; the panic attacks. The fluttering is the first warning sign; after that, the symptoms are harder to hide.

Not here, she thinks. *Not now. Please not here.*

As Lizzie passes her, heading to the gate, Moira closes her eyes. She concentrates on her inhale, then her exhale.

Please work, she thinks. *I can't do this here. I can't.*

She counts in for five, and out for five. Feels her chest relax a fraction. The fluttering subsides. She opens her eyes.

Lizzie is at the gate. She glances back at Moira. 'I'll go first.'

Lizzie doesn't hesitate. Puts the strap of her messenger bag over her head and finds a toehold on the bottom rung of the gate. Carefully avoiding disturbing the tape, she climbs over the gate to the path on the other side. She grins at Moira. 'Your turn.'

Moira steps up to the gate and climbs over to join Lizzie. Tries not to let her see that her hands and legs are trembling.

'Are you okay? I'm used to crime scenes, but for you it must be hard coming back here.' Lizzie cocks her head to the side. 'You look a bit pale.'

'I'm fine,' says Moira. She forces a smile. Tries hard to make it convincing. It seems to work.

'Well, if you're sure,' says Lizzie. She pauses, waiting to see if Moira says anything more. When she doesn't, Lizzie continues. 'As we walk, can you tell me how things looked this morning – what you saw, when and where?'

'Sure,' says Moira, relieved that Lizzie's changed the subject.

Slowly, they follow the path around the corner towards the pool. Moira thinks back and visualises the scene from that morning. 'It was still pretty cold when I got here.'

'Then what happened?' says Lizzie.

Moira inhales and can almost smell the grass, damp with early morning dew. 'The grass was wet, and it seemed just as quiet, as still, as always.'

The path starts to straighten as the pool comes into sight. Moira glances towards Lizzie and gestures towards the pool. 'This is the moment I first saw her. For a split second I thought I'd been beaten by someone else to get the first swim, but then I processed what I was seeing – that she was fully clothed and not moving, and that there seemed to be a lot of money in the water.'

Lizzie's nodding. 'Go on.'

'I ran towards the pool.' Moira accelerates, taking long strides towards the pool. Then, as the pathway broadens into the patio area around the pool she stops abruptly, pointing at the paving in front of her. 'And I had to jump away from the stones here. There was blood on them. Not much – just a few splashes leading to the edge of the pool.'

Lizzie crouches down, looking at the stone.

Moira watches Lizzie. Not sure what she's doing or how looking at the stone now is going to help. 'You've seen it in the photos.'

Lizzie scans the stone. 'Yes, I can see the trail. The CSIs have disturbed it. It looks like they've used some chemicals, probably to assess whether it came from the victim or the killer.' She stands. Looks at Moira. 'Although I think given the victim's wound, it's safe to say probability suggests that it was hers.'

Moira nods. 'I stepped up to the edge to look at the woman. It was obvious then that she was dead. So I called 911 on my phone and then waited here for the ambulance and police to arrive. It was while I was waiting that I noticed the black bag in the pool.'

'Do you remember seeing anything unusual in this surrounding area?' asks Lizzie. 'Elsewhere on the path or on the lawn or in the flower beds?'

Moira frowns. She hadn't really looked at the rest of the pool area, just focused on the woman in the pool. 'No, I don't think so. Like what?'

'Anything the killer could have discarded. The gun, for example.'

'No, nothing, I'd have said if I did. All I saw was the woman, the money, and then when I got closer after calling 911, the black bag on the bottom of the pool.' Moira pauses. Thinks back to what happened when the police arrived. 'But, a while after Detective Golding showed up, he got the uniforms searching the flower beds and surrounding area. I overheard one of them saying they were looking for the victim's phone.'

Lizzie steps towards Moira, joining her at the pool's edge. 'Damn. They've drained it completely. I wanted to take a water sample.'

'Is draining it normal?' asks Moira.

'I don't have much experience with pool deaths, not so many of them in my neck of the woods in the Thames Valley. Given the amount of blood that probably went into the water I expect the cops advised the management to do it.'

'Safer to drain it right away, I guess. They wouldn't want people swimming in it after what happened. It'd be a health hazard.'

'True. Taking the water sample was a long shot anyway.' Lizzie frowns, looking thoughtful.

'What is it?' Moira asks.

'I was just thinking about what you said earlier, how this is a strange place for a mugging.' Lizzie scans the area around the pool. 'I mean, it's fine in the daylight, but it feels spookier now that the light's fading, and after dark, with the park closed, why would anyone want to be here? The chances of two people happening to run into each other seems unlikely – it'd be a massive coincidence.'

'I don't believe in coincidence, but we know there must have been two people here, minimum.'

'Indeed. So I think they arranged to meet here after the park was closed.'

Moira senses that's not all. 'But?'

Lizzie shakes her head. 'Well, if they knew each other – say they were lovers rendezvousing here, for example – the gun seems out of place. Bringing a gun makes the murder feel premeditated, and crimes of passion are often more spur-of-the-moment, up close, and more personal – strangulation, stabbing, that sort of thing. This feels . . . different.'

Moira gets what Lizzie is saying. 'Then maybe they weren't lovers.'

'Then why would they meet here after dark?' says Lizzie, frowning.

'That's one big question,' says Moira. Knowing why the victim was in the park late last night or in the early hours of this morning is a critical piece of the puzzle. She runs her hand through her hair. 'The other is what the money was for.'

Lizzie nods. 'We need an ID on our Jane Doe. That could help.'

'For sure,' says Moira. 'And there's something else bothering me about the gun. I know it's secluded here, but we're not that far from the houses on Coral View Boulevard. Surely someone would have heard the shot?'

'Depends on the time. Mary and Archie had their golden wedding anniversary party last night. There was a firework display late in the evening. If the shot happened around that time it could have been camouflaged by the noise.'

'Do you think they knew that?'

'If they did, again, it points to premeditated,' says Lizzie. 'Shooting someone in time with the fireworks – that would take a bit of planning.'

'And inside knowledge of when the firework display was taking place.'

They're silent for a moment. Until this point they'd been working on the presumption that the killer was an outsider. But now, if their assumptions are true and the fireworks had been used to cover the sound of the gunshot, it means whoever did it had access to information about the social goings-on in The Homestead.

'We need to know the victim's time of death,' Lizzie says. 'I'll message Rick and ask if he can find out from his police contacts.'

'Good thinking.' Moira smiles. Her and Lizzie make a good team, bouncing ideas between them, testing theories and hypotheses. It seems like they've moved on from the problems of earlier – the focus on the crime scene has helped remove the lingering tension she felt. It feels like they're becoming more than acquaintances, as if they're now becoming friends. Moira's not sure whether it's a good or a bad thing.

As Lizzie turns her attention to the pool, Moira moves across the patio and on to the lawn area. Lizzie's earlier question has got her thinking. She doesn't remember there being anything else here this morning, but then, as she told Lizzie, she was more focused on the young woman and what was in the pool – and taking the pictures before the cops arrived. Now she wonders if she missed something. She closes her eyes and thinks back to that morning. Scans the scene in her mind. She remembers the young woman, the money and the bag, but nothing more. The patio around the pool is clear aside from the blood splatter, and there's nothing else on the lawn or on the two benches at the opposite end of the pool.

Suddenly, Moira has the feeling she's being watched. Shivering, she opens her eyes. She expects to see Lizzie close beside her, but

Lizzie's further away than before, crouching down on the far side of the pool, an expression of deep concentration on her face. Despite the warmth of the day, Moira feels a cold chill creep along her spine. She shivers again, and turns around.

Her breath catches in her throat.

Way in the distance, up on the hillside, beneath a crop of tall trees, something glints in the sunlight. She puts her hand to her face, trying to shield out the sun from her eyes and get a better view. She can't see clearly, but there's definitely something there. She takes a few steps forward. Squints harder.

That's when she sees it. Her heart rate accelerates.

Someone is watching them through binoculars.

16

RICK

Fetching the watch logs is taking longer than he'd reckoned on, so Rick's glad he and Philip had decided to split the work and take half the patrol list each to make the collections. It seems every member of the community watch wants to talk today. They don't get that he's on a schedule here; that the first twenty-four hours in a homicide case are the most critical.

Rick sighs as he climbs back into the jeep. Philip should have gotten the patrollers to deliver their logs to his mailbox in the usual way; it would've saved them a whole lot of time. Humans are such damn curious creatures. And some people have a real morbid fascination for details when there's been a death. Rick doesn't get it. Details are necessary to get the job done, but not things to gossip over at the golf club.

Not that you'd think that the way some people are talking. He glances back at the house he's just come from and his conversation with the owners, Melly and Rory. Shakes his head. Fresh from a round of golf and from spreading the word about the murder at the golf club, they'd tried their best to quiz him over any new developments or theories about the case. But he'd stayed like a vault. He saw through their fake angst and hand-wringing, and Rory's ranting about outsiders over on the district eleven construction site, and remembered their reactions at the Roadhouse earlier – how they were more bothered about missing a round of golf than they were about a young woman losing her life. People like that, he never will understand them.

He flicks through their weekly log that he's just collected. It's scant on detail, just the absolute minimum noted against each time slot, even though the area they've patrolled this week includes a number of Ocean Mist's premier restaurants and bars. Rick adds their weekly log to the stack of others inside the buff folder on the passenger seat. He knows Melly and Rory oftentimes patrol on foot, and has heard grumblings from some of the other patrollers that they've seen the pair enjoying a nice Merlot at one of the bars during their shift on more than one occasion. He frowns. It's tough, what with the patrollers being volunteers and all, but he knows they need to tackle the pair's behaviour. He makes a mental note to tell Philip his concerns when he's back at the house.

Rick checks the next name on his list – Dorothy – and fires up the jeep. The daylight's fading into dusk, so he switches on the lights as he moves off and hopes he's got enough time to make his last few stops before their agreed rendezvous back at Philip's place. He takes a right at the end of the street and cruises on the speed limit for a couple of blocks over to Dorothy's place on Sunrise.

He parks up at the kerb outside. Dorothy's home is a limited-edition Arts and Crafts house. There are less than a hundred of them in Ocean Mist, and less than fifteen hundred across all districts of The Homestead. From the outside it looks smaller than most of the other properties, but its distinctive brickwork and mint-green wooden cladding on the second storey make it stand out.

Climbing out of the jeep, he takes the paved path that divides the neatly mown lawn to the front door. He steps up on to the porch and uses the heavy iron knocker. As he waits, he notes the comfy-looking swing chair on the porch and the yellow flowers blooming in the planters, matching the stripes of the cushions on the swing. Everything is clean and shiny as a new pin.

'Who is it?' Dorothy's voice calls from inside the house.

Rick sees movement behind the stained glass either side of the front door's centre panel. 'It's me, ma'am. Rick Denver, from the community watch.'

He hears the sound of a bolt being drawn back. Moments later the door opens.

'Rick Denver.' Dorothy smiles. She's still wearing the pink twinset and pearls of earlier, but now instead of leather shoes she's wearing big fluffy slippers. 'Yes, of course, Philip said you'd be by.'

'I'm here to collect your weekly log.'

'And I have it right here waiting.' She steps away to the hall table and picks up an envelope. 'Everything should be in order.'

Rick takes the envelope. 'Thanks, ma'am, I appreciate it.'

Dorothy glances up and down the street before leaning closer to Rick. 'Any update on what happened to that poor woman?'

'Not yet.'

Dorothy frowns. 'Well, that's just not good enough, now is it?'

'No, ma'am.' Rick braces himself for another quizzing on what they know and what they're doing.

'Well, don't be standing here jibber-jabbering.' Dorothy makes a motion with her hand to shoo him away. 'Get back to your investigation and catch the bastard.'

Rick smiles. Dorothy's over eighty but she's got more gumption than Melly and Rory combined. He touches his forehead in a mock salute. 'Yes, ma'am.'

Back in the jeep, Rick consults his list. There are five people he needs logs from. Three he's tried already this afternoon and knows aren't around at the moment – Clint, Viola and Marilyn. Two he hasn't visited yet – Donald and Precious.

He drives back down Sunrise and heads towards Donald's place. Nothing in Ocean Mist is that far apart, but Donald's home is pretty much on the opposite side of the district to Dorothy's. It takes him ten minutes.

Drawing up outside Donald's two-storey ranch-style home, Rick realises Donald's truck isn't parked out front like it usually is. He figures he'll give the door a knock anyways, now that he's here.

Getting out of the jeep, Rick moves towards the house. The blinds are up, and through the window he can see a bunch of packing boxes piled up at one side of the room. Donald moved here about six months back and generally keeps himself to himself. He's a computer guy, always doing stuff with tech, but he joined the watch, so that makes him community-minded enough too. Rick glances down at his Apple watch. He likes new tech as much as the next guy, but he'd rather be outdoors than hunched over a keyboard for sure. Rick guesses that Donald prefers his tech to unpacking boxes.

There's no knocker or bell, so Rick raps on the door. He waits a moment. But there's no sound from inside the property, and no sign of Donald.

He tries once more. Knocks a little harder. But there's still nothing. So he turns and heads back to the jeep. Disappointed.

17

MOIRA

It takes longer than she'd thought it would.

Her legs are starting to ache now. Her breath is coming harder.

She'd told Lizzie what she'd seen; that someone was watching them through binoculars from high on the hill. She'd tried to keep her movements casual, and hadn't pointed to the place she'd seen the figure, wanting, as far as possible, not to alert them that she was coming. Then she'd set off in pursuit.

It's futile though, really, given the time it's taken to get this far – ten minutes at least, maybe longer. Anyone who'd been up here, if they had any sense and didn't want to be confronted, is probably long gone. No one has passed her, though. So maybe there's the possibility, slim though it is, that they're still on the hillside. Still watching Lizzie down below in the park. Because she'd left Lizzie poolside, and took a shortcut through to the back of the park, ducking through a gap in the hedge and on to the Wild Ridge Trail. The trees lining the start of the trail had given her camouflage. That's the moment she'd started running.

The trail is steeper than she'd anticipated, but Moira pushes herself harder. Pumps her arms faster. Lengthens her stride. Questions race through her mind in time with each footfall.

Is the blond guy watching me again?

Who are they? Why are they watching? What are they doing on the trail?

Are they the killer?

The light is fading as the sun sinks lower in the cloudless sky. She pushes on.

Now she's almost at the crest of the hill. The small group of trees is just a couple of hundred metres ahead. Their shadows seem to be reaching out across the grass towards her as she races towards them. She squints into the gloom, looking for movement. Looking to see if the person who was watching them is still here. It's hard to see in the half-light, and the shadows make visibility even poorer beneath the trees.

But there's no one.

She slows down when she reaches the trees. Alert. Still scanning the area for signs of life. If the person watching them didn't pass her on the trail, they must have taken a different route down. She runs past the trees, looking for another path. Maybe she can catch them up.

A little way from the trees the trail splits into three. The middle fork leads out across the open grassland towards the border where Ocean Mist meets the adjoining district. The grass is long and dotted with wild flowers and gorse bushes. Moira can see a long way across the wide-open space and it's empty. No sign of another person.

The right-handed path loops back around the crop of trees and disappears. She's not sure if it really goes anywhere, but runs along it anyway to check it out, just to be sure, thorough. It keeps looping around the trees, and in under a minute she discovers it just joins up with the top of the trail she used to get up here. It's a red herring.

She hurries back to where the trail divides. The left-handed path is the option the person watching must have taken. She glances around the trees again, making sure she really is alone, but there's no one here. Breaking into a run she follows the left-handed trail. She prefers walking and swimming to running, but her fitness levels are pretty good, and right now she's thankful for that.

The slope of the path starts off gentle, but that doesn't last for long, and it becomes steeper and more uneven with every step she takes. Gravity pulls at her and it feels as if she's losing her balance, but she doesn't slow down. She can't allow herself to slow down. There's no sign of the person who was watching them yet, but they have to be on this path, and she has to find them.

Up ahead the trail disappears into a small wooded area. Moira keeps running, zigzagging through the trees, following the narrow, overgrown path. Gorse bushes and brambles tear at her ankles. The fading sun flickers on-off through the tree branches like a strobe light. It semi-blinds her, stops her seeing the path clearly, but she pushes on harder. Has to catch the person who was spying on her. Can't let them get away. The questions repeat in her mind.

Who are they?

Why were they watching?

Did they kill the young woman in the pool?

The gradient of the hill is getting steeper. She goes with it. Lets gravity help her dodge around the gnarled tree roots sticking out of the dry earth like bones, and ducks under overhanging branches. She lengthens her stride. Her breathing is coming faster.

She sprints around a right-angled bend. She's almost through the wooded area now. The trail leads out of the trees and across open grassland. Her breath catches in her throat. Her heart punches harder against her ribs.

On the horizon, silhouetted against the orange-streaked sky, is a person, walking. It's a man. She can tell from his body shape. But not the wiry young guy who was following her earlier. This is someone different; broader and more athletic.

'Hey!' calls Moira. She's breathless, but her voice carries and she sees the man glance over his shoulder. His hoodie is pulled low over his face, putting it in shadow. In this fading light she can't see his features clearly. She waves. Shouts again, 'Wait up.'

He keeps walking. No. Correction, he's running now. And damn it, he's really fast.

It has to be the person with the binoculars.

I have to catch him.

Moira accelerates further. Her legs are tired, her muscles screaming to stop, but she races on, ignoring her body. She keeps her eyes focused on the retreating figure, trying to take in every detail – a possibly navy or dark grey hoodie, blue jeans, some kind of trainers, medium build.

She doesn't see the tree branch until the last moment. She ducks to avoid it, but she's too late. It slaps her across the face; a brief stinging whack that makes her gasp. Her toe catches on a tree root and she feels a sharp stab of pain in her ankle, then plunges forward, falling face first. On instinct she thrusts her arms out. Breaking the impact with her forearm.

Moira cries out as pain shoots through her elbow and up to her shoulder. Gritting her teeth, she rolls with the momentum and comes to a stop.

Did the man see me fall?

Where is he?

She scans the path ahead, but there's no sign of him now. He must have realised she was catching up with him and run faster.

Moira smacks the fist of her uninjured arm down on to the earth and shouts into the emptiness. 'Shit.'

I can't let him get away.

Scrambling to her feet, she tries to run, but she's limping now. Pain from her ankle is slowing her down. She moves as fast as she can. Ignores the increasing throbbing in her ankle, her elbow and her shoulder and scans the trail and the grassland for a sign of the man, but there's nothing. He's gone. She's lost him.

She stops and leans over, trying to catch her breath. There's a sheen of sweat across her arms, face and neck and she can feel it running down her back and into the waistband of her leggings. Her leggings are ripped across the knees and dirt from the trail is sticking to her skin. She can feel the mosquitos nipping at her flesh.

Moira curses under her breath. Shakes her head at having lost the man. Turns and limps back up the trail in the direction she's just come from. She doesn't do failure well. Never has.

She stops when she reaches the top of the hill. The sun has almost disappeared now. It's only half-visible on the horizon, the streaks across the darkening sky more blood red than orange.

Moira looks down towards Manatee Park. Even without binoculars she can make out the pickleball courts and the pools. It's too dark to see them clearly now, but earlier the man watching them would have had a good view from this vantage point. If it was the killer, from what he saw he'll most likely guess that they're looking into the murder. Moira shivers. She hopes Lizzie finished her work and is out of the park and on her way home. Safe.

Still, watching them can't have been the man's reason for coming up here, surely. If he'd seen them entering Manatee Park it would have made more sense to follow behind them; to observe what they were doing through one of the gaps where the hedge is thinner, rather than to hike up here and watch from this distance with binoculars. Also, having the binoculars seems too convenient. It doesn't add up right, unless they were up here for another reason.

Moira frowns. Thinks about why he could have been up here. Maybe she's got things wrong? Perhaps he was nothing to do with the murder? Could be he was watching wildlife, or birdwatching or something.

She shakes her head. Doubts that's the case. Thinks about the facts, the things she knows for sure.

He was up here – fact.

He was watching me and Lizzie through binoculars – fact.
He ran when I tried to talk to him – fact.

Take those three facts and it adds up to a big dose of suspicion. Of course he could just have been being nosey, but then if that's the case why did he run? It's like the wiry blond guy – why did *he* run? Are the two men connected?

Moira runs her hand through her hair, brushing out some dirt from the trail. Maybe she spooked him and they thought she killed the woman? Perhaps he was afraid, but she thinks that's unlikely. It's far more likely that he was up here watching the police and CSIs working the scene and that's why he had the binoculars. That could make him just a nosey rubbernecker, or it could be he was watching the police for a reason; because he's the killer.

Moira remembers something else that struck her as odd. When she was double-checking the person had gone, and that they weren't hiding behind one of the trees, she noticed something – a small patch of earth that looked freshly disturbed.

Retracing her steps, she moves between the trees, scanning the ground. It's harder to see now in the fading light, and she doesn't have a torch, but she can't leave this. Has to check it out. Needs to be sure that the only reason the man was up here was to watch what was happening in Manatee Park.

It takes her nearly ten minutes to find the patch of earth, and when she sees it again, she knows that something happened here. It's a small area – maybe a foot square, max. The dirt has been recently disturbed and whoever did it has tried to hide the fact by stamping the earth down and putting twigs over the area, but they've tried too hard; it looks too perfect to be natural.

Kneeling down, Moira pushes her fingers into the dirt and starts to dig.

18

LIZZIE

Alone now, she tries not to worry about whatever Moira's doing. Lizzie hadn't seen the figure on the hillside – Moira had told her not to turn around in case it tipped the person off that they'd seen them. Now Moira's gone she's fighting the urge to look. She wonders if the person up there is the same man who was lurking outside the house earlier. She shakes her head. Moira's so impulsive. The person watching them could be the killer, and it's not like Moira has any training in this sort of thing. Running off after them, it's reckless and dangerous. Lizzie doesn't like it that they're both now alone.

Lizzie scans the area around the pool. Shudders. The thought of someone up on the hillside behind her watching what she's doing sends an icy shiver down her spine. She tries to shake it off and concentrate instead on the task in hand. It's been a good few years since she was last at a crime scene, and she never thought she'd be at one again. But Philip's left her no choice, insisting that they investigate what's happened here, and although doing this isn't what she wanted, now she's let herself get involved she's determined to crack this puzzle. Because that's what every crime scene is – a picture puzzle with a few pieces missing. If you're diligent and look carefully, it'll give you most of the image, and if you're smart and focused and determined, chances are it'll yield a few leads that'll help you find the missing pieces.

That's the theory anyway, but she's feeling rather rusty, and she's anxious too, if she's honest with herself. Turning slightly, she takes a quick glance up towards the hillside, but sees nothing; no binoculars, no person watching. She takes a deep breath. Although most of the anxiety is more about being here alone than about working the scene, some of it is about Philip. It's like he's forgotten why he was asked to retire. As if somehow because a few years have passed, what happened before his retirement is no longer relevant. She shakes her head. If he thinks that, he's really burying his head in the sand. Heart problems and the rest don't just go away because you choose not to think about them. It doesn't work that way, and he should know that, after what happened. They'll always be with him, with both of them; like an unexploded bomb with the timer slowly ticking down.

Lizzie just prays nothing happens to accelerate the countdown.

In the fading light it's harder to assess the scene. If she'd been doing this for real, working with the cops, then she'd have had the big rig spotlights set up before the light changed, and a canopy erected to shield the ground from disturbance, letting her work unhindered by time and weather. As it is, she's got maybe twenty minutes before the gloom makes it impossible to continue.

Pushing thoughts of the person on the hillside from her mind, Lizzie forces herself to focus. Getting to work, she walks the scene, methodically scanning every inch – every blade of grass, each slab of stone – as she paces back and forth across the lawn and pool area. She knows the cops will have done this already, and had their own CSIs do it too, but she follows her usual process.

Leave no stone unturned. No evidence left behind.

That had been her mentor's motto, and her mentor – Dr Sally Eton – had been the best of the best. Lizzie smiles at the memory of her; tough talking, pin sharp and able to call bullshit at twenty paces. Sally had not just been her mentor, she'd been a good friend. No, more than that, she'd been her best friend. Lizzie's smile drops. She swallows hard. Now all Sally is to her is a collection of memories.

She keeps walking. Keeps looking. The grass is brittle and dry beneath her sandals. There are black powder marks on some of the stones where the CSIs must have lifted prints, or tried to lift them. There's no new evidence though, but there is something interesting.

Retracing her steps along the stone patio, Lizzie stops and crouches down. Even in the diminishing light, she can clearly make out a dark scuff mark on the stone, and it's not the only one. The marks are all around the side of the pool, spaced about two metres apart.

Opening her messenger bag, she removes a pink fabric tape measure and her notebook and pencil. She measures the length and width of the scuff and jots down the measurement in her notebook. Then moves to the side and measures the distance between the first mark and the next one – just under two yards. She writes that in the notebook too, then repeats the process for each of the scuff marks.

It doesn't take long.

Lizzie feels the nerves in her belly give way to the fizz of something else – intrigue, excitement even – as she realises what she's found. It's a pattern. Each scuff mark is the same size and shape, give or take half an inch. And the measurements of the gaps between each mark are also roughly the same, and all within about four inches of each other.

She looks at the figures written in her notebook, then back to the marks on the stone. Thinking.

What made them?
Who made them?
Why?

The marks aren't at the pool's edge, they're set back further. She thinks about the dead woman in the pool and the money floating around her.

The money.

Lizzie sets down her messenger bag on the lawn beside the patio, takes out her nitrile gloves, puts them on and then moves back to the pool. Dropping to her knees, she lies down on the stone, her shoulders level with the edge of the pool.

Glancing back, she looks at her own feet. Holding on to the pool's edge with one hand, she reaches forward with the other, as if reaching into the water.

As if she was reaching into the water to grab the money.

As she reaches out with her arm, she watches her feet. One of them moves as she stretches, the toe dragging across the stone. When she sits up and takes a closer look Lizzie sees what she suspected: from the movement, she's made a small scuff mark.

She feels her hypothesis is correct. The killer tried to get the money from the side of the pool by lying on the stone and reaching into the water. They went around the whole pool, systematically gathering as much cash as they could, while the young woman was dead or dying. The thought sickens her.

Crouching down, Lizzie measures the distance from the pool's edge to the scuff marks. Using her own height to estimate how many more inches to add to account for the person's shoulders and head being over the edge of the pool, she does some calculations.

She's five foot two; the person whose shoes made the scuff marks must be almost a full foot taller than her, putting them between six foot and six two. Lizzie notes her conclusions down in her notebook, then packs it and the tape measure back into her bag. Thinks. She didn't want to get involved in this investigation, but now she's here she can't deny that the puzzle is hooking her in. There's a real callousness to what the murderer did to the young woman – not just killing her, but sticking around to scoop dollars from the pool as she died, regarding the money as more important than the victim's life. Lizzie clenches her fists. The anxiety she was feeling earlier is still there but instead of being mixed with intrigue and excitement about the puzzle, now it's mixed with anger. She's still concerned about Philip, but she can't stand by and allow whoever did this to get away free. She wants to make sure this killer is caught.

Shifting her gaze to the pool, she wonders if there's any chance of her taking a viable sample from the small patches of water left puddled on the pool's floor. Her first instinct is it's not enough, but she decides to give it a try.

She strides around to the pool ladder. It's getting darker by the minute. The sun's light is orange and red, like a bloodstain across the sky. The birds, so noisy earlier, have fallen silent on their perches up in the trees. Lizzie knows she needs to hurry. Soon she won't be able to see a thing.

Using the ladder she climbs down into the basin of the pool. It feels weird to step on to the bottom, now waterless and barren. She takes slow steps, scanning the matt, blue-painted surface for a big enough sample.

It seems fruitless, though. The floor of the pool has some imperfections where water has puddled in tiny amounts. She keeps looking. Keeps moving across the basin. She's almost at the furthest point from the ladder when she sees a slightly bigger puddle, maybe a couple of inches across. It's a long shot, but it looks like it'll be enough to get a swab.

Lizzie glances up at the sky. The sun is sinking down below the horizon and the light has almost gone. At least the fading light means whoever was on the top of the hill won't be able to watch her so easily, but if she's going to finish this she needs to work faster. Opening her messenger bag, she removes the water swab kit she brought from home. They'd bought the kits online so they could periodically test the hot tub – Philip having heard how bad the things are for harbouring germs and bacteria. She can get a sample on the swab and test it once she's home.

Crouching down, she removes the swab from the narrow plastic container and presses it against the puddled water. It soaks up most of the water, and when she's got it damp enough, she pushes it back into the container and screws on the lid.

It's something, slightly better than nothing. But even if the swab works, whether it will show her anything of use is doubtful. Chances are the amount of chemicals used to keep the water clean will skew the data and she might not be able to get an accurate read on the ratio of water to blood anyway. And that's assuming she can find her old kit, and if she still has the testing equipment she needs.

Lizzie shakes her head. It's a whole lot of *ifs*. She knows that.

Still she packs the sample container into her bag and decides to keep looking. Taking her iPhone from the zipped section of the messenger bag, she switches on the torch app and uses the light to give the pool a final look. She's almost done when she spots it – a flash of something shiny in the far corner of the basin.

Hurrying over, she sees that there's a small filter in this corner of the pool. It's hidden by a slightly raised cover painted the same shade of blue as the pool floor, with just a tiny gap for the water to run through. Lizzie frowns. She's not sure what it is yet – just that it's something silver and it doesn't look like it should be in the filter. If it's something connected to the murder it's bad that the cops and CSIs didn't find it. They should have pulled out all the pool filters as standard procedure – they're an obvious place to check for anything small that could have been dropped. That they haven't checked is another sign that the police department isn't giving this crime its full attention.

Kneeling down on the floor of the pool, Lizzie removes a ziplock baggie from her satchel and a pair of tweezers. She opens the ziplock, and then uses the tweezers to try and lever the shiny thing from the filter. It's stuck pretty firm, and it takes a few attempts for her to waggle it free.

Her breath catches in her throat as she sees what it is. The hairclip is made of silver and diamanté, but it's not what it's made of that's making her heart beat faster; it's the symbols they make: a row of four dollar signs connected together.

Lizzie focuses the beam of her phone torch at the hairclip with the dollar signs on it and thinks about how the young woman was found – floating in the middle of this pool, surrounded by thousands of dollar bills. There has to be a connection between her and the hairclip, surely. It can't be a coincidence.

She seals the hairclip into the ziplock and then puts everything aside from her phone into the messenger bag. Hoisting it over her head, she makes sure it's fastened, then strides back across the pool basin to the ladder. It's tougher climbing back up, especially one-handed as she holds the phone in the other, the torch beam focused on the rungs of the ladder.

Back on the patio, she brushes herself down. It's time to go.

A bird in the trees nearby squawks, making her jump. There's the frantic beating of wings as the roosting birds take flight. Their cries are loud, urgent. Something has scared them.

Lizzie clutches the messenger bag to her body. It's dark now. No moon, no stars. And utterly silent now the birds have fled.

Then she hears the crack of a dried stick, and the rustle of leaves. It's coming from the direction of the trees, the same direction she needs to go in to exit – the only way in or out of the pool area.

Her mouth goes dry.

Whatever caused the birds to take flight, it won't have been Moira. She's not coming back here – they agreed to meet at Philip and Lizzie's house once they were done. And there's no reason anyone else should be here.

Heart pounding, Lizzie thinks about the slim blond man who'd been spying on them in the garden earlier. She wonders again if he's the person Moira saw up on the hill watching through binoculars. Could he have avoided Moira and come down to the pool to see what she was doing? It's possible. Very possible. He didn't look super-strong, but could Lizzie fight him off if he's out there, ready to attack? She's really not sure.

Turning towards the noise, she sweeps the torchlight from her phone across the lawn. Swears she sees something move. Her stomach flips. She grips the phone tighter.

'Who's there?' she says, hating the quiver of her voice and the anxiety in her tone.

There's no reply. Just silence and darkness and the feeling that there's someone moving towards her from the shadows.

Clutching her bag tighter, Lizzie feels very alone.

19

RICK

It happens on the sidewalk outside the home of Precious Harper. He doesn't see them at first because he's having a quick look-see at the log Precious just gave him – checking for any mention of beige station wagons or women who fit the victim's description – so he's almost back at the jeep before he's aware that they're waiting.

'You one of the patrollers?'

Rick looks over the top of the log and sees two grey-haired older guys standing in front of his jeep, blocking his path. They're dressed similar – Hawaiian shirts, baggy cargo shorts and brown leather sandals. Both have greying ginger hair. One of them wears his hair longer, almost shoulder length, and has a string of dark beads around his neck. The other's hair is cropped shorter, and rather than a necklace, he has a bunch of bracelets – leather straps, beads, and one made of knotted multicolour thread like a friendship bracelet – around his right wrist. It takes Rick a moment to realise that the men are twins. 'I sure am.'

The longer-haired guy glances at his twin and gives him a meaningful look.

The man with the cropped hair starts to speak. 'We need to know what happened in Manatee Park. We heard the police were swarming over the place this morning and there were ambulances and medics there. We have to know why.'

Rick says nothing. In law enforcement you hear all the stories – how the perpetrators of homicide and abduction sometimes return to the scene of their crime as rubberneckers. How some put themselves forward offering help. How they like to get close to the investigation and the investigators to feel part of the action, feeling clever all the while because no one has them identified. It's true these two guys look harmless enough, but then if he's learnt one thing in his career with the DEA it's to be prepared for the unexpected.

His lack of answer seems to rile the men. The longer-haired one moves his weight from one foot to the other. His cheeks flush red. 'Look pal, we have a right to know what's been going on in our community. We live here and if something bad happened, then we should be told. We're not children. We deserve answers. We're . . .'

'Fellas, I'm a resident here just like you, I don't—'

'But you're part of the watch.' The man looks pointedly at the log in Rick's hand. 'And you're collecting this . . . evidence . . . so that means you're doing things. You must *know* something.'

'I'm doing my bit as a concerned citizen is all,' says Rick, folding the log in half and tucking it into his pants pocket. 'Nothing more, nothing less.'

'So you're concerned.' There's triumph in the shorter-haired guy's voice, as if he's just got Rick to reveal some kind of state secret. 'Tell us what's going on.'

Surely these guys have the news channel, or a news app or something, thinks Rick. It's been a good few hours since the victim was found. The story should be churning on the news cycle by now. 'What do you know already?'

The long-haired man clutches at the beads around his neck, rubbing them between his fingers. 'We don't know a whole lot. They said on the radio there'd been an accident in the park.'

'But we don't believe them,' says the guy with shorter hair. 'All those police and CSIs, that was too much for just an accident.'

The longer-haired man lets go of his necklace and shakes his head. 'Can't trust nothing the news tells you.'

'Can't trust nothing the government tells you,' his brother replies.

'Amen to that,' says the guy with longer hair. He leans forward, his voice low. 'Can't trust nothing but God and what you see with your own eyes and hear with your own ears.'

Rick doesn't point out that they're asking him rather than using their own eyes and ears. He figures a smart-mouthed comment like that won't go down well with these boys.

'You look like you've seen things,' says the short-haired twin, pointing his finger at Rick. 'And we need for you to tell us the details.'

'I've seen a lot of things in my time, for sure, but I wasn't there in the park this morning, so I've got nothing to say about that.' Rick's keeping his tone amicable, but the short-haired guy's aggression is making him pissed. 'The cops are investigating. That's all I know.'

'That's a crock of shit.' He steps closer to Rick. 'You, pal, are holding out on us. You know stuff. You must know.'

Rick crosses his arms. Fixes the guy with a steely gaze. 'I ain't your pal.'

'Who was involved in the accident? Did someone die? Who died? Was it really an accident?' The man's getting all up in Rick's face. Waving his hands to emphasise each point he makes, bracelets jangling. 'Do the police have any suspects? Have they made an arrest? Are they going to?'

Rick holds his ground. Says nothing.

'Come on, man. You have to know something. She's one of the patrollers.' The short-haired guy gestures towards Precious's house.

'And if you're collecting whatever the hell that was you just stuffed into your pocket, then you must be her boss, which means you know for sure what's gone down.'

'And you have to tell us,' says the longer-haired guy, a pleading whine to his voice. He steps closer to stand alongside his brother. He grasps his necklace again, his fingers running along the beads, rubbing them in a steady rhythm.

Rick looks from one guy to the other. They stare back, all expectant. He shakes his head. 'I'm not her boss. And there's nothing to tell.'

The long-haired twin lets go of the beads. His face flushes a deeper shade of red. 'I don't believe that. Please, you have to—'

'Believe what you want, it's a free country.' Rick shrugs and turns towards the jeep.

'Not necessarily,' mutters the shorter-haired twin under his breath. He grabs at Rick's T-shirt, trying to stop him leaving. His voice is louder, almost a shout now. 'Stop bullshitting us. Tell us what's going on.'

Rick turns back to face the guy. He looks at the man's hand, still gripping his tee. Keeps looking at it until the man lets go.

The long-haired guy puts his hand on his brother's shoulder and gives it a squeeze. 'It's okay, Jack. Let him go. He won't help us.' The guy's voice breaks as he says the word help.

Jack is shaking. He's pale beneath his tan. The aggressive posturing of a few moments ago is gone; now he just looks beat.

Rick takes a breath. Pissed as they've made him, he can see these guys are real worried. Oftentimes fear makes folks act out of character. He decides to cut them some slack. 'This is about more than what happened in the park, am I right? What's really going on?'

Neither of the men speaks at first. They look at each other, something unspoken going on between them. Rick can feel the tension.

'We should tell him,' says the long-haired brother.

Jack shakes his head. 'Won't make no difference. He's not helping us.'

'He might.' The long-haired one gives his brother's shoulder another squeeze. 'And if not, if we say, then at least he'll get why . . . he'll see we're not crazy people.'

'You think?' says Jack, looking away, eyes on the tarmac. He's quiet for a long moment. Then he looks back at his brother. 'Okay.'

The longer-haired guy looks Rick right in the eye. His voice has lost the pleading whine of earlier; now it's softer, kind of wistful. 'We used to live in the city – New York City – real close to Central Park in an apartment with amazing city views and close to all our favourite spots. We loved the city. We worked there – we're both professors, I do climate change, Jack does math – and we had friends and fun and had never thought about moving.'

'Then, one weekend when we were walking in the park, we saw something,' says Jack.

His brother nods. 'We were walking our dogs when we saw a man running with a baseball bat. He was a little ways from us, but we saw what happened real clear. He ran towards this group of people having a picnic. Just charged into them and attacked, swinging at them with the bat.'

'They were screaming. The man with the bat was yelling.' Jack looks like he might be about to vomit. 'There was so much blood.'

The long-haired guy clutches at his beads again. 'There was this guy in a white shirt, he was lying on his side, blood running down his face, and the noises he made . . . the moaning . . . it was . . .' He takes a big gulp of air.

'Mark called 911 for an ambulance and the cops,' says the shorter-haired twin.

'And Jack here tried to stop the guy with the bat from hurting more people.'

Jack shakes his head. 'I tried, but it wasn't enough. The man who was attacked first didn't make it, several others were hospitalised.'

'Including Jack,' says Mark. 'The guy broke his elbow and wrist, and gave him a head injury.'

Jack looks back down at the sidewalk. 'A few of us managed to get the bat off him and keep him pinned on the ground until the cops arrived.'

'After Jack was discharged from hospital we tried to put it behind us, but we couldn't. We didn't feel safe. That city had been our home for more than thirty years, but we couldn't get past it – that man and the bat – even after they convicted him.' He frowns. Rubbing at the beads around his neck. 'At the trial, the attacker pleaded guilty. The prosecution said he'd been high, the blood test showed he had a whole cocktail of drugs in him when it happened. When they asked him why he'd done it, do you know what he said? He told the court he'd been bored and his buddy dared him. A man died because of his boredom. Because of a stupid dare.' Mark's voice has a tremor to it now. 'I've always suffered from anxiety but that . . .'

'We couldn't live there any more,' says Jack. 'It was too much.'

Mark clutches his beads tighter. 'Far too much.'

'So we sold our place and moved here. They assured us this place was safe, that nothing bad had ever happened here, that it was a zero-crime community.'

'We were finally able to relax again. But then a month back the burglaries started, and now it sounds like there's something else, something worse . . .'

'We just want to know if this place is safe.' Mark starts rubbing the beads faster between his thumb and forefinger. 'I had to take my anxiety meds this lunchtime after hearing something weird has happened in the park, it's the first time I've ever taken them here. I feel on the edge right now. I need to know what's going on. I just can't handle the not knowing. Even if it's bad, it's better to know. I really need to know. I need to feel safe.'

Rick looks at Mark. He's real twitchy; fiddling with the bead necklace, eyes darting side to side, a tremble in his voice as he speaks. He knows that he can't say anything that will make him feel safe, because nowhere is one hundred per cent safe. You can be walking down the street and get hit by an out-of-control driver, you can board the subway and get blown up by a bomb, or you can go to a park and end up dead. He can't give this man the reassurance he's after. What he can give him is the truth. 'A young woman was found dead in the lap pool this morning.'

Mark exhales hard. 'That's . . . that's a lot to process.'

'Do they know who did it?' says Jack. 'Have they caught them? Is it connected to the burglaries? Are they—'

'I understand that you're worried. I'm worried too.' Rick takes a breath. Mark isn't making eye contact – he's rubbing the beads of his necklace over and over. The other brother is the opposite – eyes on Rick, his focus pretty intense. Rick continues, 'The cops are investigating, but we're doing what we can to help. At the moment I'm collecting in all the logs made by our volunteer patrollers over the past few weeks. We're going to have a look at them and see if there's any sightings of the woman who was found in the pool.'

'And what should we do?' says Mark, his voice shaky. 'What do we do now?'

'You stay vigilant,' says Rick. 'Look out for anything unusual, and call security if you see anything suspicious.'

'And if we feel in danger?' asks Jack, the short-haired twin. 'What then?'

Rick rubs his hand over his jaw. Looks from Jack to his brother Mark. 'Then you call the cops, dial 911, and don't hesitate.'

20

MOIRA

Her shoulder aches and her ankle's throbbing but she ignores it. She doesn't want the others to make a fuss – they can't afford to get sidetracked now, not when they're getting somewhere with the investigation.

Across the table, Lizzie's talking. She looked pale when she arrived back at the house, and kept glancing around as if she was looking for someone. Moira had wanted to check she was okay, but Philip had hurried them through to the patio, where Rick was already sitting on one of the white wicker chairs, and asked for a debrief. Lizzie went first, and since she's started talking about what she found at the crime scene the colour has returned to her cheeks. Moira watches her new friend. She sounds more confident now as she reports back about the scuff marks she found on the stones around the pool, but there's something going on with her; Moira can tell Lizzie isn't feeling all right.

She needs to play it gently, though. She knows sometimes she can be too direct and full-on, and that makes people clam up. Leaning towards Lizzie, Moira asks, 'So what do you think it means?'

'Well, the scuff marks were evenly spaced, and when I tried to recreate them I managed to do it by lying on my front and reaching over the pool's edge,' says Lizzie. 'I think whoever killed the young woman tried to pull as many dollars out of the water as they could without going in, either when she was dead or while she was dying.'

They're all silent for a moment. In the light of the Moroccan-style lanterns Philip looks sombre. Rick shakes his head.

'I measured the length from the pool's edge to the marks, and from that I'd estimate the killer is about six foot two, give or take an inch,' says Lizzie. She looks at Philip. Gestures towards the patio doors. 'We should write it on the board.'

Standing, Philip takes a dry marker off the table and adds the details to the column headed 'Killer'. He taps the line above the one he's written that says 'non swimmer?'. 'If our perpetrator stayed on the pool's edge rather than entering the water, sounds like this theory could be right.'

'Could be,' says Lizzie. 'Or they didn't want any of the victim's blood getting on them through the water.'

Moira has been wondering about that. 'Did you manage to get a water sample?'

'Yes,' says Lizzie. She opens the messenger bag that's on the ground by her feet and takes out a small, narrow plastic container with a long swab inside. 'I got this, but I'm not sure it'll be viable as there wasn't much water left and I don't know the length of time between the body being removed from the water and the water being drained, or whether they flushed the pool with chemicals after draining. There's a lot of variables to consider.'

'Of course.' Moira glances away across the yard. It's pitch dark now, but you'd hardly know it. The patio lighting is on, and there are spotlights dotted across the garden. A scented candle – something lemon with a slight edge of sour – burns in the lantern on the centre of the table.

Lizzie reaches into her bag again. Pulling out a ziplock bag, she places it on the table. 'I did find this, though.'

Moira takes the bag and looks at what's inside. It's a silver hair-clip with sparkling diamanté dollar signs along it. 'Where was it?'

'In the pool, it'd got wedged in the corner filter.'

'The cops missed it?' Rick says, frowning.

Lizzie nods. 'It seems so.'

Philip runs his hand over his bald pate. Shakes his head. 'More indications they're not taking this case seriously.'

'Possibly,' says Lizzie, 'but I only saw it after the light had almost gone and I switched on my phone's torch. The filter was covered and kind of blended in with the pool floor.'

'It's sloppy,' says Philip. 'Poor work by them, very poor indeed.'

Moira doesn't disagree. Surely the CSIs should have combed every inch of the place for evidence. In pool deaths, especially those that are suspicious, she'd guess checking the filters for evidence would be high up on the list of things to do. And, as suspicious deaths go, getting shot and then drowned has to rank pretty high. It seems bizarre that the cops here don't seem to be giving much of a damn.

She puts the hairclip back on the table and looks at Lizzie. 'You think this belonged to the victim?'

'Possibly, but there's no way to tell how long it'd been in the pool.'

Moira agrees. It could be something or nothing. 'We really need an ID on the victim.'

'Agreed,' says Rick.

Philip adds 'dollar hairclip?' to the bottom of the list about the victim. He looks at Moira. 'Okay, so what else did we get?'

'Before we move on, there's something else I need to tell you.' Lizzie looks hesitant. She rotates the untouched cup of tea in front of her back and forth. 'I had the strong feeling I was being watched.'

Moira feels adrenaline start to fizz in her belly. 'When? Before or after I'd left you?'

'I felt it when you saw the person watching us, but then towards the end of the time I was there on my own, something else happened. It was virtually dark by then, and I only had the phone's torch for light, so I can't be a hundred per cent sure. But when I climbed out of the pool I thought I saw someone over on the other side of the lawn, moving by the hedge.'

'What did they look like? Was it the blond guy from before or someone else?'

'I didn't see clearly enough, it was too dark and it was just for a split second.' Lizzie widens her eyes. 'I called out but no one answered. Then I ran out of there as fast as I could.'

Moira understands why she ran, but she still feels disappointed. She does the maths on the timing – working out when she last saw the man she was chasing, and when Lizzie felt she was being watched. It could have been the same person. 'There was someone watching us from up on the hill,' she tells Philip and Rick. 'That's why I left Lizzie at the crime scene and went up on the Wild Ridge Trail. When I got there he'd gone, but I figured out the path he'd taken and almost caught up with him. I thought it could have been the young guy who's been spying on me, but it wasn't. When the man realised I was on his trail he took off at a sprint. I pursued him, but I don't know that path well, and I caught my toe on a tree root and fell.' Moira gestures to her bloodied leg and swollen ankle. 'He got away, but he'd have had enough time to return to Manatee Park.'

Lizzie pales. 'Do you think he was the killer?'

'I don't know, he could have just happened to be hiking on the Wild Ridge Trail, or he could have been watching the police and CSIs, and then stayed when he saw us going into the pool area after they'd gone.' Moira runs her hand through her hair. She doesn't believe it's a coincidence the man had been there. 'The thing is, he was using binoculars. So he was on the hill to watch something, could have been birds, or nosey rubbernecking . . . or it could be because he's the killer and he wanted to keep an eye on things.'

Lizzie says nothing, but Moira sees her eyes darting around the perimeter of the garden as if she's expecting someone to jump out at her at any moment. She keeps her gaze on Lizzie. 'What are you thinking?'

'If the man you saw on the hill wasn't the same person as before . . . It's odd that there are two men, both watching you . . . us,' says Lizzie. There's a tremble to her voice. She clasps her hands together. 'Are these men connected to the murder? It has to be likely, doesn't it, but are they connected to each other? I just don't . . .'

'We don't know they're connected to the murder,' says Philip, frowning. He sits down. Putting the marker pen on the table, he reaches out and gives Lizzie's hand a squeeze. 'It's okay.'

Lizzie meets his gaze. 'No, we don't know, but it's possible, isn't it? The killer could know I was poking about in the pool. What if they think I'm a threat? What if they—'

'We don't know anything for sure right now,' says Moira. It seems Philip likes absolutes, but it's rare you get them at this stage in a murder case. You have to work the evidence, follow where it leads. She reaches into her pocket. Feels the plastic of the bag she wrapped around her find. Pulling it out, she puts it on to the table. 'But this is something that tips the balance towards them being involved.'

'What you got there?' asks Rick, leaning forward to the table.

Carefully, Moira unwraps the plastic bag from around the phone. It's still covered with dirt – she hadn't wanted to brush it off for fear of voiding any fingerprints or DNA. The earth has got into the cracks of the shattered screen. She looks at the group. 'This morning, the detectives said they hadn't found the victim's mobile phone. It struck me as odd – a young woman like that, she's bound to have had a phone with her.' She points to the broken phone on the table. 'I think this could be hers.'

Philip stares at the phone. Rubs his forehead. 'How did—'

'I noticed the earth had been disturbed around the base of one of the trees and that leaves and sticks had been rearranged over the earth to try and disguise what had been done – it looked too perfect. So I dug down to see what it was.'

'Is there anything that connects this phone to the man you saw?' asks Lizzie.

Moira shakes her head. This is where the links are weakest. 'It's only circumstantial – he was there, the phone was found there – but if this *is* the phone of the murder victim then it seems too much of a coincidence to discount.'

Rick runs his hand across his jaw. 'Agreed, and I sure don't trust that kind of happenstance, but if it was the killer, why would he bury the phone? He could have dumped it in the trash someplace away from The Homestead, or buried it somewhere else far away from here – why do it so close to the crime scene? Especially when he knew you'd seen him.'

'Yeah, it's a weird one.' Moira's been wondering that too. Burying it so close seems high risk, bordering on foolish. 'I'm guessing he'd buried it already, and then didn't have time to retrieve it when he realised I'd seen him, or he couldn't find the spot in time, or something.'

Rick frowns. 'Yeah, sure, but it still doesn't explain why he'd bury it there in the first place.'

'We're getting ahead of ourselves,' says Philip. 'We don't have confirmation this phone is anything to do with the murder victim.'

'But it might be,' says Moira.

'Yes, yes.' Philip's tone is patronising. 'But in law enforcement you learn to investigate thoroughly, you follow protocol and the right processes, and you ensure things are evidence based, not based on hunches. As a civilian I don't expect you to understand – any policing knowledge you think you have probably comes from watching crime dramas.'

Moira bites her lip. Swallows down the reply she'd like to give. She needs him to believe she's just an average civilian.

'I think we should still treat it as if it was the victim's,' says Lizzie. She looks at Moira. 'Do you know if it works?'

Moira gives Lizzie a smile of thanks and shakes her head. 'I tried switching it on but nothing happened and I was worried to push it in case the whole thing fell apart.' She looks at Philip. His face is impassive – she's not sure how to read him. She'd assumed he'd be as excited about the phone as her. 'It should go on the murder board as a possible lead.'

'Yes, yes.' Grabbing the marker pen, Philip gets to his feet and adds 'victim's phone?' to the action log list. Then he sits back down.

Moira feels a flash of irritation. Why isn't he more excited about this? She thought he'd be enthused, yet he's looking like a bulldog that's bitten a wasp. 'What's going on, Philip? This phone could be a real lead – if it belonged to the victim it could give us her identity and some real insights into what she was doing the day she died. It can tell us who she'd been in contact with, and it might even give us who she'd arranged to meet at Manatee Park. I don't get why you're—'

'Look,' says Philip, clasping his hands together around the marker pen. 'I hate to say this, but I think we should tell the cops about the phone.'

'Really?' Moira's irritation turns to surprise. She hadn't seen that coming. Philip seemed so adamant he wanted to investigate. They've hardly got started, and he's changing his mind? She looks at Lizzie, who's nodding. She raises an eyebrow at Rick.

He shrugs. 'Could be a good move.'

Moira can't believe she's hearing this. 'But Detective Golding was such a—'

'I know, I know,' says Philip, putting his hands up. 'It's just if the phone does belong to the victim then it's a big deal. It could blow the case wide open.'

Moira clenches her fists. She hadn't wanted to be a part of their group, but they managed to persuade her and now she's hooked by the case. 'But *we're* investigating.'

'And we've done a good job and found something that could be important. *You* found something. But we're three retired law-enforcement people and an enthusiastic amateur. We've got no jurisdiction to act here.' Philip blows out hard. 'In all honesty, we've got an obligation to share it.'

Lizzie nods. 'We should tell them about the blond guy following you too, Moira. And the man you saw up on the hillside.'

Moira looks from Lizzie to Philip. She knows she's the enthusiastic amateur Philip's referring to, and although that's what she wanted him to believe about her, it still grates. Although she doesn't like what he's proposing, and she doesn't trust Golding, she supposes she sees the logic. Golding and his team have far more resources at their disposal to get the phone working. And, if it did belong to the victim, they'll be able to access the information and act on it with authority. It could get them a viable suspect, and even an arrest. Also, if they stop investigating now, she can put a bit more distance between herself and these people without arousing suspicion. She won't have to be on her guard, making sure she doesn't sound too much like she knows what she's talking about; it'd be safer for her and her situation, and help her limit the risk.

Yes, she sees the logic and the benefits. But, still, she doesn't like it.

21

PHILIP

He can see the disappointment on Moira's face – disappointment and frustration – and he understands that. He wants to keep the stuff they've discovered to themselves too, if the truth be told. But he's a stickler for the rules, always has been, even back in the day when the blokes would take the piss out of him and call him 'Follower Philip' at police training school. He'd got the last laugh, mind you. As DCI some of the people he'd trained with ended up serving under him. He smiles to himself at the memory. Then he remembers that some of them are still working; they weren't forced into retirement like him. Suddenly, rather than being his, the last laugh seems to have been on him.

Despite what happened, he still believes that rules are necessary for society to function well and not descend into chaos. You need structure to keep focused on the greater good and maintain law and order. Even those charged with upholding the law need rules to make sure they discharge their duties well. He grimaces. Even those responsible for upholding the law make mistakes sometimes.

Leaving the others sitting on the patio, Philip walks through the kitchen to the hallway. He can still hear them talking about the fruits of their afternoon of investigation. What they're doing now is outside of the rules. He knows that, and he encouraged it. Philip purses his lips. Tries to figure out where that came from. Breaking the rules is so unlike him.

He crosses the entrance hall and opens the door to his study. Switching the light on, he stands in the doorway and looks at the space – his domain: the book-filled built-ins with true crime and thrillers on the middle shelves and forensics and investigative text-books on the uppers. The big oak desk with the green leather pad in the middle, and the high-backed ergonomic chair that's the spitting image of the one he'd had at the police station as DCI.

Philip frowns. Is that what this investigation is about? Is he trying to rekindle his old life? He misses it bad; misses it like a piece of him was amputated on the day he retired. If he's honest about it he misses it as much, and maybe even a bit more, than he does his own children.

Maybe that's why he let that Detective Golding get to him.

Philip shakes his head. Was he too hasty writing off the detective bloke? The man had gone a lot of hours over clocking-off time due to catching the murder at the end of his shift; it's likely he wasn't thinking or acting his best. Could be he'd have handled their conversation better if he'd been fresher.

Philip thinks back to the conversation. Remembers how angry he was. How the tightness in his chest began the moment he heard the guy's condescending tone and ratcheted up another notch with every word he spoke. Philip doesn't think his clearest when he gets cross, Lizzie always tells him that. So it's possible he might have let his own emotions get the better of him. He hates being outside of the action, and detests being talked down to even more. The bloke got his back up. And, as a result, the investigation had seemed a good thing to do. But they've found things now – proper evidence; the phone that had been recently buried and that hairclip Lizzie fished out of the pool filter. And Lizzie could have been seen, been watched, by the killer.

Perhaps he should give the detective another chance. That's fair. Reasonable. He nods to himself. Reasonable, that's it. He's always prided himself on being fair and reasonable.

Dialling the detective's number, Philip waits for the call to connect. He tells himself to play it cool. Be calm and give the man a chance, even if he'd hung up on him the last time.

The phone's answered in two rings. 'Golding here.'

'Detective Golding, this is Philip Sweetman over at Ocean Mist.'

'Yes?' The detective's tone is frosty.

Philip presses on. Reminding himself to be calm, reasonable; to give the man the opportunity to do the right thing. 'I've got some more information I think you need to hear about. We've—'

'Let me stop you right there, sir.' Golding's words are thick with condescension. 'Like I said earlier, this is police business now and you seniors have no place trying to meddle in a—'

'But this is important.' Philip clenches his fingers tighter around the phone. He needs Golding to hear what they've found. 'We've visited the crime scene, and we've—'

'I said enough, goddammit.' Golding's voice is louder now. The condescending tone has been replaced with irritation. 'Now listen to me. You need to stop meddling and stop calling. I've got a job to do, and you need to let me do it. I don't *need* your help. I don't *want* your help. So quit calling.'

Philip's silent for a moment. Shocked. Feels the anger bubbling in his belly. The audacity of the man – the refusal to even listen – is infuriating. He hardens his tone. Bangs his fist against the oak desk as he speaks. 'You have to hear me out on—'

'Goodbye.' The way Golding says the word makes it sound more like a growl. Seconds later the call disconnects.

Philip's heart is bashing against his ribcage as if it's trying to break out. He puts his hand against his chest. He's not meant to get overexcited; the doc warned him about that, told him he needed an easy life, stress free. He clenches his fist. Presses it harder against his chest. There's nothing stress free about interacting with bloody Detective Golding.

Still angry, Philip shoves his phone into his pocket and walks back through the house to the others. He grabs a beer from the fridge on the way. Twists off the cap and takes a long drink.

He thinks again about Golding's tone; such a smug, know-it-all bastard. Thinks of the warning to stay out of the investigation that the detective gave him and the lack of respect he'd shown. Golding hadn't even given him the chance to tell him about the phone or the man following Moira for God's sake. It beggared belief. What kind of detective shuts down a caller with potential evidence in a murder case before they've even had the time to talk about what they've got? Philip takes another swig of beer.

He – *they*, as a team of four – need to keep working the case, that much is crystal clear. And he refuses to feel bad about breaking the rules for a single moment longer. Golding doesn't give a damn, and that young woman in the pool deserves justice. If the police aren't going to get it, then it's up to them. Philip takes another swig and makes a solemn vow.

No more fair and reasonable.

No more sharing of information and trying to help.

They'll solve this case and that bastard Golding can go to hell.

22

MOIRA

She can see things didn't go well from the expression on Philip's face as he stomps on to the patio and plonks himself down on his chair. Moira knew it was a long shot – after the way Golding treated Philip earlier, they all knew that – but she'd hoped for better, for his sake, and for hers. If Golding had stepped up and made Philip feel the police were taking proper care with the murder case, he'd stop investigating and she'd be able to step away from this group of ex-law enforcement types and reorientate any contact they had into something a lot more casual. She could stop watching what she said for fear of giving herself away. It'd limit the risk, and make her feel a lot less tense than she's feeling right now.

Rick leans towards Philip, earnest expression on his face. 'How'd it go?'

Philip shakes his head. His cheeks are flushed and he's holding his beer in a death-grip. 'He didn't let me speak long enough to tell him about the phone, the hairclip or the bloke spying on Moira. Told me to back off and then hung up on me again.'

'What, he didn't even . . .' Lizzie looks furious.

Moira knows the feeling. Victims of crime deserve justice, but the way Golding's behaving he doesn't seem to give a shit. 'What's the matter with the cops in this place?'

'Damned if I know.' Philip blows out hard. Takes a gulp of beer and looks at Rick.

Rick shrugs. 'Look, I've not met the man myself, but the word from my police contacts is that Golding is a known asshole. He likes the glory of a closed case, but he doesn't like the legwork. I guess that's some of what we're seeing here.'

'But I was offering him information,' says Philip. 'You'd think he'd have heard me out at least.'

'Yep,' says Rick. 'That you would.'

None of them speak. Everyone is lost in their own thoughts.

'So what's our next move?' says Rick, breaking the silence. 'You still want a crack at this thing?'

'Of course I do,' says Philip. 'We all do, don't we?'

Lizzie and Rick nod.

Moira hesitates. This could be her way out. She shakes her head. 'Look, I'm still not feeling great, and my ankle is pretty busted up. I think it'd be better if I bow out at this point and leave you guys to—'

'We need you,' says Lizzie. 'You chased after that man on the trail. You found the phone. Even if you're not feeling on top form you're still essential to the team.'

The team. Shit.

Moira takes a sharp inhale. She doesn't want to be part of a team. That's not what coming here is about. She needs to keep herself to herself. Build a new life, away from law enforcement, away from trouble. 'I just—'

'You can't back out. We won't let you,' says Philip. His tone is no-nonsense. It makes what he's saying sound non-negotiable. 'You're one of us now.'

'Well, I . . .' Moira looks at their faces. Lizzie's nodding. Rick looks keen. Impatience radiates from Philip. She knows she can't back out now, however much she might think she wants to. Because although she knows it'd be safer if she stopped investigating with them, a big part of her wants to see it through. She needs to find out who killed that young woman, and she wants them to face the consequences of their actions. She can't leave justice to someone as indifferent as Detective James R. Golding. 'Okay. I'm still in.'

'Good,' says Philip. 'And, for my part, there'll be no more trying to engage Golding in any more pieces of evidence or leads that we find. He's had his chance and he's blown it.'

'Agreed,' says Lizzie. 'The way Golding's going that poor young woman will end up an afterthought on an unsolved crime database for the next however many years. We can't let that happen.'

'Totally,' says Rick. 'We need to work this, and if we find the perpetrator we can deliver them gift-wrapped to Golding.'

'*When*,' says Lizzie. Her voice is determined. The anxiety of earlier seems forgotten. '*When* we find the perpetrator.'

'Yep. For sure,' says Rick. 'When.'

Moira likes the grit in Lizzie's voice, but from the way she's looking at Philip she can tell she's worried. Moira's not surprised. Philip's cheeks are still flushed and his skin is looking kind of waxy. Not a good sign, especially after what Lizzie told her earlier about him having heart problems. She catches Lizzie's eye. 'It's getting late, time I made a move and left you to—'

'Stay for dinner, please.' Lizzie glances from her to Rick. 'We can talk about our next moves, how we'll follow up the leads we've got.'

'If you're sure?' says Moira.

'Yes, yes, you must,' says Philip, gesturing towards their make-do murder board on the patio doors. 'We've still got a lot to work through.'

'But we'll eat first,' says Lizzie, giving Philip a stern look.

'Of course,' says Philip. 'I'll help you make dinner.'

Moira watches Lizzie and Philip take the evidence they've collected inside as they go to make a start on dinner. As they step through into the kitchen she sees Lizzie reach out and give Philip's hand a squeeze. He puts the phone in the plastic bag wrapper on to the counter, and pulls her to him into a hug. They stand, arms entwined, motionless for a long moment. Moira feels her cheeks colour and looks away. Watching them feels like she's intruding on their privacy.

'Good work finding the phone.'

Moira turns to Rick. Suddenly, now it's just the two of them out here, he seems closer than before. She can smell his aftershave, something with citrus, and feel the warmth that seems to radiate from him. 'Thanks.'

'If we can get into it, and it's the victim's, it'll be a game changer.'

'Let's hope it's a yes to both of those things.'

'True that.' Rick's looking at her with real intensity and it makes her feel a little awkward, like a teenager rather than the grown woman she is. She shifts in her seat. Tries to shake off the feeling and keep her mind on the case; on the leads they've got and need to chase down. It's hard though. And she doesn't get why.

Looking away from Rick, she glances out across the garden. The bug chorus is singing from the lawn and the flower beds. The floodlights keep the patio and the area of garden surrounding it illuminated, but beyond the reach of the lights the darkness is absolute.

Or is it? The more she looks, the more Moira sees gradients of darkness. And movement. Just beyond the neatly clipped low hedge that borders the edge of the garden, flush to the fence. What's that shape? Is it someone crouching down, watching them? Her breath catches in her throat. Her heart beats faster. Leaning forward, she squints into the gloom.

She flinches as sprinklers pop up from the lawn and there's a hiss of water as it starts to jet across the grass and the borders. Through the fine mist she can't see anything clearly. She blinks, trying to refocus, and sits up taller so she can see over the spray, but it's not enough. Jumping up, she hurries over to the fence line, scanning the ornamental hedge and the pavement and street beyond, but the shape that she thought she saw moments earlier doesn't seem to be there now.

Moira frowns. Maybe there was nothing there in the first place. Turning, she walks back over to the patio.

'Hey, you okay?'

Moira looks up to see Rick staring at her, all concerned. Sitting back down on her chair, she forces a smile. 'Yeah, I'm . . .'

'You're looking like you've seen a ghost or something.'

'It's nothing, just my imagination going crazy.' She waves his concerns away. Even if the person watching them from the Wild Ridge Trail had worked out who they were and where they lived, would he really come here? If he had been the killer surely he wouldn't risk it.

She hadn't got a good look at the person ahead of her on the trail. He was male, she was sure of that, and had been wearing a hoodie. Medium build. It had been hard to gauge his height with the sun in her eyes, but she figured it was around six feet. Lots of people fit that description, and she hadn't got a look at his face. She doubted she'd even recognise him. She'd recognise the blond guy from earlier in the day though. It bothers her that he'd been following her, and that he'd run when she'd tried to talk to him. She still doesn't know why he's spying on her.

Rick looks at her with concern. 'If you're—'

'I am.' She needs to change the subject. Doesn't want to dwell on someone being out there. It's probably just her mind playing tricks – she's tired, bruised and those codeine painkillers Lizzie gave her could be messing with her head. She forces another smile. 'How did it go collecting in the weekly logs?'

'So-so,' says Rick. 'Not everyone was home, but I've got a big enough batch to start working through them.'

'Do you think someone's hiding something?'

'Nope, I don't have any suspicions and no one acted weird in the community-watch meeting. Some were self-centred and more worried about their golf game or property prices, and a few were quick to blame the construction workers over on district eleven, but that's more about them and their prejudices than the murder. You know how it is.' Rick flicks a bug off his jeans-clad thigh. Looks thoughtful. 'Still, you never can tell about people. Best to keep an open mind, and follow the evidence to make sure. Everyone's a suspect until they're eliminated, best way not to get blind-sided.'

Moira thinks of McCord. How she'd trusted him. No matter how long you've known someone and what you've been through together, you never really *know* them. He'd taught her that the hard way. Trusting him had made her lose everything. Even so, when she replies even she's surprised at the amount of bitterness she hears in her voice. 'True – you can't ever tell what people are like.'

Rick raises an eyebrow. 'Sounds like there's a story there.'

'Yeah, a long one.'

Rick glances through the patio doors into the kitchen. Lizzie and Philip are working side by side on the far countertop, preparing a salad and some kind of meat. 'Looks like we've got some time if you fancy telling it?'

She doesn't know how she'd even begin. Would she start by telling him how she and McCord first met, how they'd become friends and what great partners they were? Or should she begin at the end, with the betrayal and the death? The guilt. The shame. And the end of everything?

Rick is looking at her with a kindly expression on his face. He's no doubt a good listener, and maybe telling someone the whole truth would help. She opens her mouth to answer, then closes it again. Who is she kidding? To tell him the story, she'd first have to tell him she'd been police, where she'd worked, what her job was, and she can't do that. She bites her lip. What happened, happened, and it was her fault. Them dying was her fault. Telling someone about it, explaining the signs she failed to see, won't change that and never can. It's impossible to scrub the blood from her hands. They're stained with it now, forever.

She meets Rick's gaze. Gives a shake of her head. 'Not really.'

He holds her eye contact for a beat longer than usual. 'Got it. Another time perhaps.'

Moira tries to keep her tone light, but it breaks as she says, 'Maybe.'

'Nearly ready.' Lizzie bustles back on to the patio carrying a large bowl of salad and a stack of plates with cutlery balanced on the top, and sets them down on the table.

'Great,' says Moira. She feels weary. It could be the events of the day, the fall up on the trail and her busted ankle, the codeine or the feelings stirred up by the conversation with Rick – whatever it is, suddenly she feels knackered.

Lizzie doesn't seem to notice. She's in full hostess mode now. Fussing over plate placement and cutlery, folded napkins and condiments in fancy wooden grinders. Moira doesn't even have napkins, and the salt and pepper she uses come from the plastic mills you buy at the supermarket.

Emerging from the kitchen, Philip fires up his top-of-the-range outdoor grill and starts loading thick-cut steaks on to it. 'Medium rare good for everyone?'

Rick and Lizzie agree. Moira does the same even though she doesn't really feel hungry. If she's honest, she feels quite weird – discombobulated, detached.

Lizzie looks at Rick and Moira. 'Wine, beer?'

'I'll gladly take a beer,' says Rick.

Moira doesn't like to drink. Avoids anything that dulls the senses and makes her less alert. She glances back out across the lawn where the sprinklers are doing their work in the darkness. She needs to be on the ball, especially at the moment. 'I'll stick with water, thanks.'

As Lizzie goes back into the kitchen for the drinks and Philip cooks, Moira picks up the marker pen on the table and steps over to the patio doors. She adds a column with the heading 'Person of interest' and lists out the description of the guy she'd caught watching her three times earlier that day: *Male. Approx five foot 8 inches. Slim. Blond, short hair. Black-framed glasses. Navy hoodie. Maroon and gold scarf. Silver VW Beetle.*

Then, from the column headed 'Killer', she makes a sub-column branching off below headed 'Suspect 1' and lists out the things she remembers: *Male. Six foot? Medium build. Hoodie. Binoculars. Wild Ridge Trail (Moira). ?Manatee Park (Lizzie). Buried mobile?*

'What about the colour of the hoodie?' says Rick.

It's a good point. As Moira turns to answer, she notices Philip looking at her and what she's writing from where he's standing at the grill. There's a frown on his face. 'You okay, Philip?'

'Yes, yes, all good.' He looks flustered for a moment. Like he's been caught out doing something he shouldn't. 'I just . . .'

Lizzie laughs. 'It's because you're writing on the glass – the board.'

'I usually hold the pen in my investigations,' says Philip.

Moira gives a tight smile. She knows she's a guest in this man's house, and agreed to help the group with their investigation, but Philip's bossy, listen-to-me tone is really grating on her. She won't defer to him. Stays put beside the patio doors. Grips the marker pen a little harder. Meets his gaze. 'So do I in mine.'

Rick raises his eyebrows. 'Is that right?'

Moira realises her mistake too late. She curses silently inside her mind. Knows that she's blown it.

Philip frowns, looking half-irritated, half-confused. 'And what investigations do you usually do?'

She looks from Philip to Rick to Lizzie, trying to think of a way to persuade them they misheard, or she meant something different; anything to put them off the scent. Fails. She'll have to brazen it out. 'I was an investigator, of sorts.'

'Exactly what sort?' says Philip.

Tell them enough truth to be plausible, Moira tells herself, but not too much. She clenches her jaw. Who is she trying to kid? Telling them anything is a risk. She has to keep details to a bare minimum. 'I was a DCI. Undercover.'

Rick's pointing at her, smiling. 'I knew it. You had to have something going on. Your instincts are way too good for a first-timer.'

'I thought so too,' says Philip. His tone is curt. He's obviously pissed off. 'Shame you didn't think to tell us before, it would have stopped me looking like a fool every time I explained things for you.'

I doubt knowing I was a DCI would have stopped you, thinks Moira.

'Why didn't you mention it when we were talking earlier?' says Lizzie. She sounds hurt and Moira can see the distrust is back in her eyes.

Damn. Moira gives Lizzie an apologetic look. 'I'm sorry. When I first came here I was trying to assimilate to retirement. It was strange not to be on the job any more and I found it easier if I didn't talk about it.'

'But you could have told me today,' says Lizzie, frowning. 'We were talking about retirement and everything. I don't get why you'd hide it from—'

'Look, I was going to tell you earlier, but Philip and Rick got back before I could and then—'

'It's not really that big of a deal,' Rick says, grinning and giving Moira a light, friendly punch on the shoulder. 'Four retired law enforcers uniting to crack this case. Who'd have thought it? We should call ourselves the retired detectives club.'

'Not all of us were detectives,' says Lizzie. 'And it *is* a big deal to me.'

'Why does it matter? You know now,' says Rick amicably. 'It can be real hard making the switch from the job into retirement. Moira's not the first ex-cop I've met who's had a hard time talking about the life.'

Lizzie shrugs.

Moira knows she's going to have to put some time into getting Lizzie back onside. The trust they'd built earlier on their visit to the Manatee Park crime scene has been eroded by the revelation of her old job.

Philip looks from Lizzie to Rick and then to Moira. Clears his throat. 'Well, I guess it's good to have you on the team, Detective Chief Inspector.'

'Thanks,' says Moira, but Philip's forced smile isn't fooling her and there's an undercurrent of irritation to his jovial tone. His nose is badly out of joint over her being ex-police, but that's just too bad. There's nothing she can do now.

Rick rubs his palms together. 'Time for us to all work a little differently then, given we've got so much expertise in the group. We need to make sure we're playing to each other's strengths.'

'Agreed,' says Moira. She gestures towards the patio door. 'And I guess that means we can all write on the murder board.'

Philip passes the spatula he's holding from hand to hand, looking uncomfortable. 'Well, usually I'd assign duties according to rank and—'

'This isn't our job. We don't need formal structures,' says Lizzie firmly. She's looking at Philip and has angled her body away from Moira, deliberately avoiding eye contact. 'We can find a way of working together that works for all of us.'

142

'True, true,' says Philip. He's still frowning, but he nods and turns back to attend to the steaks. As he flips them he says, 'We're all equals.'

Moira's glad to hear it, but she doesn't quite believe him. She's pretty sure he'd rather they agreed he was in charge, and she expects that there'll be trouble ahead – they're bound to clash over actions to take, evidence to follow up on, but she's happy to go along with things for now. She doesn't have the energy for a fight tonight. So she turns her attention back to Rick's original question. Looks over and catches his eye. 'The guy's hoodie was a dark colour, dark grey I think, but it could have been navy. It was hard to tell at that distance and with the sun in my eyes.'

'Worth including that,' he says, gesturing to the list on the glass doors.

'Totally.' She adds 'dark grey/navy' next to the word 'Hoodie' on the board. Then puts the marker pen back on the table and takes a seat next to Rick.

Philip serves the steaks.

Lizzie gives them fresh drinks. 'Dig in,' she says.

The food is good, and Moira's feeling ravenous now that it's sitting right in front of her. She's cutting a piece of steak when Philip starts with the questions.

'Where was your base, when you were on the job?' asks Philip, as he stuffs a chunk of steak covered in sauce into his mouth.

'London,' says Moira.

'Whereabouts?' he asks, still chewing.

Moira's doesn't like it when people talk with their mouth full, and she's not keen on these questions either. She can't go into detail, but she doesn't want Philip to think she's being evasive so she keeps her answers vague. 'North of the river.'

'Yes, yes,' Philip says. 'That's old Jack Mortimer's neck of the woods, isn't it?'

'He wasn't my gaffer, but I knew of him. Great character.'

'What did you—'

'Come on man, let Moira eat,' says Rick. 'She hasn't even had a bite.'

Philip rolls his eyes. 'Yes, yes, fine.'

Moira glances at Rick and gives him a smile of thanks. With the conversation paused, they eat. The bug chorus plays on around them. The ceiling fan above whirs in a steady rhythm. The night is warm and the humidity hasn't dropped much. Despite the food, Moira feels tiredness seep further into her bones.

Lizzie is the first to finish. As she sets her knife and fork down she looks across at Moira. 'I know you said the phone might not work, but I can see what I can get from it. I used to be pretty good at the tech stuff back in the day.'

'Sounds good,' says Moira. She's stuffed now. Can't even finish the last few mouthfuls of steak even though it's so good. Being around these people is draining and the weariness is getting to her now. She's already let her guard slip too far – and had to tell them she was ex-police as a result. She can't afford any more lapses of control. Needs her own space. No more talking. The dogs to stroke and a peaceful, quiet house. She looks at Philip. 'This was great, thanks, but I'm flagging. I need to call it a day.'

Philip nods. 'Yes, okay.'

Moira bites back the urge to tell him she wasn't asking his permission.

'So what's the plan for tomorrow?' says Lizzie.

'We need to collect the rest of the weekly logs from the patrollers we didn't catch up with today,' says Philip.

'And I'll make some calls,' says Rick. 'See if I can get some inside intel on what's going on in the investigation and also chase up my contact looking into the station wagon's plate, see if they've found who it's registered to.'

'Good thinking,' says Moira. Her brain is sluggish. Thinking feels like wading through treacle. But she needs a plan for tomorrow that doesn't involve being around these people the whole time. 'I was thinking I could try and get a look at the gate logs, see if they've got the driver of the station wagon on there, and also any record of a woman matching our victim's description entering our neighbourhood as a walk-in. After that I'll head over to the CCTV office and see if they'll let me see the tapes for the past few weeks.' She smiles. 'Might take a while to get through, but could be useful.'

'Good call,' says Rick.

Philip gives a curt nod. 'Agreed. An excellent idea.'

Moira forces herself not to rise to the fact that Philip's still acting like he thinks he's the boss.

'I'll find a way to test the water sample.' Lizzie looks at Moira. 'And have a go at hacking into the phone.'

'Sounds like we've got ourselves a plan,' says Moira. She's trying to be upbeat, but it's hard now. It's not late – barely ten o'clock. But all she really wants to do is sleep.

'Good, good,' says Philip, the bossy tone back in his voice. 'Get a good night's rest, everyone, then get back on it first thing. We'll reconvene here at twelve hundred hours tomorrow.'

As they all nod in agreement, Moira's already thinking about her bed. She wants to get this case solved and force Golding, this local detective who really doesn't seem to give a crap, to take action and get some kind of justice for the victim. But to do her best work, and prevent herself slipping up and revealing her secrets, she needs to sleep. It's eluded her for so long; she's only managing to doze for short periods, ever since McCord. But tonight, after everything that's happened, she feels like she might actually manage to sleep properly.

In the morning she'll chase down the entry logs and the CCTV.

In the morning she'll find the killer.

23

PHILIP

He wakes with a start. Disorientated. Confused.

What's that noise?

He hears it again. Thumping. Banging.

There's a moment of silence, and then a scraping sound as if something heavy is being dragged across the ceiling. He looks up. The chandelier light fitting is trembling. Whatever's happening, it's going on above him. The noise is coming from the loft.

Is it Lizzie? No, he doubts that. It can't be. She's never been in the loft the whole time they've lived here. Never been in the loft of any house they've had. And there's no light from the hallway leaching under the door into his bedroom; the house is in darkness. If it were Lizzie she'd have turned the lights on.

There's only one other explanation. Someone else is in the house.

Trying not to think about the ache in his chest and his jackhammering heartbeat, he throws off the duvet and quickly pushes himself up to standing. The movement's too quick, far too quick. There's a twinge of pain in his lower back, and he winces as he straightens up. It's taking him longer to get going these days and his body doesn't appreciate the urgency of this situation. Still, he can't let that slow him. He needs to know what's going on. Check if Lizzie is okay. He has to know if there's an intruder in the house.

His heart pounds harder against his ribs.

He feels a tightening around his chest.

Ignoring it, he steps into his slippers and looks around the bedroom for something he can use to defend himself. There's not much that's any use – a few framed paintings of sailing scenes on the walls, the chest of drawers against the wall at the far end of the bed with his television on it, the matching bedside tables. His gaze lingers on the bedside lamps. They're sturdy and wooden. A bit cumbersome to handle, but the best he's got to hand. Unplugging the nearest lamp, he removes the shade and bulb. It's a good weight, solid. It could do the job.

Lamp base in hand, he moves towards the door. Easing the handle down as quietly as he can, he opens the door and steps out into the dark hallway. He looks towards Lizzie's bedroom. There's a dull glow from the nightlight just outside it, but her door is closed and there's no light showing from beneath it. She must still be sleeping. That's good. He can't let anyone hurt her. Has to find the intruder.

He grips the lamp base tighter. It's feeling heavier. He chased down his fair share of criminals back in the day, but it's been years since he's done anything that strenuous and he's not as fit as he used to be. Turning, he glances the other way along the hall, and that's when he sees it.

The loft hatch is open and the ladder pulled down.

There's a light on up inside the loft.

Raising the lamp base as if it's a baseball bat ready to strike, Philip pads as softly as he can along the hallway towards the hatch. He can hear the person moving around up there. There's the sound of boxes being dragged across the boards. What the hell are they doing? What kind of burglar goes in a loft?

147

His heart's pumping. The squeezing across his chest is getting worse.

Holding tight to the lamp, he grips the loft ladder with his other hand and starts to slowly climb. His palms are sweaty, and fear makes his movements jerky, awkward. But it's not just fear he's feeling, not any more. It's anger too. How dare someone break into his house? Invade his space and his privacy? He's going to show them what's what.

The anger helps him heave himself up the last few rungs of the ladder. He launches into the loft space, lamp raised like a bat, ready to fight, charging in the direction of where he last heard movement. He lets out a war cry.

Lizzie screams and drops the box she's holding.

Philip stops. Lowers the lamp base.

His heart's pounding – he can feel it in his chest and his temples. The tightness is stifling. He feels light-headed. Sick. Can't speak. He doubles over, waiting for his body to calm. Praying for it to recover.

He hears footsteps coming towards him. Feels Lizzie's hand on his shoulder. 'Are you okay?'

Philip doesn't answer. He needs to get his breath. He focuses on his inhale and exhale for a few breaths and then straightens up a bit and looks at Lizzie. She's in a short cotton nightie, blue, teamed with a pair of old faded Converse. Her hair is down, her face make-up free. She looks about ten years younger than her true age, maybe more. Right now he feels as if he's a hundred.

Lizzie looks down at the lamp base. 'What's going on? Were you going to whack me?'

'You didn't turn on the hall light.' There's an ache deep inside his chest. He presses his hand against it, tries to rub the discomfort away. Wheezes. 'Your bedroom door was closed.'

Lizzie looks concerned. 'I didn't want to wake you.'

'But I thought you were a burglar, creeping around up here, moving things about . . .' His chest is easing a bit and his breathing is coming easier, steadier. Straightening up fully, he looks around. Last time he was up here the boxes and containers had all been neatly stacked against the far wall. Now they're scattered and chaotic. 'What are you doing up here? You never come in the loft.'

Lizzie's eyes widen. She looks at the boxes as if only now seeing the mess she's made. 'I'm sorry, love. I needed to find something and I wasn't sure where it was.'

'But it's the middle of the bloody night. You couldn't wait until morning?'

'I wasn't sleeping. Thought I may as well have a look.'

It sounds plausible, but they've been married a lot of years and she's always hated lofts. She's always made a big song and dance about the height of the ladder and spiders and dust. He's the loft guy, always has been. It makes no sense that she's willingly come up here now. 'Did you find it?'

Lizzie smiles, gesturing to the box at her feet. 'Just this minute.'

Philip looks down at the box. The top is folded over so he can't see the contents inside. 'What is it?'

Pulling the flaps back, Lizzie lifts a square silver-coloured metal trunk out of the box. 'It's my old field kit.'

He recognises it now. Remembers it sitting in the utility room of their old house, always ready to be taken to the car and off to a crime scene when Lizzie got an out-of-hours call. He runs his hand across his bald pate. Frowns. 'I didn't know you kept it.'

'I know I shouldn't have, but I couldn't part with it and they never chased me.'

Philip looks at the kit. He'd always had the impression Lizzie was pleased to leave her job. Yes, he's pretty sure she'd said she *wanted* to leave when he retired. He'd struggled with an enforced life of leisure and had envied the way his wife had taken to retirement, seemingly walking away from her career without regret or a backwards glance. But if she'd kept the kit, maybe he'd been wrong about that. Perhaps she *had* missed it, and that's why she'd held on to the metal trunk, squirrelling it away up here in the loft without him knowing. He can understand that. He knows how it feels to want to keep a bit of your old life in your new one. Reaching out, he gives her arm an affectionate rub. 'Retirement is tough. Old habits die hard.'

He feels her tense beneath his touch. A frown creases her forehead before she looks away. He's not sure what that's about, but he can guess, so he stays silent. Doesn't want to ask. It'll probably make things worse. Better not to talk about it. Lizzie made it clear earlier she was worried about him getting involved in the murder case. She's probably still conflicted.

Lizzie unfastens the clasps on the front of the trunk and opens the lid. She runs her fingers over the neatly sorted kit, then looks up and meets his gaze. She smiles, but it doesn't reach her eyes. 'Everything's here. I should be able to test that water sample.'

He smiles back. Ignores the tension between them, just as he did for all those months after he'd retired. 'I'll get back to bed then.'

24

LIZZIE

She didn't have the heart to tell Philip the truth. She's spent nearly ten years, ever since he retired and they came here, trying to forget and forgive, and she's almost managed it. These days, ninety-five per cent of the time she doesn't think about it, and for the remaining five per cent, well, she tries not to get too angry. Yoga helps. Painting does too. But now he's at it again – playing the big police chief – she can't bury her head in the sand any more. She needs to know what really happened before his heart attack and be able to spot the warning signs.

She has to be prepared.

Lizzie scans the boxes that now litter the loft space higgledy-piggledy style. She could have sworn the files were up here. Philip had them in a blue metal file case, like an over-wide briefcase, but she's opened everything and hasn't found it. He must have moved it somewhere else. She needs to work out where.

Keeping her field kit and the box it was in separate, Lizzie moves the other boxes back to their original neat positions along the back wall. She stacks them two boxes high, just as they were, then returns to the silver trunk. First she collapses the box it was packed in and leans the flattened cardboard against the end of the line of boxes. Then she turns her attention to the field kit. The metal trunk isn't very big, but it's heavy. Picking it up, she carries it over to the edge of the loft hatch. Getting it down is going to be a challenge.

First she steps on to the ladder and slowly lowers herself down through the hatch. Then she reaches for the trunk and slides it across the boarded loft floor towards her until it's teetering half over the edge. Taking a deep breath, she grips the handle on the top of the trunk and lifts it over the edge.

The weight of it almost causes her to lose her balance on the ladder. She grits her teeth. Swallows hard. Focuses on putting one foot after the other, climbing her way down.

When she reaches the landing floor and the comfort of the carpet beneath her feet, she exhales. She hadn't realised she was holding her breath until that moment. It's not a surprise though. She's always hated heights and darkness – put them together and it's the worst of both worlds. That's why she's never been up in the loft since putting her field kit there, never gone in the lofts of any of their homes. Philip had seemed shaken to find her up there.

Lizzie frowns, remembering the look on Philip's face when he'd seen her – a mixture of shock and worry. Did he buy her story about the kit? she wonders. Maybe, but she isn't sure.

She folds the loft ladder back up through the hatch and fastens the hatch door. Picking up the field kit, she carries it back downstairs to the main living space and sets it down on the island in the kitchen.

She glances at the clock. It's almost 3 a.m. She should try and get some sleep, but she doesn't feel remotely tired. Knowing there's no point trying to force it, she switches on the kettle and puts a teabag into a mug. While she waits for the kettle to boil she reaches into the pocket of her dressing gown and pulls out the old newspaper article she'd removed from its hiding place inside her old edition of *War and Peace*. She shakes her head. That's what a long marriage does to you – forces you to hide your secrets in the places your husband will never look. Philip shuns the classics; the books he reads are either crime fiction or true crime. She would have thought he'd have had enough of that in his job, but then maybe that's the attraction – getting to live vicariously through the books.

Exhaling, she sets the ageing, yellowing clipping on to the countertop. Smoothing out the creases, she takes a breath and starts to read.

Goodbye to Beloved Top Brass

On Tuesday the Thames Valley Police said goodbye to its longest-serving DCI. Detective Chief Inspector Philip Sweetman worked within the Thames Valley for his whole career. He'd been battling health issues for some time and has now decided to take his retirement and some much-deserved relaxation.

A well-known figure in our community, amongst his many achievements DCI Sweetman led the team that uncovered the identity of the Hillside Strangler, and played a leading role in breaking the 'Harvester' people and drugs-trafficking ring that was operating out of a number of farms within our Buckinghamshire countryside, which resulted in 38 convictions.

In more recent years he's focused on mentoring his team – earning him the coveted local 'top boss' award three years in a row – and on increasing police outreach and community involvement. And his efforts have paid dividends – bringing about significant drops in the violent crime statistics for the Thames Valley that have been sustained, year on year, for the past eight.

So as DCI Philip Sweetman eases into retirement, his successor, DCI Robert Keene, will be taking his place, and he has some big shoes to fill. We'll be keeping an eye on the crime stats with interest!

Lizzie shakes her head. Their local paper wasn't known for much more than local puff pieces anyway, but the article is light even by its own standards. And fabricated of course. Not Philip's service record, that's accurate enough, and it is true that his team had a lot of respect for him. Had – that's the key word. But the reason given in the article for his retirement is at best a partial truth.

The real story is very different. The media never got wind of it, but that first year during the aftermath, through to his leaving celebrations and then the beginning of retirement, she lived in fear that they would. But police protect their own, even if they've as good as fired them for something hideous. It stopped the media hounding them and their dirty laundry getting aired in public. She supposes for that she should be thankful, but in a way she isn't. Because the truth was hidden, it let Philip live the lie – the retired hero – when, really, he was anything but.

He was the villain.

She'd asked him for the details at the time. She'd wanted to know just how much of a villain he'd been. What he'd done, and why that meant he'd been forced into retirement – not trusted any longer to lead cases. Now, because of this murder that he's intent on investigating, she has to assess just how badly wrong things could go.

He hadn't wanted her to know the details at the time. At first he'd fobbed her off with the same line that had been told to the staff and the press, but she knew him well enough to know he was hiding something. And, anyway, plenty of police go back to work after recovering from a heart attack – why had he been treated differently?

So she'd kept on asking. When he'd eventually told her, a brief outline of the critical incidents – the cause and effect – had been enough for her to stomach. She'd wanted to forgive and forget. Told herself that he'd been under a lot of pressure at the time, what with it being such a high-profile case, and anyone can have an error of judgement. He'd been her teenage sweetheart. She couldn't imagine a life without him. Still can't, if she's honest. She'd thought forgiving and forgetting was the only way.

Shaking her head, Lizzie thinks back to those months immediately before and just after Philip's retirement. He'd been below par, of course, still recovering from the massive heart attack and emergency heart surgery that had saved his life, but it wasn't just that. He'd been weak and tired, but also withdrawn. And as his health improved, the dejected demeanour didn't. She'd tried to talk with him about what had happened, but he'd been in obvious discomfort each time she raised the subject, and on the odd occasion he'd let her ask a question he usually said he couldn't remember and that the things that happened around that time were all a vague blur. *'I can't remember,'* thinks Lizzie, shaking her head. Him saying that was like an American mobster taking the fifth. That's why she'd kept on pushing.

The kettle comes to the boil and she pours water on to her teabag. Pokes the teabag with a spoon. Rereads the old newspaper article. The half-truths and forced joviality of it grates on her.

She clenches her teeth. Feels a muscle pulse in her jaw.

How well do you ever know someone else? She's known Philip nearly sixty years, and they've been married for nearly forty, and yet he was still capable of doing something that blind-sided her. When he'd got home from having his heart surgery she'd moved into the spare room so he could have his own bed while he recovered. She'd never moved back. Had never been able to bring herself to, even though she knew that's what he wanted. She knows, deep down, she's never really forgiven him for what he did – for being the villain dressed in a hero's uniform.

She pulls the teabag out of the mug and drops it into the trash. The tea's stewed now, but she doesn't mind. She adds extra milk and takes a sip. The tea's fine but there's something niggling in her mind – a suspicion that she's kept buried all this time, but that now Philip's set on investigating the murder at Manatee Park, Lizzie just can't let go any longer. Because although he promised he'd told her what happened, there was something about the way he'd said it, and the look on his face as he turned away and thought she couldn't see the despair, that has always made her wonder if there was something he wasn't telling. She needs to be sure he did tell her the whole truth of what happened, and for that she has to find the files – the full story of his enforced retirement has to be inside their buff-coloured folders. It might have happened almost ten years ago, but she needs to be sure.

Lizzie shakes her head. Takes a big breath. This is ridiculous. She's a grown woman – sixty-four years old – and she knows her own mind. She's a survivor – strong, resilient. She'll handle whatever truth she finds.

She exhales, and really hopes that's true.

There's only one way to know for certain – she has to find the files. There are other places they could be aside from the loft – the garage, Philip's bedroom or the study perhaps. She needs to go through each place and do a methodical search.

Lizzie thinks for a moment. She can't go into Philip's bedroom now while he's sleeping, and the garage door tends to stick and need a hard shove – that might arouse suspicion if Philip's still awake and hears the door going. That leaves her one option that she can investigate right now.

Picking up her tea, Lizzie pads down the hallway towards the study.

25

MOIRA

Moira wakes early, blinking in the sunlight that's streaming in through the half-open curtains. Her ankle's throbbing and she feels groggy. Turning over, she squints at the alarm clock on her bedside cabinet. It's almost 7.30 a.m.

She can't believe it. Stares at the alarm clock for a couple more seconds, just making sure. She'd gone to bed around eleven last night, just a short while after Rick had dropped her home and she'd let the dogs out into the garden before feeding them. She doesn't even remember waking in the night. So it seems her usual insomnia stayed away – which means she's slept for pretty close to eight and a half hours. Moira can't remember the last time she slept for so long, but she knows it was before everything that happened with McCord.

Throwing off the duvet, she gets out of bed and limps to the shower. Her ankle has swollen more overnight, and there's an alarming purple bruise spreading up her leg from the outside of her foot. As the water cascades over her body, she bends down and presses her fingers against her ankle. Winces. It's painful. Frustrating. She's got a lot to do today. She doesn't want an injury slowing her down.

Getting out of the shower, Moira dries herself off and dresses quickly – jeans, black T-shirt and her usual scuffed purple trainers.

She feeds the dogs and gives them some attention – Pip and Wolfie get tummy tickles, then she throws Marigold's ball across the garden a few times, much to the delight of the gangly pup. She walks over to the hedge bordering the street and scans the road and pavements, but there's no sign of the silver VW Beetle or the wiry blond guy from yesterday. After a while she calls the dogs inside and locks and bolts the back door. Finding a Tubigrip in a drawer in the kitchen, Moira pulls it on to support her ankle, then takes a couple of aspirin with her coffee.

As she drinks, Moira checks the news app on her phone. She flicks past the national news to the local section, then frowns. That's weird. None of the top five local headlines are about The Homestead. There's a story about a local baseball player and his new home, a short report on a carjacking in Orlando, a story about a baby abandoned on the beach out near Tampa and a couple of articles on home improvements and crafting trends – nothing about the murder. Moira keeps scrolling, scanning more of the local news articles. She makes it to the end of the news section without finding any mention of The Homestead or Ocean Mist.

That's definitely weird. The murder of a young woman is far more newsworthy than the latest crocheting technique, surely? She makes a mental note to bring it up later with the others, and see what they think.

Moira downs the last of her coffee then looks at her watch. It's just gone eight, and she's ready to go. She sees no point in waiting. Promising the dogs a walk when she gets back, Moira slips out of the house, double-locks the door behind her and heads towards the Ocean Mist gatehouse.

The air is crisp, the humidity low, and there's steam coming off the grass as the heat from the rising sun burns away the dew. The birds are twittering in the trees. The early-morning air feels just like it did yesterday, but things are different now. There's no new *tabula rasa*. This isn't Groundhog Day. Her blank slate from yesterday is still splattered with blood and sprinkled with water-sodden dollars. It'll stay that way until finding the killer allows her to wipe it clean.

Moira shakes her head, remembering her slip-up last night, which meant she had to tell the others she'd been in the police. It was stupid and dangerous. She needs to keep her secrets more carefully and try harder to not let Philip's bossy pompousness get to her. Last night, no matter how casual he was about it, she could tell Rick had sensed she was hiding more. Maybe even Lizzie suspected something – she'd certainly been pretty pissed off that Moira hadn't been more forthcoming about her job. She's going to have a job getting Lizzie to trust her again. Moira curses, then tries to push last night from her mind. She doesn't have time to dwell on it right now. Up ahead is the gatehouse.

Each of The Homestead's districts have an entrance off the main highway with a gatehouse that's manned 24-7 by a uniformed security team. The set-up is standard; three lanes – one as an exit, two for entry – with large palm trees flanking the road on either side. In front of the gatehouse is a large sign: '**WELCOME TO OCEAN MIST AT THE HOMESTEAD – THE PLACE TO MAKE AND SHARE HAPPY MEMORIES.**' Moira grimaces at the sign. It's far too corny.

The gatehouse itself is a squat white stucco one-storey at the side of the road next to the visitors' entry lane. If you live in Ocean Mist you take the middle lane marked for residents and get an electronic pass to fix on your dashboard to activate the automatic barrier, so there's no need to join a queue. Visitors have to use the right-hand lane and stop next to the security hut to show ID and say who they're visiting. The guard then raises the barrier to let them through.

Since she moved here the biggest bugbear Moira's heard about from other residents is the security on the gates – how they don't always ask people for their names or ID, and how people have

160

sometimes been seen to drive through the barrierless exit lane to enter and security do nothing about it. She's never experienced or seen it herself, though. When she visited she was asked for her ID and the uniformed security guy in the gatehouse had made a big show about checking it over. So perhaps it depends which staff are on duty when you arrive.

Right now, everything is quiet. Half the houses are still in darkness, and she hasn't seen any cars being driven for the whole walk over here. She doubts the gatehouse is doing a big trade.

Crossing the street, she approaches the building. The lights are on, but as she looks through the window in the side door she doesn't see a guard. Usually they're looking out for cars approaching, so she wonders where they've gone. Gently, she raps on the glass with her knuckles. Waits a few moments, but no one appears.

She knocks again, a little louder this time, and waits. Still nothing. She really wants to get a look at the logs, and she's here now. Surely the guard must be inside? If they're not answering, there's only one way to find out. She presses the door handle down and pushes. Nothing happens. The door is stuck firm. Moira pushes again, harder this time. The door doesn't budge – it must be locked.

Strange. The gatehouse is supposed to be manned 24-7. Surely the sound of someone trying to get in would bring them running, but there's still no guard. Moira uses her fist to thump hard on the door.

Again, there's no answer.

She stops pounding on the door and thinks. Either the place is empty and the guard has broken protocol to step out for a while, or they're inside but not coming to the door for some reason – maybe because they've fallen asleep on shift, or hurt themselves somehow? Whatever the reason, she needs to know it.

Moving away from the door, she walks around the building to the side that borders the entrance lanes. She stops beside the large viewing window and peers inside. The gatehouse looks neat and tidy. There are three desks, one immediately the other side of the window and two more further back in the room. They all have computers on them. The desk closest to the window has a half-drunk mug of coffee and a Lee Child novel splayed open. The chair has been pushed back from the desk. Someone is in there, she's sure of it.

Moira cups her face and squints through the window, scanning the room inch by inch.

It takes her a moment to see him. He's hunkered down towards the back of the room, hiding behind one of the desks further from the window, trying to stay out of sight.

Moira shakes her head. The Homestead pride themselves on great security – it was one of the things they pushed hardest when she spoke to them about possibly moving here. She's pretty sure guards shouldn't be hiding from residents.

Banging on the glass, she shouts, 'I can see you.'

The security guard peeps over the top of the desk. His brown hair is sticking up all tufty at the front. It makes him look like Beaker from *The Muppets*.

'Yes, you,' says Moira, gesturing to the door. 'Open it.'

The guard's cheeks flush red and he stands. He's young, barely twenty, with patchy stubble and a tall, lanky and slightly hunched stance. It makes him look even more like Beaker.

'Come on,' says Moira. Gesturing again to the door.

As the young guard shuffles across the room, Moira heads back around the building. She hears the door lock click, and a number of bolts being drawn back. Then the door opens a few inches, just wide enough for the guard to peer through.

'Didn't you hear me knocking?' says Moira. She knows he did, of course, because he was hiding, but wants to give him the chance to explain.

162

The young guard nods. 'I thought you were the killer.'

The murder might not have been reported on the news app, but it seems the staff are aware of what happened. Moira raises her eyebrows. 'Do I look like a murderer?'

The young guy shrugs. 'I don't know. I've never seen one before.'

It's a fair point.

'I live here. Can I come in?'

He shifts his weight from foot to foot. 'Well, I don't—'

'You want me to tell your boss about how you weren't at your post when I came by? How you were hiding?' Moira glances towards the road. 'Anyone could have driven on in and you'd have been none the wiser about who they were. Think your boss will be okay with that?'

The young guard swallows hard. 'No, ma'am.'

'So I'll come in then.' It's a statement, not a question.

The guard steps back from the door, opening it wider. 'Okay.'

Moira is pretty sure allowing a resident into the gatehouse for no good reason is against the rules, but she doesn't say anything. Instead, she steps inside.

The security guy says nothing. Looks awkward.

'So what was the hiding about?' asks Moira.

He looks down, his cheeks colouring redder. 'Nothing, ma'am.'

'You were hiding behind a desk and the door was bolted. I'd say that's a little more than nothing.'

His voice is barely audible. 'I was afraid.'

'Of the killer?'

The security guard meets her gaze. 'I heard a young woman was chopped up in one of the swimming pools. Blood everywhere. I didn't want to end up like—'

'I get that it's worrying,' says Moira. 'But you're a security guard. Your job is to protect this community.'

'But what if the killer wanted to get me?'

'Why would they?'

'Could be I saw them.'

'Did you?'

He shrugs. 'Maybe. I don't know. I see a lot of people.'

Moira tries not to show her frustration with the guy – she needs him on her side. 'I could help.'

The lanky security guard frowns. 'How?'

'I've heard from the neighbourhood patrol that a station wagon was seen over near Manatee Park on the night of the murder, and nearby a few nights before that.'

The guard looks confused. 'Okay?'

'So I thought if I could just get a quick look at your gate log, I could see when else the vehicle has been—'

'I can't let you do that.' He's shaking his head. 'It's against the rules.'

Moira fixes him with a hard stare. 'I'd guess hiding away and not keeping eyes on the entrance is also against the rules.'

He looks down, avoiding eye contact. 'Yes, ma'am.'

'So if you'd want your supervisor to hear about it . . .'

'I need to use the restroom,' says the young guard. 'The logs are on the computer filed by year. The password is password.'

'Thanks,' says Moira.

The guard says nothing. Then shuffles across the room towards the door at the back that Moira assumes must be the loo.

Once he's gone, she gets to work. Sitting down at the computer, she jiggles the mouse to interrupt the bouncing The Homestead logo screensaver, and the password prompt appears. She types in password and the computer unlocks. It doesn't take her long to find this year's log. Double-clicking to open it, she finds the search function and types 'beige station wagon'. The results come back almost immediately: no matches.

Damn.

Moira thinks for a moment. Then she remembers. Before she'd left Lizzie and Philip's place last night she'd taken a picture of their makeshift murder board on the patio doors – worried that a freak rainstorm might erase it overnight and they'd have to start again. At the time she'd thought she was probably being over-cautious. Now she's pleased that she was. Pulling out her phone she finds the picture, and enlarges it until she's able to read the car registration plate they'd got for the station wagon. Reading it off her phone, she types it into the computer.

The new results appear – one match. Better than nothing. She clicks the link to take her to that page of the log. The record is from over a month ago. It shows that the station wagon entered The Homestead Ocean Mist community at 9.32 that evening. The spaces for the driver's name and the person in Ocean Mist they're visiting are blank.

Moira blows out hard, frustrated. The record doesn't give her much. All it tells her is that the beige station wagon had been here at least one more time than they previously knew about, and a few weeks earlier than they'd originally thought.

Behind her, she hears a click as the door to the restroom is unlocked. Swivelling round in the chair, she sees the lanky security guard emerge, wiping his damp hands on his uniform.

Moira points to the screen. 'Why are these fields blank?'

The young guard crosses the room and peers over her shoulder. 'I guess this one was picked up on the automated plate reader, rather than the guard entering it manually.'

Moira cocks her head to the side. 'How so?'

'If a guard is in the john, rather than the visitor having to wait, they can switch the system to auto. That means if a visitor shows up, the electronic plate reader over the gate will register the car and open the barrier, rather than them having to wait until the guard has finished their business.'

'But you miss out on the key information.'

'We're working solo here after 9 p.m. until 9 a.m. You have to use the restroom sometime.'

Moira thinks about the fuss made by the sales team over the high level of security at The Homestead – how they knew about every vehicle, and every person, within the complex at any one time. She shakes her head. 'So, what, protocol doesn't matter between 9 p.m. and 9 a.m.?'

The guy raises his hands. 'I just work here. I don't make the rules.'

'It's not good enough.' Moira holds his gaze until his cheeks blush and he looks away. Good. He should be embarrassed. The sales bullshit is one issue, but the slapdash way they're running security means there's no way of building a fully accurate picture of who has entered the community.

The guy runs a hand through his hair. 'Look, I'm sorry, okay. I'm not—'

'There's only one entry for the station wagon,' says Moira. 'But I know it's visited Ocean Mist at least two more times. How's it not on the log?'

'If they drove in through the exit the registration plate wouldn't have been recorded,' says the security guard.

'And you think they could have done that a couple of times without being noticed?'

He looks a bit shifty. 'Well, sure, if they came after nine in the evening and when the guard was using the restroom.'

Moira clenches her fists. Tries to hold her temper – she can't afford to have a go at this guy or he might clam up completely, but damn, these security people are seriously crap. 'And so he could have been here a lot of nights, and slipped in and out unnoticed?'

'I guess so.'

Moira curses under her breath. The killer could easily have exploited the system to enter and exit unseen and unrecorded. There's little merit to be gained from the logs, aside from knowing the driver of the beige station wagon had started coming here at least a month before the murder. She thinks for a moment, then pulls out her phone and makes a note of the date the wagon was recorded entering – from memory it seems to be around the time the burglaries started. She'll check that with the others later.

'Is there anything else I can help with?' The young guard is looking twitchy. He keeps glancing out through the viewing window towards the entry lanes.

Moira guesses he's worried someone will see her sitting at the computer. She decides to cut the guy some slack. She doubts she can get much more from him. 'No, you've been helpful, thanks.'

He gestures towards the computer. 'Are you going to tell the police our records aren't complete?'

She shakes her head. 'No.'

He smiles. There's relief on his face.

Standing up, Moira moves back towards the door. 'Lock this behind me, if it makes you feel safer. But do me a favour and don't go hiding again when people come by. We need you with eyes on the gates at all times, okay?'

'Yes, ma'am.'

'Good.' Moira pulls open the door and steps out into the cool morning air. She hears the door lock behind her and the bolts being slid back into place. She shakes her head. Doesn't doubt that he'll be hiding from the next person who knocks on the door, just like he did with her.

The security here isn't top-notch, as promised. It's bullshit. Just like the illusion of zero crime. Residents here have bought into it. Hell, she almost did herself. But it's a lie.

Moira frowns. Recalls how the murder hadn't registered on the news app, even by this morning. Pulling out her phone, she checks the local news again, scrolling through all the stories from yesterday. She finds no mention of Manatee Park and the murder of a young woman; as far as the reported news goes, nothing bad has happened here. It's the opposite of fake news – it's a news void.

She thinks about the lax security and the saccharine-sweet marketing messages, and wonders how far The Homestead will go to keep their lie about zero crime alive.

26

RICK

The day starts with two hundred push-ups, a five-minute plank and a half-hour spent lifting weights. He converted the garage into a home gym the first week he'd moved here. He has no time and no mind for a communal gym full of sweating and huffing bodies. Working out has become like a religion. It brings him peace; it's not a shared experience. Back when he first came here, with Alisha's loss still so new and raw like an open wound inside his heart, he'd used workouts as a way to numb the pain. The rawness of that pain has receded to a dull ache nowadays, but he still needs his own private space.

After he's showered, he has a black coffee and eats eggs over easy on a couple of pieces of wheat toast. He's almost done when his cell phone buzzes – the name of his police contact is lit up on the screen.

Grabbing his cell, Rick answers the call. 'Hey, buddy. What've you got for me?'

Rick's glad Hawk's been quick. They trained together back in the day, and were co-workers in the same team for a time before Hawk had gotten a job based out in Miami. They'd stayed in touch, and have met up for a few beers on a semi-regular basis since Rick retired out here. Hawk is a good guy – discreet and well connected with the police precincts around the state. He also likes to know about everything going on, which made it easy to persuade him to help out.

'I had a few drinks with my guy in Homicide last night. Found some stuff you might be interested in.'

'Hit me.' Rick takes another gulp of coffee.

'So it took a hell of a lot of liquor to get the man talking, but once he did there was no stopping him. He seems real shaken by the crime scene. The way the vic was found in the water, what with them dollars and all, seems to be messing with his head.'

'Why d'you say that?'

'It's hard to say,' says Hawk. 'A feeling, I guess. And he kept muttering things like "It ain't right" when he was telling me about stuff.'

'Weird.' Rick drains the last of his coffee. Homicide detectives see a lot of bad stuff. He can't imagine the scene in Manatee Park would rank that high in terms of depravity. 'What did he say about progress?'

'They're still waiting on the autopsy so time of death, cause, and all that will take longer but, on the crime scene, he said there were some oddities. Like the money, it was a weird amount – almost five thousand dollars, but not quite.'

Rick can hear Hawk chewing gum. He's never seen the guy without gum in his mouth. 'How much?'

'Four thousand, two hundred and sixty-seven dollars. Weird, huh?'

'For sure,' says Rick. The amount works with their theory – that the killer lay on the side of the pool and grabbed all the dollars they could before leaving – but he doesn't tell Hawk, and instead he says, 'Anything else?'

'Yeah, there was a rucksack – a leather, fashion-type piece rather than something practical for hiking – sunk on the bottom of the pool.'

Rick remembers Moira saying about a bag in the pool, but that she'd not managed to get a proper look. 'You know what was in it?'

'That I do.' Hawk pauses. Chews his gum.

'And?'

'Apparently it was a bunch of random stuff – a gold mantle clock, a few pieces of nice jewellery, some antique silverware like milk jugs and creamers, a set of rare baseball cards. Good stuff, quality, you know? But not stuff that fits together.'

Rick does know, and he knows how they fit together. All those things are items that'd been taken during the recent burglaries. 'The cops have any theory on that?'

'Not so far.'

He clenches his teeth. How can the homicide squad be so far behind? The contents of the rucksack connect the homicide to the thefts that have been reported in Ocean Mist over the past month – they could run a search of their database and see the link. It's an obvious move, one of the first they should have done. Rick shakes his head. It's as if the cops in Homicide are deliberately dragging their heels. 'Well, thanks, I appreciate you passing this on to me.'

'No problem. One last thing, I ran that plate, the one for the old wagon.'

Rick waits. He can hear Hawk's still working his gum hard.

'It came back with the name of a young punk from out of state, but I figured you'd be interested anyways. He has himself a bit of a rap sheet.'

'Yeah?' Rick says. Interested.

'Nothing major, but there's a couple of DUIs, and a bit of trouble a few years back with thefts, small stuff – the high-school football trophy is the most notable item.'

'Any indication of violence?'

'Not that he's been arrested for.'

'Okay. You said this guy is from out of state, whereabouts?'

'DMV has his address as a place in Maryland.'

That fits with what Donald said – that the car had a Maryland plate – but it's a long way from Maryland to Florida. 'Can you give me a name?'

'Sure I can, buddy, as it's you.' There's a rustle as if Hawk's turning the page of a notebook. 'The guy's name is Michael Graften.'

'Graften?' says Rick. He knows a Graften here at Ocean Mist – Miss Betty is one of the oldest residents. 'You sure about that?'

'Positive. I'll message you a photo of his licence.'

'Appreciate that.'

'And remember you owe me a ticket to the game.'

'Already got you covered. Next home game there's a pair of seats just behind the dugout with our name on them.'

'I'll let you know when I've got more. Autopsy isn't likely until late today, or could be tomorrow.'

'Call me when you've got something.'

'For sure.'

Rick ends the call and puts his cell in his pants pocket. Picking up his coffee mug, he takes it over to the sink, rinses it out and sets it on the drainer. Hawk said the beige station wagon with the Maryland plate is registered to a guy with the same family name as Miss Betty. Betty's place is over on Albatross Heights Boulevard, the opposite side of the Ocean Mist district to Seahorse Drive and the head of the Wild Ridge Trail, the places the vehicle had been spotted parked up by Donald and Clint. Interesting. And something that needs checking out.

Taking his keys off the hook by the back door, Rick opens the door and hurries out to the jeep. The cops might be dragging their heels on the investigation, but Rick's always been a 'do it now' kind of a guy.

He's got questions. Miss Betty might have answers. There's no time to waste.

172

27

MOIRA

It takes her a moment before she realises it's him. He's parked at the side of the road, tapping away at his phone. He's too engrossed to see her. Stopping on the pavement next to the jeep, she clears her throat and says, 'Hey.'

Rick looks up with a start. He smiles when he sees it's her. Puts his hand to his forehead as if saluting a higher-ranking officer. 'Good morning.'

She's about to answer when his mobile beeps. He looks at it and fires off another message.

Moira waits until he's pressed send before asking, 'Any developments?'

'I've got a possible lead on the owner of the station wagon. I was just updating Philip. I'm heading there now, he's going to meet me.' Rick puts his phone into his pocket. The jeep's windows are down and his quiffed white hair looks tousled by the breeze. He shifts in the driver's seat towards her, elbow resting on the window frame. 'Any sign of that guy who was following you yesterday?'

Moira shakes her head. 'Not so far. Maybe he got scared when I banged against his window and chased his car down the road.'

'Could be,' says Rick, nodding. 'And how's that ankle holding up?'

'So-so,' she says. 'It's annoying really. I've been to the security hut, wasn't that useful except to show how rubbish the security on our gates actually is, now I'm on my way to try and charm the CCTV guy into letting me see the tapes.'

Rick jerks his head towards the passenger seat. 'You want a ride?'

Her automatic reaction is no, but she stays silent for a moment. Thinks. She's already walked to the gatehouse and back, and taken the dogs out for their morning run. The CCTV office is a good thirty minutes on foot from here and, in truth, her ankle's worse than so-so, it's throbbing and seems to be getting more swollen. Moira knows she should be resting it rather than walking. 'Okay, thanks.'

'Jump in. I'll update you on the drive over.'

Moira moves around to the passenger side and manoeuvres herself up on to the seat. Her ankle throbs faster from the move-ment. She grits her teeth. She can count the number of times she's accepted lifts from people before on the fingers of one hand, but in the last day she's been driven about by both Philip and Rick. It feels like she's losing her independence.

As she fastens her seat belt, Rick puts the jeep into drive and pulls away from the kerb. Moira turns to him. 'So tell me about this lead on the station wagon.'

'Seems the owner could be a relation of Miss Betty. She's one of Ocean Mist's oldest residents, lives on the other side of the district over on Albatross Heights Boulevard.'

'The gatehouse had the station wagon's plate registered as enter-ing Ocean Mist late evening a month ago, but nothing for the two times your patrollers said they'd made sightings.'

'Figures, if the guy's been staying with Miss Betty.' Rick turns the wheel, taking a right on to Wave Street. 'They have anything about who the driver was visiting in the gatehouse log?'

'They didn't even have the guy's name.'

Rick gives a long whistle. 'You're right, that's bad. How'd it happen?'

'Seems that security gets lax on the late shift. People who arrive after nine at night and before nine in the morning are less likely to be asked for their details. The security guard can switch the system over to automatic plate record so they can go to the loo. My guess is they put it on and take a nap.'

'And that's what happened the night the station wagon entered Ocean Mist?'

'Yeah. The automatic plate reader logged the registration in the system, but the fields for driver name and who they were visiting were empty.'

Rick brakes hard as a small tabby cat makes a run for it across the road. He waits until the animal is safely across the lawn and on to the front porch of its house before continuing. Glances at Moira as he steps on the gas. 'And when the plate was registered in the system around a month ago, what date was that?'

Moira tells him.

'Well, damn.' Rick runs his hand through his hair. 'That there's a whole lot of interesting. Seems the first time we've got a record of him arriving in the neighbourhood is two days before the first home got burglarised.'

Moira pulls her hoodie around her. It's warm outside now, but inside the jeep it's freezing. The air conditioning is cranked up to the max, and even though Rick's got the windows open she's feeling cold. 'Coincidence?'

Rick shrugs. 'Perhaps.'

'I don't believe in coincidence, not when crime's involved.'

'Me neither, which means talking to Miss Betty, and finding out if she's had any visitors recently, is my number one priority this morning.'

They drive in silence along Wave Street. The houses here are similar to Moira's own Country Classic, but as they make a left turn on to Sweetwater Drive the buildings change. Along this road they're more Boston colonial style – strong, square silhouettes with impressive front porches and weatherboard cladding. Each one is painted a slightly different shade: greys and beiges, pale pinks, blues and greens.

'Good real estate along here,' says Rick, as if reading her mind. 'Top dollar.'

She remembers seeing a couple of homes like this for sale on The Homestead website before she'd picked out her house. They'd been more than double what she'd paid. 'Out of my price range.'

'Just as well,' says Rick. 'The houses are big, but the yards are real small. No good for your dogs.'

Moira sneaks a glance at Rick while he's concentrating on pulling out on to Sandcastle Street. He's pretty hot really – strong jawline, attractive face. Jesus. She pushes the thought away. She's so not wanting anything like that. Yesterday she'd told Lizzie she was happy alone, that she didn't want a man in her life, and she'd meant it. A relationship needs trust to work and she's all out of that. She doubts she'll fully trust anyone again. And, given the situation, how could they trust her if they knew the truth? She shakes her head. No. It's a non-starter. Anything romantic would be doomed.

'You doing okay?'

She turns and meets Rick's gaze. 'Why'd you ask?'

'Looked like you were doing some serious soul-searching then.'

Moira doesn't answer straight away. She can't tell him what she was thinking about, obviously. Needs to get her mind back on the investigation. 'You know the murder hasn't been reported in the media yet?'

Rick raises an eyebrow. 'I did not know that, but then I guess I don't look at the news so much these days.'

'It's not on the local news channel or the news app, national or local.'

'Well, I guess they focus more on Miami and Orlando – the main hotspots and places those on vacation are most interested in.'

'Maybe, but it's a murder in a retirement community. Surely that warrants some attention, especially in a place like this that markets itself on being super-safe?'

'Yeah, you'd think.' Rick indicates and pulls over beside a squat-looking one-storey red brick. He parks up the jeep. Looks thoughtful.

'What is it?' says Moira.

'You know, thinking on it, I don't remember the burglaries hitting the news anytime.'

'Not even your local paper?'

Rick shakes his head. 'Nope, don't think so. Might have been something on the community Facebook page, but that could have been one of the residents posting.'

'Didn't that strike you as odd?'

'Not so much at the time, you know, the burglaries were pretty small fry in the grand scheme of things.' He runs his palm over his jaw. 'But now, if the murder isn't on the news, taking the two together, it does seem weird.' Rick shrugs. 'Or could be, like I said, they'd just rather use their column inches and news segments for the stuff going on in Miami and Orlando.'

Moira's not so sure. It feels wrong to her. With both the burglaries and the murder not getting reported it seems like there's a news blackout on crime from The Homestead, and that can't be a good thing. She needs to know what's going on.

She adds it to her list of things to look into.

28

PHILIP

Rick's eight minutes late. Philip drums his fingers on the steering wheel of the Honda and looks across the street towards Betty Graften's place. It's a pretty house with its weatherboard cladding painted pale grey, glossy black front door, plant pots on the porch and along either side of the steps. Immaculate. Just as The Homestead likes its residents to keep their homes.

He checks his watch again. Rick's ten minutes late now. Ridiculous. Pulling his mobile from his shirt pocket, he taps out a message: You're late?

He's just about to press send when a jeep pulls up behind him, and a few seconds later Rick jumps out. Shaking his head, Philip deletes the message.

'I've been waiting ten minutes. You said you'd be here.'

'Sorry,' Rick says, striding towards him with his hands open in apology. 'I saw Moira on the way over, she was limping pretty bad, so I took a detour to the CCTV office to drop her off before I came on. I'm here now.'

'Well, yes, I suppose,' says Philip, unable to shift the begrudging tone from his voice. 'Any progress update from Moira?'

'Yeah, she found out the station wagon entered Ocean Mist for what seems to be the first time, if the gatehouse log is to be believed, two days before the first house got burglarised.'

Philip feels a tingle in his palms. The one he always gets when a piece of the puzzle drops into place. 'That's interesting. Fits with the theory that the thief isn't a resident of The Homestead.'

'Or wasn't until recently,' says Rick, gesturing towards Betty Graften's house.

'True,' says Philip. 'We need to get in there and ask Betty a few questions.'

'Lead on,' says Rick.

Philip heads towards the Graften house, pleased that Rick recognises he's the one in charge of their investigative group. He's not sure about Moira, having got the distinct impression yesterday that she felt she should be their leader. He frowns. He still doesn't understand why she'd not said something about her police career before last night. It'd been a bit of a bombshell, especially for Lizzie. Moira seems pleasant enough, he supposes, but she's a bit too secretive for his liking. He'll have to keep an eye on her.

They step up on to the front porch and Rick rings the bell. They move a pace away from the door, so as not to be too close when Betty Graften answers. Even when questioning someone who might be linked to a suspect, Philip likes to show respect.

The door is painted black and solid wood, so there's no way to see what's going on inside. Philip waits for what seems like an eternity, but there's still no answer. He glances at Rick, who shrugs, and he's about to knock again when he hears the latch being twisted and the door opens.

'Can I help you?'

The person standing in the doorway isn't at all what Philip expected. She's too young for a start, at least fifty years too young. 'Isn't this Betty Graften's place?'

'Sure it is.' The young woman smiles. 'I'm Martha, Miss Betty's help. I'm new, started just last week, so I don't know many people around here yet. Are you friends of hers?'

'I'm Rick, an old friend of Miss Betty's,' says Rick, smiling as he removes his shades and props them on the top of his head. He gestures to Philip. 'And this is my friend Philip. It's been a while since I last visited with Miss Betty, a month at least. Is she free for visitors this morning?'

Martha nods. 'I'm sure that'll be no problem. Why don't the pair of you come on into the great room and take a seat. Then I'll go find Miss Betty.' Martha leans towards Rick, lowering her voice. 'She's in the backyard, tending her roses. Can't have a single one that's gone at all brown or wilted, and with this heat, well . . .' Martha shakes her head. 'She won't let me help out, you know how she can be.'

Rick laughs. 'That I do.'

Philip follows behind Rick as Martha leads them to the great room. Now he's had a chance to have a proper look at her, he realises he should have guessed she worked rather than lived here – her outfit is a loose-fitting pink tunic and trousers, like nurses wear, and she has one of those little upside-down watches attached to her tunic so she can see the time when she looks down.

'Here you go,' says Martha, opening the door to a large, light lounge. 'Here's the great room, please take a seat and I'll go fetch Miss Betty for y'all.'

Philip thanks her and steps into the room. It's huge; you could fit half of his and Lizzie's home in this room alone. 'Blimey,' he says under his breath.

'Yep,' says Rick, perching his bulk on a dainty-looking chaise longue. 'Miss Betty was heir to a cookie fortune and when her father died she took over as chief executive, even though that was in a time when it was almost unheard of to have a female in the top job. She diversified the company, expanded the brand, increased their profits and made them into the household name they are now. Then, and it must only have been five years ago, she moved to be chair of the board and appointed a new chief executive. That's when she moved here. She's one hell of a lady.'

Philip's impressed. It can't have been easy running a company as a woman back then, and from the clean lines and stylish furnishings in this room he can see she's a person of great taste. He's looking forward to meeting Betty Graften. 'How did you . . .'

He stops talking as the door to the great room opens, and he stares at the woman who enters. She's taller than he expected – around five foot ten at least – and despite her age there's no sign of a stoop. She moves gracefully towards them, smiling. With her high cheekbones and short white hair teased into a style that frames her face, Miss Betty reminds him of two of his favourite actresses – Dame Judi and Helen Mirren.

'Rick, honey, it's real good of you to come visiting.' Her smile drops a little as she scans the coffee table. 'Has Martha offered you some sweet tea? No, I bet she hasn't, has she. Really, that child has so much to learn.'

'I'll get it right away, Miss Betty.'

'Thank you, Martha, yes you do that. And fetch the good cookies as well. On a plate, please, as we discussed.'

'Yes, ma'am.'

Miss Betty turns to Philip. 'And you must be Rick's friend?'

Philip lurches to his feet. Holds out his hand. 'I'm Philip, I run the community watch with Rick.'

'Lovely,' says Miss Betty, and she gestures back towards the chaise longue. 'Sit, please.'

She lowers herself on to one of the couches. 'Now. From the lack of warning and the early hour, I'm guessing this isn't a social visit?'

Rick nods. 'Sharp as ever.'

'No point if I'm not,' says Miss Betty. 'So tell me, is it about the homicide in the park?'

'You know about that?' says Philip, unable to keep the surprise from his voice. It seems like this place, on the very edge of the Ocean Mist district, wouldn't get the gossip from lower down the hill.

'I'm old, but I'm not stupid,' says Miss Betty sternly. 'I make sure I stay appraised of all the neighbourhood news. It would be foolish not to.'

Philip blushes. Before he can reply the door opens and Martha hurries into the room carrying a tray of three tall glasses of what looks like iced sweet tea, and a plate of cookies. He can smell the cookies from here. *Chocolate chip*, he thinks. His stomach rumbles, even though it's barely two hours since breakfast.

'You're right, it's connected to the homicide,' says Rick, nodding his thanks to Martha as she hands him a glass of sweet tea. 'Some information has come up that we think you can help us make sense of.'

Miss Betty puts her hand to her chest. 'I can help you with something to do with the homicide? Now that is an interesting development. Please, do tell me how.'

'Do you know someone who drives a beige station wagon?' says Rick.

'Well, of course I do. My grandson, Mikey. He's staying with me a while, has been for a few weeks now.'

Rick's expression is serious. 'Is he here now?'

'Yes, I believe he is. Although he doesn't usually rise until noon.' Betty frowns. 'It's one of his behaviours I'll be sure to change while he's here.'

'I didn't see the station wagon parked in the front,' says Philip.

'Well, no, obviously. I can't have that godawful-looking thing near the house, that would just . . .' She shudders. 'So I told him, I said, if you're going to stay here a while, you'll have to find some other place to park that vehicle.'

'Do you know where he parks it?' Rick asks.

She flaps her hand at him. 'I don't know and I really don't care, just as long as the thing isn't spoiling my property.'

Rick smiles. 'It's pretty beat-up, huh?'

'Ugly as sin,' says Miss Betty, laughing.

Rick doesn't laugh. 'Do you know where your grandson was two nights ago, Miss Betty?'

She stops smiling, and her eyes narrow. Her voice has an edge of steely frost to it when she asks, 'Is that when the homicide took place?'

'Yes, ma'am.'

Miss Betty sighs, and fiddles with the heavy gold bangles around her wrists. She looks conflicted. After a long moment she says, 'So what you're really asking me is whether my grandson is a murderer?' She glances from Rick to Philip. Exhales hard. 'And if you're asking me that question, well, I suppose there is something you should know.'

29

MOIRA

The CCTV office is another squat one-storey stucco building; just like the gatehouse but minus the big glass window. It's set back a little way from the road, and looks out of place compared to the row of neat Spanish-style properties that line the rest of the street. As Moira walks closer, she sees that the blinds are drawn in all the windows, and wonders if she's got the opening times wrong. The office is supposed to be manned 24-7 – it says so in the sales brochure. Although she's learning fast that the marketing spin and the reality of The Homestead aren't always one and the same.

Glancing around, she checks that there's no sign of the silver VW Beetle or the wiry blond guy who'd been watching her. There's no sign of him or the vehicle; no sign of anyone. She shakes her head. It's weird. He was obviously spying on her yesterday morning, but after she spotted him lurking outside Philip and Lizzie's place, and called him out and chased after him, he seems to have disappeared. She wants to know why.

Focusing back on the job in hand, Moira walks around the side of the building to the entrance. It's shaded here; there's a high wall a few feet from the building that's keeping the passageway cool. Moira's glad of it. The sun is at full rise now, and the temperature is soaring. Even though it's just moments since she climbed out of Rick's icebox of a jeep, she can already feel the sweat on her skin.

The door to the office is ajar. She hesitates. There's a keypad beside the door, and a button to press to speak on the intercom. She's not been here before, but from the signage beside the keypad it looks as if the door is supposed to be kept locked. She wonders why it's open today. Rick told her the guy who works here, Hank, is a resident too. Rick said he's part of the community watch and is a thorough guy, good with details; so him leaving the door open seems unlikely. But then perhaps it was the person who did the night shift who didn't close it properly on their way out. Could be Hank doesn't realise it's open.

Moving closer, Moira pushes the door with her toe and it swings open. 'Hello?'

There's no reply. Inside it's gloomy. There are no lights on, and the windowless hallway has no natural light. She steps inside. A few feet ahead there's a line of yellow-and-black tape across the floor with the words '**Do Not Cross**'. A sign on a stand beside it is a notice to visitors – 'no entry beyond this point unless accompanied by a member of the security team'.

Moira glances along the corridor again; there's no one here. Attached to the pin board on the wall to her right there's a collection of health and safety-related posters. A little way along the corridor there's a door with the sign '**Store**', and another a few feet along the hallway from that labelled '**Meeting Room**'. At the end of the corridor there's a door with a sign saying '**Surveillance Suite**'. She heads towards it.

Treading lightly, she takes care to step around the metal filing cabinets, their tops piled high with dusty folders, lining the wall space along the left side of the hall. The place seems deserted, but it shouldn't be. As she gets closer to the Surveillance Suite she becomes aware of a musty smell mixed with something metallic. Moira doesn't like it one bit.

She reaches the door. Hesitates, thinking what to do – should she barge in or knock first? Was the door left open by accident or for another reason? Moira makes her decision and raps her knuckles on the door. 'Hank, you in there?'

There's no response. Moira holds her breath and listens hard.

All she can hear is silence. Her heartbeat bangs harder in her chest. Hank should be here. He should be answering.

Something is very wrong.

30

PHILIP

He nods, encouragingly, and wishes Miss Betty would stop with the dramatic pauses and tell them whatever it is she thinks they should know about her grandson. This is a murder investigation, not a tea party. Philip's had enough of the theatrics.

Rick leans forward, towards Miss Betty. 'We're listening.'

Miss Betty stares at them for a long moment, then laughs out loud. 'Will you quit looking at me with such serious faces? I'm just messing with you. Mikey wouldn't hurt a fly.' She beckons them closer. 'Between you and me, my grandson is far too wet. He needs to toughen up. There's no way he'd have had the balls to kill someone.'

Philip clenches his fists. This woman isn't taking things at all seriously. Her grandson is a murder suspect. This isn't a time for jokes. He doesn't hide the irritation in his voice. 'You didn't answer the question.'

She turns to him. Cocks her head to one side. 'Well, no I didn't. Because I think it's really a rather stupid one.'

'Humour me, if you will,' says Rick. He shoots Philip a look – back off.

Philip feels heat flushing his neck and face, but stays quiet. Bloody woman. She might look like a film star but she needs to drop the diva act.

Miss Betty looks from Philip to Rick. 'Okay, fine. I don't know where he was two nights ago. Out somewhere I'd expect, as he's out most nights. I don't monitor his movements that closely.'

Philip doubts that. Betty Graften seems like the type who'd monitor the movements of everyone in her household. And it seems strange that her grandson is driving around in an old station wagon, especially if she hates it so much he's not allowed to park it near the house. He obviously comes from money. Why doesn't he have a decent car?

As if reading his mind, Miss Betty leans closer towards him. 'You're sceptical, Philip? Well, that's okay. But, you see, I expect my grandson to make his own way in life. I'm happy enough to let him come and visit with me for a while, but I don't believe in handouts. People shouldn't just be given everything on a plate. They need to understand the value of money, it's important, so their trust funds don't kick in until their twenty-fifth birthdays. Mikey has been out most nights since he arrived here. I assumed he'd gotten himself a job.'

It's one way to explain it, thinks Philip. 'Very wise.'

'Yes, I thought so.' She looks at Rick. 'I assume you'd like to ask him some questions?'

'We'd sure appreciate that, Miss Betty.'

'Of course.' Betty raps the bottom of her walking stick on the wooden floor three times. 'Martha? Where is that girl?'

Martha comes scuttling into the room. 'Miss Betty?'

'Fetch Mikey. Tell him he's got some visitors.'

'Yes, ma'am.'

Philip takes a sip of his sweet tea. It's really very good.

Rick clears his throat. 'While we're waiting for your grandson, there's something else perhaps you can help us with. The security gatehouse has a record of Mikey arriving about a month ago, but after that there's no record of him leaving or arriving. I'm assuming he has though, so I—'

'I gave him my auto-device for the barrier,' says Miss Betty. 'I don't have a car any longer so I have no need for it myself. I told him to put it in the wagon.' She shudders as she says the word 'wagon'.

Rick nods. 'Makes perfect sense.'

'Yes, it does,' says Miss Betty. She glances at Philip, as if expecting him to disagree.

Philip says nothing. He wonders if the gatehouse has a log of the residents' comings and goings. He doesn't remember anything in the paperwork they signed about their movements being logged, but that doesn't mean it wasn't there. There was so much paperwork involved in becoming a resident. As he's making a mental note to check, he hears the door behind them open. Turning, he sees a young, dishevelled-looking bloke hurry into the room.

'Gram, you wanted me?'

Mikey Graften is nothing like Philip had expected. He looks shifty for starters. And although he's slim and tall like his grandmother, he doesn't have her poise. He stands slightly hunched over, which rather than making him look smaller, as Philip expects he's trying to, exaggerates his long frame and makes him look more like a weeping willow sapling.

'Mikey, these gentlemen want to talk to you,' says Miss Betty, gesturing towards Rick and Philip.

'What about?' Mikey crosses his arms over his stomach. His gaze flits from his grandmother to Philip and then Rick.

'About the young woman that died in Manatee Park,' says Rick, getting out his phone and showing the picture of the dead woman to Mikey. 'We think you might have known her.'

'I . . . oh Jeez, it's just, it's not . . .' Mikey looks pained, like he might vomit. He runs his hand through his hair, tugging on the top.

It looks even messier now, thinks Philip. It's the sort of look his daughters would call 'bedhead'. Personally he thinks the boy should damp it with some water and give it a good comb. 'We've got an eyewitness who puts her in your car a few nights ago, son.'

Mikey looks down. He shakes his head. 'This can't be happening. It can't. I just . . .'

'Tell us what happened,' says Rick.

'Are you the cops? Have you come to—'

'These are good people,' says Miss Betty, putting down her glass of sweet tea and fixing Mikey with a steely gaze. 'They help keep this neighbourhood safe. So you're going to tell them everything you know, and you're going to tell the truth, otherwise I'll cut you out of my will and then you'll be stuck driving that godawful car forever.'

'Yes, Gram.'

'Good. So speak. Tell them.'

Mikey hugs himself tighter and looks away from the picture on the phone that Rick is holding up. 'I know – knew – her. I mean, we'd only known each other a few weeks, but I . . .' He shakes his head. His eyes are watery. 'We were kind of dating.'

'Kind of?'

'We talked, and hooked up, you know, and we just kind of vibed.'

'You vibed?' Philip shakes his head at the absurdity of the word. 'What the hell is that?'

Mikey looks uncertain. 'How'd you mean?'

190

'He means, could you tell us about her,' says Rick, shooting Philip a look that says 'steady'.

Philip drowns his irritation with a gulp of sweet tea. He should be leading the questioning. This is *his* investigation. Rick shouldn't be telling him to back off. He takes another gulp. The ice has almost melted, so the tea is more diluted now. It's spoiled it really. Philip puts it down on the side table. The bang as it hits the coaster is louder than he'd intended. Mikey flinches from the sound. Miss Betty raises an eyebrow.

'Her name's Kristen Altman and she's a croupier at the Flying Mustang Casino over in Conaldo Plains.'

Interesting, thinks Philip. Conaldo Plains is another district of The Homestead, Ocean Mist's neighbour to the south. It's a bigger neighbourhood and home to a big square with several casinos, a theatre and some fancy eating places that The Homestead residents have nicknamed Little Vegas. 'How did the pair of you meet?'

'In a place called Showtime Grill over in Little Vegas. I needed a drink in someplace more lively than here, and she had just gotten off shift. We were drinking the same bourbon. We got talking and . . .' He shrugs. 'Vibed.'

Philip can see Rick watching him; his expression a warning to take it slow. Philip ignores him. He's the senior-ranking officer here. He'll ask whatever questions he damn well likes. 'The night she died, did you see her?'

Mikey looks down at his shoes. 'I was meant to, but she never showed. We agreed to meet at the Wild Ridge Pavilion just after midnight. She was working until eleven thirty, so when she wasn't there on time I thought her shift must have dragged over. But I waited until 1 a.m., and then, when she wasn't answering my calls and messages, I decided to go home.' He shakes his head. 'I was real mad at her for not showing up. I feel bad about that now.'

'Do you have anyone who can vouch for your whereabouts that night?' Philip asks, although he can already guess the answer.

Mikey shakes his head again. 'I was home for the first part of the evening, so Gram and Martha can vouch for me up until around eleven, but after that I was alone.' He tugs at his hair again. 'It looks bad, doesn't it? I know it looks bad. But I didn't hurt her. I'd never do anything like that, and I wouldn't . . . I just couldn't . . . You believe me, don't you?'

Philip watches the lad break down in tears. He almost feels sorry for him, but he remains silent. He has to be neutral – unemotional and detached. It's the only way to stay objective.

'You need a minute?' asks Rick, his tone softer than earlier, less businesslike.

Mikey wipes his eyes on the back of his hand. Nodding, he gulps the air. 'I need a smoke.'

'In the yard then,' says Miss Betty, firmly. Her lips are pursed into a thin line.

Philip watches the lad run from the room and thinks Miss Betty's right: the boy doesn't have it in him to murder someone. He glances back at Miss Betty. She looks almost disappointed.

31

MOIRA

It happens fast.

The door jerks open and there's a figure, a man dressed in black with a balaclava over his face and his hoodie pulled up, standing in front of her. Before she has time to react, he shoves her in the chest.

Staggering backwards, Moira grabs for something to help her stay upright – the wall, anything – but her fingers clutch at air. He shoves her again, and she's falling. She bangs her hip on a metal cabinet as she drops. Her bad ankle twists. The pain vibrates through her body.

Seizing his chance, the masked figure pushes past her, heading towards the exit. Moira lashes out, trying to stop him, but he dodges round her. The grey messenger bag slung across his body looks full to bursting. It bounces as he runs.

Scrambling to her feet, Moira sets off in pursuit. 'Stop, you can't . . .'

The man turns, and his eyes widen. He grabs the folders from the nearest filing cabinet and flings them into her path. Moira jumps over the bulk of them. Loses her balance as she slips on some papers scattered across the floor, but stays upright. She keeps her eyes focused on the man, taking him in. He's broad and athletic. Too broad to be the slim guy with the Beetle, but a close match for the man she saw on the trail last night. Ignoring the pain in her hip and her bad ankle, Moira pursues him.

She can't let him get away.

But she's losing ground. He's out of the building and away, slamming the door behind him. Reaching the exit Moira yanks the door open and rushes outside. She spots him. He's at the wall. He's going to escape.

'No!' she yells, sprinting after him. Her limp getting more pronounced with every stride.

He grips the creeper growing over part of the wall. Uses it to pull himself up, scaling the vertical brick as nimbly as a cat. He's at the top when she reaches him, climbing over with a leg either side.

Moira clutches at his leg, twisting his foot, trying to pull him from the wall. He kicks at her but she clings on, leaning down so that all her weight is on his foot, tugging him down. She feels him move, slipping from the wall. Pulls harder.

She doesn't see it coming.

Something hard slams into the side of her head. Pain ricochets through her skull. Her grip on his foot releases.

Looking up, she sees the messenger bag flapping open. The man's arm is raised and what looks like an old-fashioned hard drive, with blood across one side, is swinging towards her. Moira lets go of his foot and raises her arms to try and protect herself but she's too slow. The pain comes again, more intense this time.

Then the darkness takes her.

32

RICK

Rick leaves it a couple of minutes, then puts his sweet tea down on the side table and tells Philip and Miss Betty he's going to check on the kid. He heads to the backyard. The yard space is bigger than any other he's seen in Ocean Mist; there's a kidney-shaped pool with a line of white sunloungers along one side, a large patio with an outdoor kitchen and grill, and a huge stretch of lawn that runs all the way to a line of tall oaks at the back. It's real pretty.

It takes him a moment to spot Mikey. He's a way across the yard on the other side of the pool, sitting on the bench seat inside a cute little summerhouse built in the same white weatherboarded style of the main house. Hunched over, Mikey's head is in his hands. Even from this distance, it looks as if his shoulders are shaking.

Rick feels real bad about showing him the photo. It was a scare tactic is all. Go in hard with the picture of the dead woman – shock him into complying. But he'd misjudged the play. Mikey is no tough guy. All it did was freak him out.

He walks around the pool to the summerhouse, stopping on the threshold to the building. 'How're you doing?'

Mikey flinches when he hears Rick's words. Doesn't look up. 'I'm okay. You can go back to the house.'

'You sure about that?' Rick steps inside. He stops a few paces from the kid. He still can't see his face, but he can tell from the way he's breathing, and moving, that he's fighting back tears – trying to get control of himself.

'I . . .' Mikey straightens up. Rubs his eyes with his hands. His face is red and blotchy from crying, and his eyes are real bloodshot. 'I didn't kill her.'

Rick holds the kid's gaze. All he sees is sadness. Sure it could be for himself rather than Kristen Altman, but Rick's always been a good judge of character; he usually calls these things the right way. 'I know.'

'Then why are you out here?'

'There's stuff you know that might help us find the person who did kill her, stuff you might not even think of as important. I need you to tell me about her, about what you did and what she liked and really, everything.'

Mikey frowns. 'But you're not police, Gram said. So what are you? A PI or something?'

'Or something.' Rick can see the kid's reluctant to talk. Lots of folks are like that. Oftentimes it just takes a little patience. Rick glances back towards the house. Patience is something it seems Philip doesn't have much of. He shakes his head. He's glad he's got Mikey on his own; between Miss Betty's obvious irritation with her grandson and Philip's misjudged pushiness, being inside is unlikely to help get the kid to open up.

Sitting down on the bench seat a little ways along from Mikey, he gestures towards the kid's smoke. 'You got another?'

The kid looks surprised, but pulls a soft pack of Marlboro Reds from his pocket and holds it out to Rick.

Rick takes one. 'Can I get a light?'

Mikey hands Rick a silver Zippo. Rick takes it and lights the cigarette. Hands the Zippo back and inhales. He feels the heat as

196

the smoke fills his mouth and hits the back of his throat. Stifles a cough. Jesus, he hates these son-of-a-bitches, but he's learnt that making a shared connection with the person you need information from pays dividends, and oftentimes doing what the informant is doing is the best way to fast-track building trust. He breathes out the smoke and leans against the side of the building. 'You think you can tell me about Kristen?'

'I'll try.' Mikey swallows hard. Takes a breath. 'I wasn't looking to meet anyone. I only intended staying here a week or so, to get my head together. Gram's great and all, but she's . . . she's a lot, you know?'

Rick nods. The house might be luxurious, but it has a rigid, static feeling to it, like a museum. And he'd seen the way Miss Betty treated the kid. It couldn't be easy living under her roof for long. 'Sure.'

'But Kristen, she was really something. She was so on it. She had all this energy and was always coming up with crazy schemes. She was just so alive . . .' He looks away across the yard and cusses under his breath. Turns back to Rick. 'I can't believe she's . . .'

Rick tries to keep his tone light. Doesn't want to spook the kid. 'What sort of schemes?'

'The money-making kind. She was always telling me I needed to think big. That I could be something, you know, with my music.'

Rick says nothing. He doesn't know about the music, but wants the kid to stay focused on Kristen, not divert into talking about his hobby.

'We just needed to get to Nashville, that's what Kristen said. Then everything would happen.' Mikey looks past Rick into the distance. He smiles, as if reliving a memory, then wipes his eyes with his hand again. 'She was real clear that we'd need a wedge of money to help us get set up there, what with it being a fresh start and all, but then we'd make ourselves some luck and I'd play my

197

music and get discovered, and then we'd be like Johnny Cash and June.'

'Did she ever tell you how much money you needed?'

'No, but it was quite a bit from the way she talked. Five, maybe ten thousand.' He rubs his eyes. 'We fought about it. I said let's go now, we can sleep in the car if we need to before we get started, but she wouldn't have it. She said she wanted to do things right. Have a little style.'

'Did you fight like that on Seahorse Drive one night earlier this week, around midnight?'

Mikey shrugs. 'Probably. Like I said, we argued about it a lot.'

'Is that why you think she didn't meet you two nights ago? You'd had another fight?'

'No, we hadn't been fighting that day. She suggested we meet up that evening. Said she had something to tell me and that I was going to be all kinds of excited. I tried to get her to tell me on the phone, but she wouldn't. I called her, and sent a bunch of messages, but she held firm the whole day. All she'd say was that after that night our money problems would be over and we could be in Nashville by the end of the week.'

Rick thinks about the money floating in the pool beside Kristen's dead body. *What were you up to?* he thinks. *What did you do that got you killed?*

Mikey's looking at him, head cocked to one side. 'You think you know what happened?'

Rick thinks about the burglaries. They started around the time Mikey showed up. Sure, people do bad things for love, lust and money, and there's at least one or two of those things going on here, but it doesn't seem that Mikey would be behind the thefts; the thefts on his sheet were stupid things – school trophies, not house burglaries. Betty's right, he's just a kid trying to find his way in the world, not a criminal. And unless he's the most talented actor Rick's ever met, he really doesn't seem to have it in him.

But Kristen, on the other hand, she could have known something or even been involved – the make-money-quick schemes and the desire to get out of Florida are both interesting factors. It doesn't quite fit right, though. There's something, a puzzle piece, that's missing. He meets Mikey's gaze. 'Not yet, but I mean to find out. You've been real helpful.'

'I just want you to get whoever did this to her and make the asshole pay.'

'Amen to that,' says Rick. 'And with a bit of luck it'll happen.'

'Not luck.'

'Excuse me?'

'Kristen always said luck and fate are bullshit. She said people make their own luck.' Mikey gives him a sad smile. 'I hope you make yourself some luck in this investigation.'

'Well, I'll—'

'Police. Freeze.' The shouted commands drown out Rick's words.

He hears the sound of boots stomping against the baked earth. Turns to see a squad of police charging towards them across the yard, weapons drawn and raised.

'Stay where you are!' yells the closest officer. 'No sudden movements!'

More cops in full body armour pour through the yard gate and across the patio and lawn. Their sights are pointing at the summerhouse, and Rick and Mikey.

Rick glances at Mikey. The kid looks terrified, like he might bolt. 'Don't do anything stupid. No sudden moves,' says Rick. 'Just listen to whatever they say and do that.'

'Hands on your head! Hands on your head!' yells the closest cop, his Glock moving from Rick to Mikey. 'Do. Not. Move.'

They do as they're told. Rick's tempted to point out the absurdity of giving an instruction that requires movement alongside one to stay still, but he holds back. He doesn't know these cops, and it could be that there's a trigger-happy son-of-a-bitch among them. Better to be safe and leave the smart-mouthed comments for later.

Mikey's shaking. Crying. 'Oh Jeez, oh Jeez. What do I do? What the hell do I—'

'Stay calm and ask for a lawyer,' says Rick, keeping his voice low so the cops can't hear him. 'Don't answer any of their questions until your lawyer is with you.'

Next moment the first cops are on them. Rough hands pull them from the summerhouse and push them face down on the lawn. Rick doesn't resist, but still he's shoved hard. The jolt as he lands on his stomach vibrates through him. He feels a knee in his back, pressing him down. His shoulder muscles feel like they're tearing as his arms are yanked behind his back. Next he feels the snap of metal around his wrists. He doesn't waste his breath trying to reason with these cops in the here and now. Knows it's better to wait until they feel they've contained the situation and gotten the kid and the nearly seventy-year-old senior sprawled on the ground in cuffs.

Jeez, though. These Florida cops have no kind of finesse or sense of proportion; instead they're mistaking the use of excessive force for a job well done. From the sound of their voices, and the things they're saying, they're real proud of themselves.

They don't even realise it's a shit show.

33

MOIRA

Her head feels like it's been split in two. She opens her eyes and winces from the light. She's lying on concrete, slumped against the wall. Her bad ankle is throbbing. Everything else aches.

Moira puts a hand to her head. There's a damp stickiness beneath her fingers. Wincing again, she closes her eyes for a moment, thinking she's going to vomit from the pain. She takes a couple of breaths and the nausea passes. Opening her eyes she looks down at her fingers and sees that they're covered in blood.

She curses. Hates that the masked man got the better of her.

Hates that he got away.

She scans her surroundings. Wonders if anyone saw anything, and if they've alerted the police. From what she's seen, she doubts it. The neighbourhood here is really quiet. No cars are passing, and there's no one walking along the street or tending their neatly mown front gardens. If she wants help she's going to have to call someone or ring the bell of one of the closest houses.

It's then that she remembers Hank, or rather the absence of him. She hadn't seen him in the Surveillance Suite, but there'd only been a second or so before the intruder attacked her. She shivers. If the man attacked her, what has he done to Hank? She needs to find out.

Using the wall for balance, Moira stands and starts to limp back towards the CCTV office. She feels light-headed and her legs are as wobbly as a kitten on a trampoline. The sunlight and the movement are making her headache worse.

Entering the building, she steps around the folders and papers scattered across the floor by the intruder and heads towards the Surveillance Suite.

'Hank? Are you here?' Her voice sounds over-loud in the quiet hallway.

There's no answer.

She reaches the doorway to the Surveillance Suite. It's gloomy in here, with the blinds covering the windows, but it's clear the place has been ransacked. Files have been pulled from the shelves and computers are littered over the desks, their wiring spewing out from their plastic bodies like multicoloured intestines.

Moira keeps moving further into the suite. Blinking to help her eyes adjust as she scans the space looking for Hank. Seven strides into the room she stops.

Her heart rate accelerates. She feels a wave of nausea.

Over on the far side of the room, below the bank of screens that line the far wall and beside a large desk cluttered with several takeaway food containers and a half-drunk mug of coffee, Hank is lying on the floor.

His glasses are smashed. He isn't moving. There's a lot of blood.

Moira hurries to him. Kneeling beside him, she checks for a pulse. 'Hank, can you hear me?'

He doesn't answer.

She searches again for a pulse, struggling to listen for Hank's when her own heart is hammering at her chest and temples so hard. She takes a breath, but can't seem to get enough air. She gulps.

Please don't let me have a panic attack.

She closes her eyes. Tries to do what the doc taught her. Knows she can't panic. She has to focus. She has to see if Hank's okay. She tries to take a shallower inhale. Doesn't gulp. Keeps her eyes closed.

Her heart rate starts to feel steadier, and when she inhales she's able to breathe in the air she needs. The panic is leaving her. She exhales, and takes another breath. Feels calmer. Then, opening her eyes, she tries to find Hank's pulse again.

There. She feels a faint pulse this time and relief floods through her.

Leaning down, she checks that Hank's breathing. Yes. Slow and shallow, but he is breathing. That's good, but things are still serious. Moira doesn't want to move him. From the location of the blood she guesses he was hit on the head from behind. The intruder must have crept up on him and taken him by surprise. He's wearing headphones, the big noise-cancelling ones. If he'd been listening to music or a podcast or something he wouldn't have heard the intruder coming. The poor guy wouldn't have stood a chance.

She pulls her phone from her pocket and dials the number. As she waits for it to connect she looks again at the computers on the desk. Every one of them is damaged, and there are holes where their hard drives should be. All around Hank's body there are crushed USB sticks – back-up copies of the CCTV footage, she assumes. She's too late; any evidence the cameras caught is gone.

The call connects and starts to ring. The noise seems to vibrate in her brain. She swallows hard as another wave of nausea floods through her. Her vision starts to distort. The phone feels heavy in her hand. Her fingers start to shake.

Fighting nausea, Moira hopes she doesn't lose consciousness again.

34

RICK

His cell phone is buzzing in his pants pocket, but Rick can't answer because of the cuffs. Above him there's a whole lot of shouting and drama. Lifting his head up from the lawn, he counts five sets of boots and one pair of leather slip-ons – six people – five cops and a friend. Two of the voices are far louder, and angrier, than the rest and he knows both of those – Philip and Detective Golding.

Rick looks across at Mikey who is spreadeagled in the dirt a little ways from him. There's a clump of earth above his right eye from where his face has been pressed into the ground, and the kid's looking wide-eyed and terrified. His whole body is shaking. Rick holds the kid's gaze and mouths, 'It'll be okay. But remember – no lawyer, no talking.'

One of the cops notices Rick talking. He prods him in the ribs with his boot. 'Hey, shut it.'

Rick ignores the cop. Keeps his eyes on Mikey until the kid nods.

'Do. Not. Kick. Him. That is an assault on a senior citizen.' Philip's voice is louder now. Rick watches as the leather slip-ons step closer to one of the pairs of boots. 'You move away from him this minute. And you, you uncuff him. He's a guest of Betty Graften, the lady who owns this property. What the hell do you people think you're doing? This man is a—'

'No one is getting uncuffed until I give the order.' Detective Golding's voice is equally angry. 'Mr Sweetman, you shouldn't be out here. Go inside with the others.'

'I will not leave until you uncuff this man. There's no reason to hold him.'

'I'll be the judge of that.'

'Then tell me the grounds you're holding him on? Is he a suspect? Are you going to charge him? It can't be for resisting arrest because you've got me, and two more witnesses in the house who watched what happened, and what we saw was a heavy-handed abuse of—'

'Mary mother . . .' Golding exhales hard, then turns and barks an order. 'Do it.'

Moments later, Rick feels the cuffs being released.

'Get up,' says a male voice – the one that a few minutes earlier was screaming at him to get on the ground.

Rick's glad to be free of the cuffs, but his shoulders are aching real bad from the ten minutes or so they've been on. He presses his hands into the ground and pushes himself up to standing, wincing as he straightens up.

'You all right?' asks Philip.

Rick rubs his wrists where the cuffs have been. 'Yep.'

Golding glares at Philip and then Rick. 'You've got what you wanted, now get out of here.'

Rick holds Golding's gaze. It's the first time he's seen the man and he already knows he doesn't like him. He's met cops like him before – full of macho bullshit, and more concerned with their own image than the truth. 'The kid didn't do it.'

'I've got evidence to suggest otherwise.' Golding gestures to Philip with a dismissive wave of the hand. 'And your buddy here gave it to me.'

'A licence plate, that's all you got?' Rick frowns. 'It ain't enough.'

'That's for me to decide. I'm the detective here, not you . . . seniors.' Golding says the word seniors as if he's talking about dog shit. 'You need to go back to your pickleball, or have an afternoon nap, or whatever it is you do with your time.' He steps closer to Rick and Philip. 'But whatever you do, just make damn sure it's nothing to do with my case, because I don't ever want to have to run into you both again, you hear me?'

Rick says nothing. He glances at Philip, who is also silent. He can see Philip's jaw is clamped tight and there's a bright red flush spreading up his neck to his face. Rick can tell Philip's suppressing the urge to tell the detective exactly what he's thinking. It's for the best that he doesn't. Oftentimes you need to pick your battles, and squaring up to Detective Golding right now isn't a fight worth having. It's better to be smart, to work the evidence more, and beat the asshole to solving the case.

Golding shakes his head. Turning to the officers standing over the kid, Golding gestures towards Mikey. 'Get him out of here.'

As Golding strides back towards the cop cars, the two uniforms closest to the kid grab his shoulders and haul him to his feet. As they frogmarch him towards the yard gate, Mikey looks over his shoulder. His eyes are pleading with Rick's. 'You've got to believe me. I didn't kill her.'

'Ain't that old timer you need to be worrying about,' growls the taller of the cops, giving Mikey a hard shove in the back. The kid stumbles.

Rick pays no mind to the comment. Keeps his eyes on Mikey. 'Remember what I told you.'

The kid nods. Rick watches, squinting into the sun, as the cops take him away. A kid like that, he's not going to find jail easy. Miss Betty is going to need to use any influence she has to get him out fast.

'That bloody Golding,' says Philip. His face is still beetroot red. 'We can't let him get away with talking to us like that. So dismissive, like we're on the scrapheap and incapable of being able to—'

'Yeah.' Rick remembers the call to his cell while he'd been cuffed. Taking it from his pocket, he checks the screen: *1 missed call – Moira.* Looking up, he sees Philip watching him with an irritated expression on his face. Rick raises the cell phone. 'I need to make a call.'

As Philip stomps across the yard after Golding, the uniforms and Mikey, Rick presses Moira's name on his call log and dials her back. He waits as it rings.

He's just about to end the call when it's picked up.

'Rick?' Moira sounds out of breath. 'Did you get my message?'

'No, I . . .' He looks at the cell phone's screen, but all it's showing is that he's on a call with her now. Had she messaged him? He doesn't think so. 'I just saw you'd tried calling so I dialled you back and—'

'Maybe I didn't press send, but I thought I . . .'

'Are you okay?' Rick asks. There's something about Moira's voice that sounds different, frailer somehow, when frail is the last word he'd normally think of to describe her. 'Did you get the CCTV footage?'

'Hank got attacked, I . . . didn't manage to stop them.'

'Are you hurt?'

'I'm okay.'

'You don't sound okay.' Rick starts walking back towards the house. 'You still at the CCTV office?'

'I called 911, they've despatched a car and an ambulance. Hank's—'

Rick breaks into a run. 'You safe?'

'Yes, yes I think so.' Her voice sounds weaker.

'Okay, stay where you are. I'm on my way.' Rick ends the call. He sprints across the yard and into the house. There's no sign of Philip or Miss Betty. Hurrying through the house to the front, he opens the door. They're standing out front, on the pathway at the bottom of the porch steps.

Martha and Miss Betty are talking with one of the uniformed cops. Miss Betty is shaking her head vigorously. 'No, I refuse to allow you to go inside my home, not when you've just dragged my grandson out on to the street like a criminal.'

'Like I said, we've got a warrant, ma'am,' says the cop. 'So with all due respect, you have to let us do our job.' He gives the signal to the rest of the officers and they swarm around Miss Betty and up the porch steps.

Rick steps aside to let them pass. They hurry past him, yanking the front door open and disappearing inside the house.

Miss Betty raises her hands to her chest and seems to sag at the knees. Martha, fast as lightning, takes a hold of Miss Betty and helps her stay upright. For a moment the older lady looks as if she might be too much for the young woman, then she recovers her strength and stands again unaided.

She fixes the cop with a steely gaze. 'Officer, your behaviour here is beyond awful. You've taken my grandson, and now you're violating my property. I'm going to take this up with the commissioner. He's an old family friend and I'm sure he won't take kindly to—'

'I don't mean you any disrespect, ma'am, but I have to do my job. The search will be fast, and then we'll be out of your hair.' The cop touches his hand to his forehead in a makeshift salute, then follows his officers into the house.

Miss Betty doesn't look pleased. She turns to Rick and Philip. 'Why aren't you stopping them?'

'We can't,' says Rick. 'They've got a warrant. Legally, you have to give them access.' He turns to Philip. 'Look, I talked to Moira. Things went bad at the CCTV office. Hank's been attacked, and it sounds like Moira's injured. Cops and medical are on their way. I'm going there now.'

'I'm coming with you,' says Philip.

Rick looks back to Miss Betty. 'Call your grandson a lawyer, Miss Betty. And make sure they're real good at what they do. He's going to need it.'

'You think he killed that girl?' says Miss Betty.

'No, I don't. But he's going to have a hard time proving that to the cops.' Rick looks from Miss Betty to Martha. 'Keep me in the loop on whatever happens, and I'll do the same. If you need me, I'll be on my cell.'

'You're leaving right away, when I've got a house full of police doing who knows what to my private belongings?' Miss Betty says, clenching her fists. 'What kind of gentlemen are you? Why aren't you staying here and helping me? How can you—'

'I am helping you, ma'am,' says Rick, trying to keep his tone even. 'I'm helping you and your grandson, because I'm going to find out what the hell is going on and prove Mikey isn't the murderer.'

35

MOIRA

Moira's eyes don't want to stay open. She feels as if there are weights on her lids, pushing them down, no matter how hard she tries to stay alert. Forcing herself to move, she shuffles closer to Hank. He's still unconscious and his skin has a greyish, waxy look to it that can't be a good thing. She checks again that his pulse is still there and is relieved when she feels it, but as she counts the beats her relief mingles with concern. Hank's pulse is slower and weaker than it was a few minutes earlier. She glances towards the door to the Surveillance Suite and hopes help arrives soon.

She looks at Hank's ashen face. Putting her hand on his arm, she tries to muster her most convincing voice. 'Hang on in there, Hank. Help is coming.'

His eyes flicker.

'Can you hear me, Hank? It's Moira. I'm a new resident here. I found you. You've been injured. Help is on the way.'

Hank's eyes open, darting from side to side, unfocused. His lips start to move. He's trying to say something. Moira leans closer. Listens hard. But she can't make out his words. 'What's that?'

Silence.

She looks at his face. His eyes are closed. His mouth is slightly open. He's lost consciousness again.

Moira curses under her breath. Then she hears voices in the corridor. She thinks she recognises them, but the woozy feeling is back and she feels strange, discombobulated. She swallows back the nausea. Raises her head.

'I'm in the Surveillance Suite,' she calls. Her voice sounds odd, weaker.

The footsteps come closer, get louder. The noise of them feels like a pneumatic drill bashing into her brain. Just as she thinks she can't take the noise a moment longer, Rick rushes into the room with Philip not far behind.

Rick stands above her, looking even more like a hulking giant from her viewpoint on the ground. The worry clear on his face. 'You okay? What happened?'

'I'm fine.' Moira gestures towards Hank. 'He hit Hank harder, he needs the medics now.'

'Did you call 911?' asks Philip, bending down to pick up one of the crushed USB sticks.

'Of course I did, I'm not a bloody idiot.' Moira doesn't try to hold back her anger; she hasn't the energy or the patience. Philip needs to not ask stupidly obvious questions. 'The guy had a mask on, but I think it was the same person I saw on the trail last night – similar body type and gait. He took the hard drives.'

'And destroyed the rest,' says Philip, grim-faced, as he inspects the smashed USB stick in his hand. 'He must have—'

'Shush.' Moira holds up her hand to silence him. Listens. There's a siren and it's getting closer. She looks at Rick. 'Can you go outside and guide them to Hank?'

'Sure,' says Rick.

She closes her eyes as he hurries back down the hallway to greet the blue lights. The pneumatic drill inside her mind seems to double down on its efforts, and the effect makes the urge to vomit stronger. When she opens her eyes again she sees Philip poking about at the computers on the desk and muttering something unintelligible.

Moira ignores him. She thinks back to the previous evening – how she'd had the feeling that someone was watching her and Rick as they talked outside in Philip and Lizzie's garden. And how she'd thought she'd seen movement over by the hedge. She'd checked it out and when she'd seen no one she'd told herself she was being paranoid, but maybe there *had* been someone there – not the blond from before, but the guy she'd seen on the trail.

She thinks back to that part of the evening. The four of them had planned their next moves and talked about the CCTV cameras. She'd said she was going to make a visit to Hank at the CCTV office the following morning. What if the killer had heard her and decided to remove the evidence first? What if she caused this to happen? She looks down at Hank – still out cold – and shivers. She doesn't want to be responsible for more hurt, more death, but now Hank's blood is smeared across her *tabula rasa* too.

'They're in here.' Rick's voice is in the hallway and coming closer.

Moments later three paramedics and several uniformed police officers burst into the room. Two paramedics go to Hank and get to work. The third kneels in front of Moira.

The paramedic is a tall, athletic-looking woman with her long blonde hair tied back in a neat ponytail. 'Ma'am, we need to take a look at you. Are you able—'

'Yes, I'm fine.' Moira pushes herself up to standing. Waits a moment as her vision swings, the room seeming to tilt at an angle before it rights itself again.

'Okay then,' says the paramedic, looking unconvinced. 'You want to come with us to the ambulance and we'll check you out?'

Moira glances at Hank. There's an oxygen mask over his face and the other paramedics seem to be doing some vitals checks. She supposes there's nothing more she can do. 'Yeah, okay.'

It takes a while to get to the ambulance and she has to use all her concentration to stay upright and keep putting one foot in front of the other. An assistant paramedic – a short, muscular guy with close-cropped black hair and a receding hairline – offers to help her, but she declines, so he hovers around just behind her, waiting to catch her if she falls, she assumes. She's vaguely aware of a gurney being wheeled down the hallway towards the Security Suite. Fear grips her around the chest. 'Is Hank okay?'

'My colleagues are helping him,' says the blonde paramedic. 'He's in good hands.'

They reach the end of the gloomy hallway and step out into the daylight. The medics help her navigate along past the spot of wall where the attacker got away, and out to the parking lot. It's not empty any more; now there are two ambulances and several police cars. Moira stops. She can guess what comes next, and she doesn't want to do it.

'Let me help you inside,' says the blonde paramedic. 'It's a bit of a step.'

Moira shakes her head. Then immediately regrets it as the nausea threatens to overwhelm her. 'No, I'm okay, I don't need to—'

'With all due respect, you're not okay, ma'am. I need to treat that head wound, and I can't do it standing out here.'

Unlike yesterday, Moira doesn't have the strength to argue. With the paramedic's help, she climbs up into the ambulance. Her vision swirls from the movement and she reaches out to the trolley bed to steady herself.

'They need your help.' It's Philip's voice, outside the ambulance.

Moira turns as he appears at the door. He's red-faced and his breath is coming in gasps. He looks at the blonde paramedic and her muscular assistant. Gestures back in the direction of the building. 'Hank . . . your colleagues say he's crashing.'

The female paramedic grabs some kit from a side locker and gestures at a metal box, which her assistant picks up. The writing, in capitals, on the box reads *'DEFIBRILLATOR'.*

'Stay here and don't touch anything, okay,' says the blonde paramedic to Moira, as her assistant jumps out of the ambulance. She follows him, then turns, pointing at Philip. 'You too.'

Moira clenches her fists. She doesn't want to stay here. She wants to go and help. She tries to push herself up to standing, but her vision blurs and the world seems to tilt. Sitting back down, she slows her breathing. Knows she has to let the medics do their job, she'd just be in the way. She hates it though, this feeling of being so useless.

'Well, here we are again,' says Philip, having got his breath back.

Idiotic man, thinks Moira. 'Where's Rick?'

'Still inside with Hank.' Philip glances back towards the building. 'It doesn't look good. Poor chap.'

If only I'd got here earlier, thinks Moira. *If only I'd listened to myself more last night and checked out if we were being watched. If only. If only.*

Philip runs his hand over his bald pate. 'You know—'

'Can you give me a minute,' says Moira. 'I can't talk right now.'

He looks crestfallen, and she knows that she's hurt his feelings, but she can't deal with him banging on about whatever it is he was about to say. She closes her eyes, and a long moment later hears footsteps as he moves away from the ambulance. She takes a deep breath in and blows out in a long exhale. It helps. Makes her feel a little calmer.

It doesn't last long. She hears the squeal of tyre rubber on tarmac as a car pulls into the lot, then the squeal of brakes as it stops close to the ambulance. A car door opens and slams shut.

214

An American voice that she kind of recognises growls, 'What in hell's name are you doing here, Sweetman?'

Moira's eyes snap open. It sounds like Detective Golding.

Philip's voice is different when he answers the detective – like he's putting on a posher accent and a more pompous tone. 'I was attending the scene of—'

'Don't tell me, I know the reason. It's cos you're a goddamn busybody meddler.' Golding's voice is getting louder. 'I told you to stay the hell away from my investigation, Sweetman. I warned you that you'd not want to force my hand to—'

'You warned me?' Philip sounds angry. 'Are you trying to threaten me? Why would you—'

'Take it however you want.' Golding's shouting now, his fury clear in every word. 'Just stay the hell away!' There's a loud bang on the wall of the ambulance.

Moira flinches. The noise feels as if it'll split her head in two. She swallows down another wave of nausea. Keeps listening.

'I can do what I want,' says Philip, his tone getting more pompous. 'I'm an experienced police officer and I live here. I'm entitled to—'

'You ain't entitled to do shit.' There's a hard steel core to Golding's tone now. The volume's lower, but the level of menace is dialled up to the max. 'I know all about you, DCI Sweetman – or rather, *ex*-DCI Sweetman. I did my homework and got in touch with a friend over in the UK who put some feelers out, because I was thinking to myself: what kind of senior meddles in homicide cases? Well, now I know *exactly* what sort of man does that. I know what you did, and why the British police force had to get shot of you fast.' The detective's words have become a hiss. 'Getting involved in my investigation won't save you; there ain't nothing that's going to do that. You killed that little girl and we both know it. So don't try and play the big saviour here, because you're nothing

215

but a liar and a fraud, and if you get in my way again, I'll make sure all your friends here in this senior community know. Hell, I might even let it slip to the journalists that hang around the precinct too – something fun for them to look into on a quiet news day.'

Philip doesn't reply. Seconds later Moira sees Golding stride past the ambulance towards the CCTV office. She doesn't see Philip again. Wonders if she should try and talk to him, then decides against it. She's not sure she's stable enough on her legs to climb out of the ambulance anyway.

So she sits in the ambulance and waits. Thinking. Her mind's whirling at a hundred miles an hour trying to make sense of what Golding had said – that Philip hadn't just retired, that he'd been forced out; that he killed a child. She can't make sense of it. Her brain seems sluggish in making connections, like it's on go-slow. It's frustrating.

She closes her eyes.

It's too bright in here. It feels as if the light is boring into her brain.

She feels so very tired.

Moira wakes with a start. Feels spaced out, disorientated. Jarred awake by the rattle of the gurney. Opening her eyes, she sees the paramedics flinging open the doors of the other ambulance and loading the gurney, with Hank strapped on to it, inside. The two original medics, who were treating Hank before he started crashing, climb into the other ambulance. The blonde paramedic and her assistant medic come back inside with Moira.

'How's Hank?' asks Moira, as the other ambulance pulls away, and the lights and siren start.

'Not so great right now, but he's hanging in there,' says the blonde paramedic as she moves across the ambulance to Moira and leans down, peering at her head wound. 'You should have some stitches.'

216

'Can you do them here?'

'No, ma'am, you'll need to come with us.'

Moira feels her adrenaline flare. She needs to stay on the case, not sit in a hospital unable to do anything. There's so much going on – Philip and the revelation from Golding, and Hank being rushed to hospital. 'I can't do that. Can you fix it with some butterfly strips?'

The paramedic frowns. 'I could, but it's not the optimum solution here, if you come with us to—'

'Thanks, but no.' She gives her what she hopes is her most charming smile, although given that she's feeling so weird right now it's possible it's closer to a grimace. 'Patch me up with the strips. Please.'

The paramedic says nothing for a few moments. Then nods. 'Okay, ma'am, but I'm noting down that they were your choice.'

'That's fine with me.'

She gets to work, putting some antiseptic wash on to a cotton pad and pressing it against the wound on Moira's forehead.

Moira winces at the stinging sensation. 'I got off lightly compared to Hank.'

'Perhaps,' says the paramedic, peering at the wound. 'But this is pretty deep. You sure you won't take a ride to hospital with us?'

'I'm sure.'

'Well, okay then.' The paramedic discards the cotton pad into a cardboard kidney-shaped tray and picks up the butterfly closure strips. With speed born from a lot of practice, she tapes the wound closed. 'There you go, all done.'

'Thanks.' Moira eases herself off the gurney. Her head is throbbing and standing feels weird, like she's outside of her own body and looking down at herself. Still, she manages to sign the paperwork that the paramedic puts in front of her, then takes a couple of steps towards the door.

217

'Your face is going to bruise up real bad,' says the paramedic. 'Best to have some anti-inflammatories ready.'

'Will do,' says Moira, holding tight to the handrail as she steps down from the ambulance. She scans the parking lot. Philip's nowhere to be seen, but she spots Rick a little way across the lot, leaning against the side of his jeep.

He rushes to help her. Takes her elbow and guides her to the passenger side, practically lifting her on to the seat. She doesn't fight his help. She needs it.

Rick looks worried as he stares at her head. 'You sure you shouldn't be in hospital?'

Moira shakes her head, and tries to ignore the nausea as her vision goes hazy again. 'It's just a nasty scratch, I'll be fine.'

Rick looks unconvinced, but he fires up the jeep's engine, and she's thankful for that. She closes her eyes, and as she does the conversation between Philip and Golding replays in her mind. Golding said Philip was a liar, that he killed a child, and that he was fired because of it. That's a long way from the story Lizzie told.

She needs to know who is telling the truth.

36

LIZZIE

There's something wrong. Philip's trying to hide it, but Lizzie knows the signs. She doesn't think it's because of what happened to Moira, either. It's something else, and it's happened since he left this morning.

Lizzie looks at Rick. 'It feels weird without Moira here. How was she doing when you dropped her home?'

'Playing the tough cookie. She was feeling rough, anyone could see it, but she was real determined not to let it show. I offered to give her a hand with the dogs and all, but she said she'd be fine and I didn't want to push it.'

'I'll check in on her later,' says Lizzie. 'See if she needs anything.'

She sneaks a glance at Philip. He's holding his mug in both hands and staring into the coffee. It seems like he isn't even listening to what Rick's saying. *No*, she thinks, *he's not worrying about Moira, but he's been off since he returned an hour or so ago. There is something else going on with him. Maybe it has something to do with the investigation.* 'What did you guys find?'

Rick doesn't answer right away. Instead he looks at Philip to see if he's going to jump in. Philip stays silent. Keeps looking into his coffee mug. Rick gives a shrug, and turns back to Lizzie. 'We found a whole bunch, but I'm not sure where it leaves us.'

'How come?'

'Well, for starters, we know that Betty Graften's grandson, Mikey, is the guy that Donald saw arguing with the victim, and that he'd been dating her for a few weeks. He told us her name – Kristen Altman – and that she was a croupier at the Flying Mustang Casino over in Conaldo Plains. He also—'

'Hold on, we should be keeping track of this on the board,' says Lizzie. Getting up, she picks the dry marker off the table and walks over to the patio doors. She takes the lid off the pen and turns back to Rick. 'Keep talking. I'll make the notes.'

'So Mikey Graften says he was due to meet the victim the night she died, and that she'd messaged him earlier that day saying that after that night all their money worries would be over. He says he waited for her in the spot they'd agreed, but she never showed.'

Lizzie frowns. 'And you believe him?'

Rick exhales hard. 'The kid's pretty messed up about it. Seemed like he was telling the truth to me. I don't think he killed her, but Golding does. He showed up while we were still talking to the kid and arrested him.'

'Does he have evidence we don't?' asks Lizzie.

'I doubt it.' Rick glances at Philip, who doesn't look up. He looks back at Lizzie. 'Golding said it was off the back of the plate sighting that he was bringing the kid in. It shouldn't be enough to hold him long.'

'What about the CCTV?' asks Lizzie.

'Nothing left, from what I could see. The hard drives had been ripped out of the computers, and all the USB backups destroyed.'

'So Moira and Hank got injured for nothing.'

They sit in silence for a minute.

'How did things go here?' asks Rick. 'You find anything useful?'

Lizzie glances through the patio doors into the kitchen. Her testing kit is sitting open on the countertop. The water-testing equipment is drying on the drainer rack beside the sink. She shakes her head. 'Nothing of use, I'm afraid. The sample was non-conclusive – there was too much cleaning agent in the water.'

'Worth a try.'

'I guess,' says Lizzie. 'I'm still working on the phone. I haven't managed to get it to work yet, but I'll keep trying and maybe I'll get lucky.' She glances at Philip. He hasn't spoken for ages. She keeps staring at him until she catches his eye. He looks away fast as if he's been burnt.

Rick notices. He stands up. 'Look, I should get going.' He looks at Philip. 'I'll do another round of the volunteer patrollers in the morning and collect the last few logs.'

Philip sounds distracted when he speaks. 'Good, good.'

Rick frowns but doesn't say anything; instead he turns to Lizzie. 'Thanks for the coffee, Lizzie. Let me know if Moira needs anything, I'm more than happy to help out.'

Lizzie smiles and thinks what a kind and uncomplicated man Rick is, not like her husband. She feels a pang of guilt almost before the thought is fully formed. 'Of course.'

She waits until Rick's disappeared around the side of the house and she's heard the back gate open and then click shut. Philip's still staring into his mug at the half-drunk coffee. *It'll be cold now*, Lizzie thinks, *and he hates cold coffee*. She gathers her and Rick's mugs up and heads inside to the kitchen. She's at the sink, washing out the mugs, when Philip joins her.

Lizzie turns off the water and turns around to face him. 'Did something happen today?' She tries to keep her tone conversational, but even she can hear the telltale quiver of worry. She keeps her eyes on Philip's face, even though he's avoiding eye contact.

'It's nothing,' he says, putting his mug in the dishwater and turning towards the hallway.

Lizzie moves fast, blocking his path. 'What's going on?'

Philip shakes his head. 'It's—'

'Don't tell me it's nothing, because I know it can't be nothing. You're never silent unless there's a problem, and you've hardly spoken a word to me or Rick for the last hour.' She stares at him until he meets her gaze. 'Tell me what's happened.'

There's a long pause. Then Philip says softly, 'Golding knows.'

Lizzie frowns. 'I don't—'

'He knows why I left the force.' Philip's voice is so quiet she can barely hear him. 'He knows about the girl. That I was made to retire.'

Lizzie feels like a bus has just slammed into her chest. The memory of the day he'd come home after they'd found the child's body and told her he'd made a terrible mistake. She'd pushed him to tell her what had happened, and he'd resisted for a while, but in the end he told her that he'd missed a vital clue and it had led to them discovering the child too late. He'd cried in her arms. Sobbed for hours. Then, later, after the heart attack and agreeing to step down from being DCI, when she'd asked him, he'd said he'd rather not talk about it. That he'd made an error of judgement. That he'd gone out to lunch rather than following up on a tip-off, and that had delayed them locating the kidnapped girl. Now she looks at his dejected stance and the way he can't meet her gaze, and her suspicions return. Did he tell her the whole story, or has he been hiding something all this time? 'What does Golding know?'

Philip shakes his head. 'I don't know exactly, but enough. He says he has a contact in the UK force who told him all the details and if I don't stop getting in his way he'll tell everyone here, maybe the media too.'

Lizzie breathes in fast. If that happens, their happy life here is done. 'Then we need to stop.'

'I won't stop,' says Philip. He looks at her with angry intensity. 'That bastard can't make me—'

'You'd have everyone here know what happened? If people find out, we could lose our friends, everything we've built here . . .'

'Was what I did so bad?' Philip's voice is raised now. His face is red.

'You tell me,' says Lizzie. 'Was it?'

They stare at each other for a long moment. Both angry.

Philip's the first to look away. He shakes his head. 'I don't remember.'

'How very convenient,' spits Lizzie. She's furious now. It's obvious he's lying.

'Look, I . . . I made a mistake. It was an awful thing, a tragedy, but I . . .'

Lizzie hugs herself. Feels like she's going to explode. 'First you don't remember. Now you say it was a mistake. If it was just a one-off error of judgement, why did they fire you? They knew you'd been under extreme pressure, they knew the volume of tip-offs was massive once the reward was offered. Surely they could have moved you to a desk, or put you into another unit, but they didn't, they pensioned you off. Why?'

Philip says nothing but she can tell from his expression that she's right – he's hiding something. His silence infuriates her. It's like he doesn't care or respect her enough to tell her the truth. She swears under her breath.

She knows a child died because of Philip and because of it he was forced to retire. If that gets out they'll have to move – their friends here will shun them and the shame will be too much. Emotions rollercoaster through her – anger that Philip caused this, hurt that even after all these years he won't tell her everything that happened, and, if she's honest, the rising frustration with herself for standing by and staying with him. She glares at him. 'You owe me the whole story. You've owed me that for nearly ten years.'

'I . . .' Philip shakes his head. Opens his mouth, then closes it again. 'I'm going to do some reading.' He steps around her.

Lizzie doesn't try to stop him. Doesn't waste her breath trying to make him talk to her. It's pointless. She can see that from the expression on his face.

Till death do us part, that's what they promised each other in their wedding vows. She takes their vows seriously, always has. But now, she wonders if it's enough; if it's enough for her to stay with him. The way he's behaving isn't the way the man she spoke those vows to used to behave, and he seems a long way from the idealistic, public-service-committed man she fell in love with all those years ago. Has he really been hiding something from her for the last ten years? If he has, does she even know him at all?

If he keeps hiding the full story from her she's not sure that their relationship will survive this.

She's not sure she wants it to.

As Philip walks away from her, Lizzie thinks about the blue metal box file. That's where Philip kept everything to do with his police career. When they moved here he'd put it in the loft, but she knows, having searched for it last night, it's not up there any more. Since then she's gone through the garage and the study, but not found the metal filing box. There's one more place she can look, and that's Philip's bedroom, but she ran out of time before he came back. Now she's going to need to wait for him to go out before she can search. Whatever happens and whether he tells her or not, she *will* find out the truth of why he was forced to retire for one error of judgement in an otherwise highly decorated career. And she will discover how that poor child died.

37

MOIRA

She wakes with a start; an unfamiliar movement in the bed jerking her into high alert. It's too dark to see anything but she can feel something moving, pinning her legs to the bed. Her breath catches in her throat. Her heart pounds almost as hard as the throbbing in her head. Groping around for the light, she switches it on and grabs the glass from the bedside table, ready to defend herself against the intruder.

She laughs when she sees who it is. Pip, her earnest little sausage dog, stares dolefully back at her. He's lying across her legs. Shaking her head, she puts the water glass back on the bedside table. 'Did I wake you?'

Pip responds by rolling over on to his back for a tummy tickle. Moira obliges. There's something so comforting in the feel of a dog's fur beneath your hands. Slowly her heart rate returns to normal. Pip sighs with happiness. The noise causes Marigold, the young Labrador, to raise her head from its resting place on Wolfie, the terrier's back. Wolfie doesn't stir, just snores a little louder.

Moira remembers now. Last night, still feeling woozy and vulnerable from the attack earlier in the day, she'd let the dogs sleep on her bed.

'Night-night, baby,' she says to Pip, giving his tummy one last stroke before turning off the light.

Moira lies back on the bed. Her head's still pounding, and her body feels like it's been run over by a truck. This isn't how she'd anticipated her retirement to be. She came here to start a new, less complicated, life. Instead, she's had the crap knocked out of her and got more injuries in a couple of days than she's had in the past couple of years. This place is meant to be a safe place – a sanctuary – a place where good things happen. Yet it seems to be more dangerous than the trouble she left London to escape.

She shudders, remembering how when she'd read the marketing material for The Homestead she'd laughed and mocked the advertising bullshit. A place where only good things happen doesn't exist, yet that's what the marketing brochure claimed. It's nonsense, of course – humans always screw things up, no matter how perfect a place is. People are incapable of only doing good.

Yet ever since she's got here, the overwhelming narrative of The Homestead – in the local news, the community news and the social media pages – has been positive. She'd started to wonder if maybe the security was so good and the vetting process to live here so strict that trouble found it hard to enter. Then the burglaries started, and now there's been a murder, proving bad things are able to happen here just as much as anywhere else: yet the narrative hasn't changed. Something weird is going on.

Moira reaches across and takes her phone from the bedside table. Pressing the screen she blinks in the blue light as it illuminates. First she scans the local news sites – radio, TV and web – but finds nothing relating to The Homestead. She switches to The Homestead News website and scrolls through the articles on the pickleball championship series, and the new garden over in Wild Spring Fields. She's almost given up when she finds a small news article: Tragic Accident in the Park.

She scans the text, picking out the keywords – Manatee Park, swimming pool, young, unidentified woman. The piece is more puff than facts, and passes the incident off as an accidental drowning, but it's clear from the date given that it's referring to the murder. There's nothing about the money or the fact that the woman had been shot. The most important details have been left out.

Moira feels uneasy. What's reported certainly isn't anything close to the whole truth. It seems like misdirection or some kind of arse-covering move, but by who and why?

Switching to the Facebook app, she opens The Homestead community page and searches for mentions of the murder or so-called accident. She scrolls through the posts from the various special-interest groups talking about tennis tournaments, quilt-a-thons, the pickleball championships, a trip to a local vineyard and a weekend excursion to St Pete Beach. There are posts from different residents asking for recommendations on local restaurants, home-maintenance help and someone who can install an aquarium. But there's nothing about the murder. She's staring at the screen, thinking how odd it is that there's a total absence of discussion about it, when a new post appears at the top of the feed.

> Peggy Leggerhorne to The Homestead community: [PLEASE DON'T DELETE AGAIN] Does anyone know WHAT HAPPENED at Manatee Park? My husband, Dougie, says someone DIED? Is that true? Does anyone KNOW who it was?

Moira frowns. If Peggy Leggerhorne is asking the moderators not to delete her message again, they must be taking down posts on topics they don't like – and it looks likely that the subject of murder is one of those topics.

As she watches, comments start to appear beneath Peggy's post. Interesting. It's barely six in the morning, but it seems as if plenty of the residents are awake.

> TexasPete58: I heard a girl died

> SamanthaLovesCats: Someone died? Who?

> MarkGrecian: It's just a rumour is all

> DorothyKnits: It was a young woman. She was in the pool.

> TeaAndCake44583: I heard something about an accident in the pool at Manatee

> MarkandJack: It was murder

> BlakeGotterton: This can't be true

Moira hasn't finished reading the comments when the thread suddenly disappears. She scrolls up and down the page, but can't find it. Comes out of the app, and then goes back in – still nothing. She's just about to post a question to ask what's happened when a notification flashes up:

The moderator has turned off posting and comments.

It seems overkill if it's due to Peggy's discussion post – there wasn't anything inappropriate being said, and they were talking about something that had happened in the community. Moira thinks about the lack of news reports on the murder. Perhaps the problem is that they *were* talking about it happening in the community. Opening up Messenger, Moira taps out a message.

Moira Flynn: Hi Peggy, I just saw your post but it's disappeared now. Do the moderators usually delete things like that?

Peggy replies almost immediately.

Peggy Leggerhorne: All the goddamn time! I just wanted to know what's going on but I've posted three times about the death and they delete it every time. It was the same when I posted about getting burglarised – they deleted that too!!

Moira Flynn: I'm so sorry to hear you got burgled

Peggy Leggerhorne: We were the first home it happened to. We're on Stingray Drive. If they'd let us post about it on the group maybe others could have gotten more preventative measures in place and saved themselves the heartbreak of getting burglarised

Moira Flynn: Who moderates the group?

Peggy Leggerhorne: Homestead management. I thought they'd be asleep now but no!

Moira stares at Peggy's reply. It's interesting that the management run the community Facebook page. She clicks back to the page and looks up the moderator list. There are three of them, two women and one man. In their profile pictures they look like they're all young – probably in their twenties – and have the super-wide smiles of a Disney cast member. They're all wearing turquoise The Homestead T-shirts. Only one of them has a green dot beside their name, indicating that they're online right now – Brad Winslow.

Moira inhales sharply. She recognises him. It's the guy. The turquoise T-shirt has replaced the maroon and gold scarf and navy hoodie, and he's not wearing his black-framed glasses in the photo, but the slim face and blond hair are the same. Brad Winslow was the man with the silver VW Beetle who was spying on her two days ago.

Why did you follow me, Brad? Moira wonders. *And why did you delete Peggy's post?* She puts her phone on the bedside table and lies back in the darkness. There's something really odd going on here: he'd followed her for most of the day after she'd found the body, but after she'd chased him off he hadn't seemed to return. Online, there were Peggy's posts about getting burgled and the murder being deleted whenever she posted them, the lack of news coverage about the burglaries, and the fact that the Manatee Park murder hadn't appeared in any telly or radio broadcasts and was only on one newspaper site online, and even then it had been reported as an 'accident'. *That's far too much to be pure coincidence.* Instead it points to The Homestead meddling in how the news is portrayed and shared inside and outside the community. Moira just doesn't get why.

She reaches out to Pip and strokes his silken head. He snores louder.

It's as if The Homestead is able to block bad news getting reported. And deleting residents' posts when they're trying to share information and find out what's going on in their own community isn't okay. It's like Big Brother is watching their every move and deleting the things they don't like – editing the narrative of The

Homestead in a kind of *Stepford* community or *Truman Show*-type situation.

Moira shudders. That's really not okay. It's creepy.

This is real life; real things – bad things – are happening, and the residents are entitled to know about them. Hank could have died today. A young woman has already lost her life.

Finding the killer isn't enough now. Moira also needs to know why the management of The Homestead are censoring what their residents say, and if they are somehow manipulating the news.

She thinks back to when she was sitting in the ambulance earlier and the conversation between Detective Golding and Philip. Remembers the venom in Golding's voice, and the fear in Philip's.

She needs to know what's going on.

38

RICK

He's barely gotten a couple of streets from home when his cell phone starts ringing. Easing his foot off the gas a little and driving one-handed, Rick reaches into his pants pocket for his cell and answers. 'You're talking to Denver.'

'It's Hawk.'

'Hey buddy. What've you got for me?'

'A bunch of stuff as it goes, it's like your Christmas came early.'

Rick smiles. He knows Hawk will try and squeeze him for another game ticket, but if the intel's good that's fine with him. 'So tell me about it.'

'ID first – your Jane Doe is officially confirmed as Kristen Altman. Twenty-three years of age. Her most recent address is an apartment in The Homestead staffers' building – Golden Springs. She has a driver's licence but no vehicle registered with the DMV. Her birth certificate has her as a native of Pennsylvania.'

'Twenty-three.' Rick lets out a long whistle. Shakes his head. Twenty-three years old – the woman was barely more than a child.

'Yeah. Bad business for sure,' says Hawk, chewing on gum as he speaks. 'Listen, I got the read-out from the autopsy. She was shot with a .22 calibre. The wound was in her chest but up towards her shoulder and it missed her vital organs. It wasn't fatal, not immediately.'

'But?'

'But she was in the pool. She would have lost a hell of a lot of blood and gotten real weak. The medical examiner said the cause of death was drowning, but from the wound and the blood ratio in her body, she was shot before she hit the drink.'

'Damn.' Rick shakes his head, distracted. He makes a left and turns into Philip and Lizzie's street.

'Yeah. And here's where it gets messed up. The gun that shot the vic – they think it was most likely her own. She had a .22 calibre registered, an old-school purse-sized thing with a pearl handle. When they searched her apartment they found a half-used box of ammunition but the gun wasn't in her metal gunsafe.'

Rick frowns. 'And they didn't find the gun at the crime scene?'

'Nope. It hasn't turned up yet.'

'Let me know if it does.'

'Will do. One other thing, the young punk who owns the station wagon, well, word is that Detective Golding has a real hard-on for him. He's likely going to be charged with the murder today.'

'On what evidence?' Rick pulls the jeep over to the kerb outside Lizzie and Philip's house and puts it into park.

On the other end of the call, Hawk works his gum. 'Circumstantial from what I've heard. But there's pressure to close the case and move on. And Golding's a player, you know, he does what's wanted.'

Rick blows out hard. He hates it when detectives let their career become more important than the truth. 'The kid's innocent.'

'Then you better prove it,' says Hawk.

Yeah, thinks Rick as he ends the call. He'd better. And fast.

Time is running out.

39

MOIRA

She's up at seven thirty. The sun is already warm; the dew long burned off from the grass. She takes the dogs for a run out on the grassland behind her house for forty minutes, then feeds them and grabs herself some watermelon for breakfast. She aches everywhere, worse in her bad ankle and her head. That won't do, she needs to do things today, can't sit about. She takes the highest-strength painkillers she has with two mugs of strong coffee drunk one after the other. Within twenty minutes the throbbing in her head has subsided enough for her to contemplate driving. Which is good, because she's got a plan.

First stop is The Homestead office. It's over in district one – Homestead Hills – the first section of The Homestead community that was built. It'll take almost fifteen minutes to drive to it from home and they'll be opening at nine. Moira's aiming to be first in line.

The journey's uneventful, but she's glad to have an automatic car – with her ankle, driving a manual gearbox would be impossible; she'd never manage to press down the clutch. As it is the automatic does its thing, and there's minimal traffic. She cruises under the 'WELCOME TO HOMESTEAD HILLS – THE HAPPIEST RETIREMENT COMMUNITY IN FLORIDA' sign that stretches over the highway like a bridge and clenches her teeth. Checking her watch she sees that she's several minutes earlier than planned.

She parks out front. Like all the official buildings on The Homestead the office is a single-storey cream stucco, although this one's bigger than the security hut and the CCTV office combined. There are lights on inside, and she can see people moving about through the windows. On the side of the office between the windows and door there are two full-height billboards. One features a grey-haired couple with the wording 'THE HOMESTEAD – BECAUSE YOU DESERVE YOUR HAPPY EVER AFTER' and the second has a picture of three grey-haired ladies laughing in the swimming pool with the words 'THE HOMESTEAD – A PLACE TO MAKE AND SHARE HAPPY MEMORIES'. Moira remembers her last memory of the pool at Manatee Park and shakes her head.

At nine o'clock she gets out of her car and walks to the office. The sun is hot on her skin and she starts to sweat. Her limp is still pronounced as she tries to keep the pressure off her bad ankle. Even with the painkillers it feels like fire every time she puts her weight on it.

The automatic door slides open as she approaches. Inside the air conditioning is already turned up high. There's a long curved counter with three people – two women and a guy – wearing bright turquoise polo shirts with The Homestead logo across the pocket seated behind it. The women are closest to the door and they smile in unison as she enters. The third – sitting furthest from the door – remains focused on his screen. Moira heads towards him.

'Good morning,' he says cheerfully, as he turns towards her.

Moira gives him a quick smile, and watches as the smile fades from his face.

'I . . . I should . . .' He moves back from the counter. Looks as if he's going to run.

'Don't,' says Moira, her tone strong, authoritative. It's definitely him. She recognises him from his picture on the community Facebook page, from their encounter by Manatee Park, outside her house, and in the street outside Lizzie and Philip's place. He's got a name badge pinned to his polo shirt beneath The Homestead logo. 'You owe me an explanation, Brad Winslow.'

The Disney prince-type smile is gone. Maybe it's because he recognises her, or maybe it's due to the bruising on her face. Maybe it's both, because now he looks more like a frightened deer in headlights. Still, even though his voice has a quiver to it, he seems to be sticking to his script. 'How can I help you today?'

'Why were you following me two days ago?'

'I wasn't—'

'Don't lie to me, Brad.' Moira looks across at his colleagues, and then peers back behind the counter towards the back room. 'Or maybe I should speak to your supervisor. Tell them about you spying on me, and how you were very bad at it.'

He shakes his head. 'Don't. There's no need, I . . . I was told to watch you. And I was told I mustn't let you see me. They wanted me to make sure you were doing okay. Nothing more.'

Moira crosses her arms. 'And I'm supposed to believe that?'

'Honestly, it's the truth. You'd discovered that poor young woman. The management were worried, especially as you're a new resident. They asked me to watch you for a little while and make sure you were okay.'

It sounds like bullshit to Moira, but he seems to believe it. 'Why did you stop watching me then?'

He looks down. 'Because you spotted me that third time.'

'So you didn't care about my well-being after that?'

'No . . . no, I . . . you scared me. All that shouting and banging on my car window like that. I thought you were going to hit me. You were so angry.'

'Yes, because you were spying on me.'

'Well, it seemed like you could take care of yourself okay, so I told management you were fine and that you'd got your friends supporting you, and I stopped. I kind of had to anyways, because my cover was blown.'

Moira shakes her head. Stifles a laugh. 'Your cover was blown from the first time, outside Manatee Park, when I saw you crouched down beside your car watching me and you took the picture.'

Brad's cheeks flush red. He sounds defensive when he speaks. 'I'm an administrative and social media manager. I don't know how to do surveillance.'

She holds his gaze for a long moment. His story is plausible – odd but plausible. And he doesn't seem to be a credible threat. She decides to continue with her other questions. 'As you clearly know, I live over in Ocean Mist and I want to know why you delete residents' posts on the community Facebook page?'

He looks more concerned. 'I—'

'Early this morning there was a post asking about the murder at Manatee Park. Why delete it?'

Brad glances in the direction of his colleagues. Lowers his voice. 'It's company policy. We can't let hearsay or rumours spread through the community page. We're authorised to delete any posts breaking rule eight.'

'I don't know what rule eight is, but that post wasn't spreading hearsay, it was talking about something that actually happened.'

He shakes his head. 'No, it was misinformed. Yes, there was an accident in the pool at Manatee, a tragedy, but not a—'

'That's bullshit, Brad, and we both know it.'

Frowning, he turns to the computer on the desk and clicks through a few screens. Reads something and then turns back to Moira. Gives her a fake-looking smile. 'With all due respect, I think you're mistaken, ma'am. I've got the incident report right here and it's telling me there was a tragic accident when a swimmer—'

'Just stop.' Moira holds up her hands. 'Your incident report is wrong. As you know, I found the woman's body in the pool and called the cops. She was murdered. I saw the blood from the gunshot wound myself.'

Brad gulps at the air like a landed fish and fans his hands at his face, which is getting redder by the second. His smile is non-existent. 'But I . . . I wasn't told . . .'

'Who filled out the incident report?' asks Moira.

His gaze flits to the screen, then back to her. 'That's above my pay grade. I'm afraid I can't . . .'

'I didn't think so.' The two other assistants behind the counter are watching her and obviously listening in. And Brad's looking increasingly uncomfortable, shifting his weight from side to side and glancing towards his colleagues. Moira senses she's got as much information from him as she's going to get, for now at least. 'But thanks, you've been helpful.' She leans in closer. Lowers her voice. 'And don't even think about spying on me again.'

Brad tries to give a Disney-prince smile. It doesn't work and the result is a flaccid half-grimace. 'No problem. Have a great day.'

Moira turns and walks towards the exit. A few strides before the door she stops and looks back at Brad. He flinches as their eyes meet. 'By the way, what's rule eight?'

Brad hesitates, and then answers in a tone full of fake enthusiasm. 'All posts must be positive in spirit.'

She'd figured that much, but it's useful to have it confirmed. They're controlling the message, and keeping the *only good things happen here* narrative alive, even though it's fake news.

Saying nothing, she turns and walks away.

As she steps out of the building into the heat and bright sunlight she thinks about what she's discovered. Faked incident reports,

238

especially when the police are involved, are a serious business. How can The Homestead get away with it? It makes no sense, just like the lack of media attention and Detective Golding's extreme reaction to them trying to help. It's all connected, it has to be; it can't be a coincidence. She just needs to figure out how.

40

PHILIP

He hates tension. Tries to ignore it. But Lizzie isn't making it easy with her long accusing looks and over-loud sighs. That's why he's brought his coffee into the study and shut the door. This way he doesn't have to see the disappointment on her face every time she looks at him, and he can avoid answering her questions. He really doesn't want to have to answer her questions. If enough time passes maybe she'll stop asking and things can go back to the way they were. He liked the way they were.

Right now he needs to focus on the case, and the patrol logs. He's looking for something that could have been missed, or didn't seem important, first time around. If the Graften boy didn't do it – and Rick's pretty sure that he didn't – they need a new lead. Philip is good at this sort of thing, he always has been. He knows he can find them a lead. He just needs to put his mind to it.

Sorting through the log reports, he picks out the ones done by patrollers who were in the areas, or bordered the areas, where the burglaries and the murder took place. There are four patrollers in that group – Clint, Pamela, Clayton and Donald. Once he's separated their reports from the main pile he settles back in his chair and starts reading. There's a month's worth of logs from each patroller – around fifty pages each in total – so it's going to take a while.

He's finished reading Donald's reports and is right in the middle of Pamela's when his attention is broken by a knock against the open door. Tutting, he tries to ignore it and keep reading.

There's a louder thud. Dammit. 'Can't a man get any peace?' mutters Philip.

Tutting again, he looks towards the door.

Lizzie's standing there. She hovers just inside the doorway holding a mug. 'I brought you coffee.'

Philip doesn't want coffee. Even though it's not yet noon he's already reached his four-cup limit. But he doesn't want to refuse it and risk upsetting Lizzie more. 'Thanks.'

She hands the mug over without a further word, but she doesn't need to speak for him to know how she's feeling. Her posture is stiff, her movements jerky. And the way she looks at him as he takes the coffee makes him feel like a criminal. Philip looks away. He knows it's all because of the retirement nonsense. Why can't she just drop it? It was so long ago and they've been happy here – he doesn't understand why she has to rake it all up again.

Bloody Golding. He caused this. Philip curses himself for telling Lizzie what the detective had said. He'd forgotten how weird she'd gone after his retirement party, how she'd hinted that there must have been something more to prompt his hasty retirement rather than just an error of judgement and his heart attack. She'd given him the cold shoulder for a few weeks, but then they'd made their trip out to Florida and things had improved, and she seemed to have forgotten about it. That's when he knew they needed a big change – a new start, in a new environment. That's why he'd persuaded her to move here.

'What are you doing?' she asks.

'Searching through the field logs of the patrollers – looking for anything that might have been forgotten.'

'Good idea,' says Lizzie. Her voice is deadpan, no intonation. 'Have you—'

The doorbell chimes. They both look out towards the hallway and the front door. Neither of them move.

'You can get that,' says Lizzie.

Philip looks at the patrol notes in his hand. 'Can't you . . .'

Lizzie sighs. Shaking her head she moves away towards the front door.

Damn and blast, thinks Philip. Setting the notes down, he gets up and follows. He catches up with her at the end of the hallway as she's opening the door. She shoots him a frosty look and he almost retreats. Then he sees who it is at the door and puts a hand on Lizzie's shoulder and smiles. He tries not to notice Lizzie flinching at his touch. Puts it from his mind. Presenting a good front, a united front. That's important.

'Morning,' says Rick, stepping over the threshold. 'What's going on?'

Philip wonders for a moment if Rick's sensed the problem between them already. Then Lizzie smiles at their friend and puts on her poker face, and Philip feels relief. If she'll pretend things are okay with Rick, maybe in time she'll do the same with him.

'I'm working on the phone Moira found,' says Lizzie. 'And Philip's been going back through the patrol logs.'

'Any luck?'

'The phone's still a work in progress.' Lizzie looks at Philip, but doesn't meet his gaze.

'I'm working through the reports,' says Philip. 'I've got a lot of pages to get through.'

Lizzie closes the door behind Rick. 'What about you, anything new?'

'I just got a call from my police contact. The autopsy happened yesterday. The cause of death was drowning, as we'd been thinking

242

it could've been. The gunshot wound would have caused the victim to lose a lot of blood, but it didn't have to be fatal. As things went, she must've bled out in the water. Lost consciousness and . . .' Rick shakes his head.

'So she must have stayed in the water for a reason,' says Lizzie. 'Just like we suspected.'

'Sure looks that way,' says Rick.

Philip runs his hand over the top of his head. 'What about the gun, did they find it?'

'Nope. Not yet. They know it was a .22 and, although they don't know for sure until the murder weapon turns up, they've got a working theory that she was shot with her own weapon.'

'She had a gun?' asks Lizzie.

'Yep. A pearl-handled .22 was registered to her and it's missing. They searched her place. *Nada.*'

A girl with a gun – Philip knows that shouldn't surprise him; this is America after all, it's not unusual for a person to own a gun, but it does put a twist on things. 'Any chance she fired it?'

'At the crime scene, I don't think so.' Rick runs his hand across his jaw. 'My contact would've said if they'd found gunshot residue on her hands.'

'Let's hope so,' says Lizzie, as she turns and heads towards the kitchen.

Philip and Rick follow her. Philip wonders if Rick can sense the frostiness between him and Lizzie. The man's sharp, ex-DEA; despite them both trying to put on a good show surely he'll notice the lack of eye contact and the tension. It's embarrassing. Things between a husband and wife should be private – they shouldn't show their grievances in public.

Philip feels tension rising in his chest as he remembers how angry Lizzie was last night. He's never seen her that cross before, not in all the years they've been married. It'll blow over, won't it? He hopes so. He hopes she'll calm down soon.

'Did your contact know anything else that's useful?' says Philip, as they enter the kitchen.

Rick leans against one of the countertops. 'The victim had a rental apartment in the Golden Springs accommodation block for Homestead staffers. She didn't have a vehicle registered with DMV. I need to check it out properly, but I reckon her fastest route walking from her job at the Flying Mustang Casino to her apartment would be along the Wild Ridge Trail and through Ocean Mist to her place in the Golden Springs staffers accommodation complex on the edge of district eight – Whispering Palms.'

'As a croupier she'd work all kinds of hours,' says Lizzie, pouring coffee into three mugs. 'Those casinos are open twenty-four-seven.'

'Yep, for sure,' says Rick, nodding thanks to Lizzie as she hands him a coffee. He looks back to Philip.

Philip wonders how Lizzie knows about the casinos. She's never been there. As far as he knows she's never been inside any casino. He can't ask her now though. He looks at Rick. 'How come the victim lived in staff accommodation in a different district to the casino? Surely she'd want to be close to her place of work.'

'It's a good question,' says Rick. 'Maybe the staffers' block in Conaldo Plains was full when she started.'

'Could be.' Lizzie doesn't sound convinced as she plonks a coffee mug on to the counter next to Philip without making eye contact. 'Worth checking that out.'

Philip wonders if Lizzie's cross that he didn't bring the coffee she just made for him through. Shakes his head. Rick's contact has a lot of new information; maybe Golding is finally giving the case some proper attention. 'The cops seem to have made good progress.'

'Yep, they have. Although aside from the autopsy, we kind of gave them their best lead – from the licence plate of the station wagon they found the person she was closest to and he told them the victim's identity,' says Rick. 'What about you? Are those patrol reports giving you any theories?'

'Not really.' Philip tries not to be put off by the fact that Lizzie still isn't even looking at him. 'But we know the cameras were taken out in the areas the burglaries took place. I'm thinking that maybe the patrols saw something that they didn't think important back then, but could give us a lead now.'

'What kind of thing?' asks Rick.

Philip shrugs. 'I don't know. Something. I mean, we know Clint and Donald both spotted the victim and or the station wagon in the weeks leading up to her death. And now we know where she lived it's likely she walked through our streets on her way to and from work, often at unusual hours. The burglaries and the murder happened in or near the areas that Clint, Donald, Pamela and Clayton patrolled, and that could've been part of her route.'

'Could be she saw something,' says Rick.

Philip recalls the strange list of items that'd been found in the victim's backpack when it was recovered from the bottom of the pool. He thinks of the assumptions they've made. 'Or it could be we're looking at this wrong – she could've been the burglar.'

Lizzie cocks her head to one side. Looks at Rick. 'It's possible. The timings work. Could be even if she didn't do it, she is at least in on it.'

'What, and she was killed by the other person or people involved?' says Rick.

'Maybe,' says Lizzie, taking a sip of coffee. 'It's a theory worth exploring.'

Philip tightens his grip on the mug he's holding. The alternative theory was his idea, but Lizzie's only talking directly to Rick.

He's her husband, and he's standing right here, but she won't even acknowledge him. He stares pointedly at her, but she doesn't look his way. Dropping his gaze, he takes a breath.

'True,' says Rick, seemingly unaware of the rising tension. 'If we go talk with the patrollers of the areas that got burgled it might jog their memory a little more. And I still need this week's patrol reports from Clint. I was going to get his log and then head over to the Flying Mustang Casino to try to talk to some of the victim's work colleagues, but how about I ask Clint about any other sightings while I'm there? I can visit the other patrollers too.'

'I'd been planning to talk to them once I'd read the patrol logs,' says Philip. He puts his mug down on to the countertop harder than necessary. Doesn't care that it makes a loud noise as the mug impacts. The patrol-log stuff was his idea. He doesn't want Rick stealing his thunder. 'So I'll come with you.'

41

MOIRA

Moira puts the car into park and turns off the gas. She doesn't get out right away, but sits for a moment, getting her thoughts together. She didn't get much sleep last night, and when she did drift off she found herself reliving bits of the day. One thing she'd dreamt about was the argument between Golding and Philip. In it, she'd noticed something more than just the anger and threatening tone in Golding's voice – there'd also been an undercurrent of fear. Now she's awake she doesn't know if that was real or imagined, and whether her mind was distorting what had happened.

Moira rubs her forehead. She doesn't understand why Golding would fear Philip, especially when he seems to have information on him that would be damaging, and therefore lets him hold power over him. But then, right from the very beginning, Golding has done everything he can to get them to back away from his investigation and belittle them as doddering old retirees. It makes no sense. If he thinks so little of them, why does their presence at crime scenes antagonise him so much?

She looks towards the hospital entrance. It doesn't look like the NHS hospitals she's used to in the UK. This place, with its fountains and beautiful landscaping, looks more like a five-star hotel than a medical treatment centre. She looks at the message Rick sent her with the address on and double-checks the room number – 243. That's where Hank is. And she needs to speak to him.

Following the signs to reception, Moira steps into the double-height atrium and again can't believe she's in a hospital. There's no smell of antiseptic here. Instead there's a mahogany reception desk and a four-foot-high silk flower display. Everything is polished and stylish. The signage looks like a hotel rather than a hospital, and the floors are some kind of wood or laminate.

Moira asks for directions to Hank's room and then takes the lift up to the second floor. There's a smaller silk flower display in the foyer area as she exits the lift. Up here there are more indications that this is a hospital – a nurse in scrubs is hurrying along the hallway, and Moira can hear the beeping of a machine in the room adjacent to the lift area. She inhales and detects a very slight odour of disinfectant.

As she pauses in the foyer, looking for signage that will point her in the direction of room 243, a bald guy in a security uniform and an earpiece approaches her.

'ID please, ma'am.'

She does as he asks, and hands over her driver's licence.

He takes the photo card and looks from it to her several times. 'What's your business here, Ms Flynn?'

'I'm visiting a friend. He's in room 243.'

The security guy is still looking at the licence. 'Admitted when?'

Moira starts to feel anxious. Wants to grab the licence from him and get going. She swallows back the nerves. Keeps her tone even. 'Yesterday. He'd been attacked and I found him. So I want to check how he's doing.'

The guard looks at her face for a long moment. Hands the licence back to her. 'Seems your friend wasn't the only one who got beat.'

She nods. 'Yeah.'

The security guy gives her a kind smile. 'Well, I'm real sorry about that. I hope you and your friend both make good recoveries. For 243 go halfway along the hall, then make a right and it's the fifth room along.'

'Thank you.' Moira tucks her licence back into her wallet.

'No problem, ma'am.'

She follows the security guy's directions and finds Hank's room. Standing outside, her hand hovers above the door handle. She isn't here in any official capacity, and she doesn't know Hank well enough to visit him as a friend; they've only said hello a couple of times before in passing and he probably won't even remember she found him yesterday. She hopes he doesn't see her visiting him as an intrusion of his privacy.

Moira gives the door a quick knock and pushes it open.

Aside from the medical equipment – a drip and a heart monitor – the place looks like a fancy hotel room with pale walls, oak furniture and a comfortable-looking ergonomic bed with crisp linen and a thick blanket. Hank's sitting in the bed, his attention focused on the football game that's playing on the wall-mounted television.

As Moira steps into the room he mutes the sounds and looks over at her. He's wearing a new pair of glasses – a spare pair, she assumes, but his face is a patchwork of purple and black bruising, and there's bandaging securing a dressing to the back of his head. Even so, his eyes are bright, and aside from the beeping heart monitor and the drip he doesn't seem to be hooked up to many machines.

Moira softens her posture, doing her best to look non-threatening and non-official – hands by her sides, she rests her weight more on her uninjured leg and gives him a big smile. 'Hi Hank, I'm Moira. I'm not sure you recognise me, but I'm a resident at The Homestead. I wanted to stop by and see how you're doing.'

Hank holds her gaze for a couple of beats before speaking. 'They told me when I woke that I had myself a guardian angel.' He smiles and tries to sit more upright, wincing from the pain of the movement. 'From the state of you, all beat up like me, I'm thinking that's you.'

Moira isn't sure she likes the analogy, but she nods. She hadn't really given herself a proper look in the mirror that morning – just washed her face and put on her moisturiser – but she can feel the bruising down one side of her face and the tightness of the skin around the butterfly strips. 'It was me that found you. I tried to stop the person who attacked you leaving, but . . .' She gestures to her bruised face.

'Guess I'm saying a big thank you then. The docs said I was lucky I got found and brought here when I did. I lost a lot of blood, you see.' He gestures to his bandaged head. 'Could've ended different.'

Moira remembers how he'd looked when she'd found him – lying there so still and pale, a puddle of blood spreading out from his head wound. 'How are you feeling?'

'Like a monster truck used me for sparring practice. How about you?'

She smiles. 'Yeah, similar.'

'Did you get a good look at the asshole who got the drop on me?'

Moira shakes her head. 'Not really. He was wearing a mask and a hoodie so all I got was the basics – height and all that. Did you see him?'

'Nope. Never even heard him.' Hank blows out hard. His frustration is clear on his face. 'Asshole must've sneaked up on me while I was working. One minute I was checking the tapes were streaming right and having my first coffee of the day, the next thing I knew I was waking up here.'

250

It's as Moira suspected, that he was hit from behind, but it's still a disappointment that he didn't see the guy any better than she had. 'You mentioned tapes, do you use them as backup to the digital recordings?'

Hank shakes his head, again wincing from the movement. 'Sorry, it's a figure of speech. It's not tape we use these days, hasn't been for years, but I'm old school. I still think in terms of tapes and reels even though it's all on the computer now. It's saved on the computer itself then we back up on to the flash drives.'

Moira remembers the smashed USB sticks on the floor and the gaping holes in the computers where their hard drives had been ripped out. Everything ruined. 'Then it's all gone. They stole the computer drives and smashed the flash drives.'

Hank clenches the bedcover in his fists. He shakes his head and winces, cursing under his breath. For a moment he looks dejected. Then he looks back at Moira. He taps his finger to the side of his head. 'Good job I've still got my memory then.'

Moira feels a flare of hope. 'What did you see?'

Hank gestures for Moira to sit on the visitor's chair beside the bed. 'It was after the cops called me to say they wanted the CCTV footage for around Manatee. I told them the cameras are switched off at Manatee once the park closes in the evening until it reopens in the morning, the only exception being if there's a party or something planned. But I told them I'd have a look at the other cameras and see if there was other footage that'd be worth a look. I was pulling it together for them, trawling through the footage, and I noticed a few things that seemed off.'

'Like what?' says Moira, moving her chair closer to Hank.

'So for starters the cameras around the streets close to Manatee were out the night of the murder. They'd been working just fine the night before, but that night they were only showing snow, which means someone vandalised them. I searched the footage around a big radius from the park, but saw no one in the area around the times the cops wanted footage. No one aside from the Graften boy, Mikey.'

That doesn't sound good for Mikey's defence, thinks Moira. She knows Rick thinks he's innocent, but the little evidence there is all seems to point towards him.

'Anyhow, I'm not a quitter, and something was bugging me. When the cops on the video call held up a picture of the victim to their camera to see if I recognised her, she seemed kind of familiar.'

'Had you seen her here in Ocean Mist?'

'That's the thing, I couldn't remember at first – I see a whole lot of people sitting in my chair in front of the bank of screens, day in, day out. But as I was trawling through the tapes it hit me.' He chuckles, and gestures to his bandaged head. 'No pun intended.'

Moira smiles to humour him, but wishes he'd get to the point.

'I'd seen her recently, on another evening.'

Moira remembers what Rick had said about the young woman being spotted in a car with Mikey Graften. 'Was she in a station wagon on Seahorse Drive?'

Hank frowns. 'No, not there, it was a different part of the neighbourhood.' He pauses, thinking, then nods. 'It was over near Crystal Waters Boulevard. I remember because I saw her when I was watching the tapes live, eating a snack. Nutter Butters – really good – and I was on the night shift. Must have been around one in the morning. Pitch dark. Nothing much else going down on the screens. Then suddenly she was hustling along the sidewalk and I thought to myself, *Where are you going so late, lady?*'

Moira leans forward in the chair. 'And where did she go?'

'I don't know.' Hank shrugs. 'I watched her to the end of the street, but then she took a turn into Stingray Drive, and the cameras are out along that stretch, so I lost her.'

Moira feels the hairs on the back of her neck stand to attention. Stingray Drive – she's heard that road mentioned already today. Peggy Leggerhorne said she lived on Stingray Drive and that hers was the first house that was burgled. Moira knows the thefts have been going on for around a month. If the murder victim was in the same location as the burglary, there could be a connection between the crimes. 'Can you remember exactly when that was?'

'Let me think.' He shuffles back against the pillow and closes his eyes.

Moira watches him. She stays silent, willing him to remember. The beep of the heart monitor seems to get louder. The click of the drip makes her flinch.

Hank opens his eyes. 'It was a few weeks ago for sure. And I can remember I'd been pissed about having to work the night shift and having to miss the game – my team was playing and it was a critical time for them.'

Moira nods. Tries to keep her impatience from her expression.

'The game was against the Dallas Cowboys, so that would have made it . . .' He closes his eyes again as if looking at a fixture list in his mind. Grins. 'It would have been the nineteenth of last month.'

The nineteenth. Moira makes a mental note. 'That's really helpful, thanks.'

'No problem.' Hank smiles. 'Anything for my guardian angel.'

42

LIZZIE

She inhales slowly as the front door clicks shut behind Philip and Rick, glad to be alone in the house for a change. Clearing away the mugs, she loads the dishwasher, then goes back to the kitchen table and the mobile phone that Moira dug up on the peak of the Wild Ridge Trail. When she started working on it yesterday, first she'd cleaned the dirt off as best she could and fitted the snapped pieces back into the order they seemed to have started off in, but the screen had remained blank.

So then she took it apart again and thought about other things she could try. Damp from the earth had leached into the whole phone and she'd wondered if it'd affected it. She'd dismantled the phone and removed the SIM card, placing them into ziplock bags of rice. They've been in there long enough now. It's time to put the whole thing back together.

Lizzie hopes it works. If the phone belonged to the victim it could give them a lot more leads. Removing the pieces and the SIM from the ziplock bags, she lays them out on a kitchen towel. Moving steadily, she snaps the pieces into place and adds the SIM, checking her work against the diagram she pulled from the internet of how it should look. When it's done she presses the button to switch it on.

Nothing happens.

She tries again. Holds the button down for longer.

The screen remains blank.

Lizzie curses under her breath. Thinks. If it was the victim's phone it wouldn't have been in the ground that long, but there's no telling how much charge it had at that time. Maybe it needs power. Maybe the damage has left it unable to hold a charge. Getting up, she carries the phone across the kitchen and plugs it into the charger next to the cooker. The phone's casing is cracked, and it's difficult to get the charger inserted, but after a bit of tilting and jiggling she manages it. She flips the power on and watches for the screen to register the power connection. Nothing happens. She presses the buttons to do a hard reset, and then watches the phone for a few minutes longer, but the screen remains black.

Lizzie sighs. She's done all she can with the phone, but it's not looking hopeful. She'll leave it plugged in for a bit and see if that makes a difference. If not, they're going to need to find another avenue to pursue.

Glancing out to the hallway, Lizzie makes a decision. Nerves fizz in her belly but she knows this is what she has to do next. Getting up, she hurries out of the kitchen and along the hallway to Philip's bedroom.

She pauses in the doorway. This room is so Philip. Neat, with everything in its place – from the creaseless blue duvet and pillow set on the double bed, to the books lined in height order on the bookcase and the bedside tables with matching lamps, coasters and tissue boxes. The room smells of his aftershave – Old Spice – and clean bed linen. Lizzie feels like a trespasser, but she steps inside.

The blue box file is sitting at the back of his wardrobe, surrounded by pairs of shoes. With her heart pounding in her chest, Lizzie reaches into the wardrobe and lifts it out. There's a lock on the front clasp, but it isn't locked. Her fingers shake as she undoes the clasp and lifts the lid. There's one file inside – an A4 buff folder that's stuffed about two inches thick.

Lizzie opens the file and starts to read.

43

MOIRA

She parks on the street and double-checks the address against Peggy Leggerhorne's message – 233 Stingray Drive. She hasn't told Peggy she's coming – didn't want to give Peggy the chance to tell her not to – so she feels a bit bad, but she'll get over it. She's on the trail of something important, she's sure of it, and she just needs to get clear on the sequence of events.

Climbing out of the car, Moira walks up the neat path that borders the driveway and then cuts across the front of the white weatherboard-clad house to the porch. The steps up to the porch are lined with pots of flowers in full bloom – pinks, reds and a dotting of cream. There's a double-seated swing bench on the porch with a blue gingham seat pad and pretty embroidered cushions in different shades of blue arranged neatly along the back. The front door is pale grey. Moira raises her hand and knocks firmly.

The door opens almost immediately. It stops at about six inches open, a brass door chain visible across the gap. A silver-haired lady who looks to be in her mid to late eighties peers through the crack between the door and the frame. 'Hello?'

Moira suspects she's been watched from the moment she pulled up outside. 'I'm Moira, we've been talking on Messenger.'

Peggy stares at her for a long moment without speaking. 'I didn't think you'd come here. I thought you asked for my address to know the location of the burglary. I don't—'

'I'm really sorry to turn up unannounced, but I'm working with Philip and Rick from the community watch – we're doing our own investigation into the murder at Manatee Park.'

Peggy frowns. 'The one that the management are trying to hush up?'

'Yes.'

'Is that how you got those injuries?' asks Peggy, gesturing towards Moira's face.

'I disturbed an intruder at the CCTV office yesterday. He'd attacked Hank, the guy who works there, and hurt him. I tried to stop him getting away, but, well, he did this and knocked me unconscious.'

'Sounds like you were very brave.' Peggy moves closer to the door, but she's still looking worried. 'Thing is, we don't like people coming inside, not after what happened.'

'I understand,' says Moira, giving Peggy what she hopes is a reassuring smile. 'We can talk right here if you like.'

Peggy looks unsure. She leans away from the door, her hand on the chain.

I'm losing her, thinks Moira. She tries again. Last chance. 'I appreciate this might be difficult but can you tell me about the burglary and how it happened?'

'I try my best not to think about it.'

'It could help solve the burglaries and the murder at Manatee Park.'

Peggy bites her lip. She glances back into the house and uses sign language to say something to her husband, then steps out on to the porch and pulls the door closed behind her. 'What do you need to know?'

'Everything you can tell me. Why don't you start from the beginning?'

Peggy nods. 'It woke me up, the noise of them breaking in, but it didn't wake Arnold, my husband.' She leans closer, her voice hushed. 'He's deaf; they said eighty-eight per cent of his hearing had gone when they last tested him. He sleeps like a log, unlike me.'

'Do you know what time it was?'

'I do, because when I opened my eyes the alarm clock display was right in front of me. It was 1.03 a.m. on the nineteenth. I remember thinking I'd had even less sleep than usual before waking. Then I heard the breaking of glass and knew there was someone who shouldn't be inside our home.'

Moira feels the hairs on the back of her neck stand on end – the Leggerhornes were burgled the night of the nineteenth, and Hank said he'd seen the murder victim walking along Stingray Drive around 1 a.m. on the nineteenth. 'What happened next?'

Peggy shakes her head. 'Nothing on my part, I'm ashamed to say. You always think that if someone breaks into your property you'll act to protect what's yours, you know, fight back.' She exhales loudly. 'I didn't do that. I wasn't brave like you were yesterday with that intruder you found. I stayed in bed. Hugged my husband, who was still sleeping. And prayed that the intruder wouldn't come upstairs and hurt us.'

'And did they?'

'No. I could hear them moving about downstairs, and I think they thought about coming up but when they stepped on the first couple of stairs they creaked really loudly. The intruder left soon afterwards.' She shakes her head. 'I guess they'd got enough and didn't want to risk us finding them in the house.'

'Did they take much?'

Peggy closes her eyes for a moment. When she opens them her eyes are watery. 'They took the silver my mother left me when she passed, a gold mantle clock that had been in my family for five generations, and Arnold's service medals. We kept our emergency fund in the kitchen drawer – around five hundred dollars in twenties and tens – they took that too.'

'Did you report the items stolen to the police?' asks Moira.

'For sure,' says Peggy. 'And they made a note of them but didn't sound hopeful about us getting them back.'

Moira remembers Rick telling them the list of items that had been in the victim's backpack – they'd included antique silverware and a gold mantle clock. They could have belonged to Peggy and her husband, but Moira doesn't say that. Instead she says, 'I'm so sorry.' The words don't feel enough.

'Just find who did it.'

'I intend to.'

'Good,' says Peggy. 'You said before that you're investigating the murder at Manatee Park, but you're asking me about us getting burglarised. Why?'

Moira doesn't answer right away. She thinks about what she's learned that morning. Kristen Altman would have been in the immediate vicinity of the Leggerhornes' house at the exact time the burglary was taking place. It's unlikely to be a coincidence; Moira doesn't believe in them – especially that late at night. Either Kristen Altman was involved in the burglaries or she was a witness. If they solve the murder, they'll solve the burglary cases too.

Moira looks Peggy straight in the eye and tells her, 'Because I think your burglary and the murder victim are connected.'

44

LIZZIE

The loud shrill of the doorbell makes Lizzie jump and she almost drops the file she's holding. She's sitting on the floor in Philip's bedroom, in front of the open wardrobe and blue file box. She doesn't get up.

Go away, she thinks.

The doorbell goes again. The person outside keeps their finger on it for longer.

Lizzie sits tight, waiting, hoping for them to go away.

Then her mobile starts ringing in the pocket of her cardigan. She takes it out and looks at the screen. It's Moira. It keeps ringing.

Lizzie presses answer. 'Hello.'

'Are you at home? I'm outside. I've found something important and I need to look at the patrol logs.'

Lizzie looks at the folder in her hand. Thinks of what she's discovered. She's still reeling. Doesn't want to see Moira. Doesn't trust her after the revelation that she'd been a DCI.

'Lizzie?' There's urgency in Moira's voice. 'Are you there?'

She wipes her eyes. Presses her fingers against her forehead. If Moira's found something important she can't ignore her call for help; if she does then she'll be just as bad as Philip. She clears her throat. 'Sorry. Yes, I'm here. Hold on.'

Hanging up, she puts the folder back into the file box and closes the clasp. Carefully she lifts the box back into the wardrobe and arranges the lines of shoes around it, just as it had been. Swallowing back the nausea she's feeling, she closes the wardrobe and hurries to the front door.

The sour taste is still in her mouth. She's not sure it'll ever go away. She yanks open the door, taking her rage for Philip out on the handle. Moira is standing on the front porch. Lizzie inhales sharply as she sees her. 'Oh my God. Your poor face. Are you okay?'

'It's fine,' says Moira, stepping around Lizzie and coming inside. 'Looks worse than it feels.'

Lizzie can't imagine that's true. She closes the door behind Moira. Tries to think of something to say, but she can't, she feels frozen. All she can think about is what she saw in the folder. What she knows now; the truth about Philip that he's kept hidden from her all these years.

'Are you okay, Lizzie?' Moira is looking at her with concern.

She feels her eyes get watery and blinks, forcing the tears away. She doesn't want to get emotional. She just needs to help Moira with the case. Fears that she can't trust her with anything personal. 'I . . .'

Moira puts her hand on Lizzie's shoulder. 'What's happened?'

Lizzie shakes her head. Says nothing.

'You can trust me, Lizzie,' says Moira. 'Please, let me help.'

Lizzie holds Moira's gaze. Folds her arms around herself. Maybe it would help to speak to someone. Moira looks so sincere. She wants to trust her, really she does. Hopes she's not making a mistake. 'It's Philip.'

Moira frowns. 'Is he okay? Did something—'

'Philip was responsible for the death of a child, a young girl. That's why he had to retire.'

'I thought it was because of ill health?' says Moira, her frown deepening.

Lizzie drops her gaze. She takes a breath then looks back at Moira. 'That was the story, and it was true in part – he wasn't well enough after the heart attack and the surgery to go back to his job full-time. But he could have been more desk based, or done something part-time, but they forced him out, and if he'd refused to resign they were going to discipline and fire him instead of retiring him like a hero.'

'What did he do?'

Lizzie sighs. 'It's not what he did that's the problem. It's what he didn't do and what he didn't tell them . . . or me. There was a high-profile case he was working before the heart attack – the abduction of a young girl. It consumed him. He worked all hours, I hardly ever saw him, and when I did he was distant and didn't want to talk. He looked sick – pale and clammy a lot of the time – but he insisted he was fine, just a bit tired from all the long hours.'

'Was that normal for him?' asks Moira.

'Sort of, he always got tunnel vision on cases he worked, but being distant and looking so pale was different. He usually liked to talk things through – said it helped him crystallise his thinking.' Lizzie shakes her head. 'But not that time. The only thing he said to me was that he felt he wasn't seeing everything.'

'And then?' Moira's voice is gentle, encouraging.

'A tip came in through the tip line that'd been set up. It was solid, they fast-tracked the checks because of the urgency, and then they passed it to Philip, as DCI in charge of the case.' Lizzie bites her lip.

Moira nods. 'What was the tip?'

'The location where the girl was being held.'

Neither of them speaks for a moment. Then Moira asks, 'What happened?'

Lizzie feels the rage churning in her stomach. The nausea is getting stronger. She tries to swallow it down. 'Nothing. He didn't do anything. I read the first interview transcript with him in the file. He said that he read the email with the tip details, but he was due to leave for lunch and decided to deal with it afterwards. So he left it and went out for lunch, or that was his original story anyway. It was over two hours before he was back at his desk and passed on the tip. Three hours before the team arrived at the location mentioned.'

'And she was gone?'

'No. The child was dead. The coroner put her time of death within the hour.' Lizzie blinks back tears. Her voice falters. 'If Philip had acted on the tip straight away she would still have been alive when they got to her.' She feels anger flare inside her. Blinks back the tears. 'He told me at the time it was a lapse in judgement. That he was tired and there were so many tips coming in they couldn't follow everything up immediately. He felt awful, I know he did, but I always felt like he was holding something back from me.'

'And was he?'

Lizzie nods. 'He'd led me to believe that he was stuffing himself at lunch as that poor child was dying, and that's why he was forced to retire. He said it was because his actions made him negligent in his duty. He could have saved her, but he didn't.' She clenches her fists. Can't keep the anger from her voice. 'That he as good as killed her himself.'

'Mistakes happen in the field,' says Moira, gently. 'It's not good, but it happens. There are so many variables and—'

'Mistakes that kill people?' says Lizzie, narrowing her eyes.

Moira doesn't quite meet her gaze. 'Sometimes.'

'But that isn't the full truth of what happened here.'

Moira says nothing.

Lizzie continues. 'A few days after they found the child dead, Philip had the heart attack. I blamed the pressure of work and guilt about the young girl's death, but it wasn't just that, it was the stress of an internal investigation into what happened and him knowing what they'd find. That and the fact he had been having serious health problems for months and hiding it.'

Moira frowns. 'Didn't you know about—'

'No, all I knew was that he didn't look great and seemed tired all the time, but I had no idea what he'd been battling and for how long. He'd hidden it from me and the kids, and he'd hidden it from his employers too.'

'He could have been trying to protect you.'

'That's not what he said when Internal Affairs interviewed him. He'd known that if he'd told the police doc what was going on they'd have put him on immediate medical suspension. He knew he wasn't fit to work, and that him staying in post could seriously compromise an investigation.' Lizzie clasps her hands together. 'He knew it, and yet he didn't say anything. Not even to me. Even though he could have died.'

'What was wrong?' asks Moira.

'His heart was totally screwed. He'd been having tests and been under observation for a while apparently. That's where he was that lunchtime when he didn't follow up the tip – he was at the John Radcliffe Hospital having tests for two hours, not eating lunch as he'd told everyone.' Lizzie pauses. Takes a breath. 'In the end he told the Internal Affairs investigator the whole thing. I read their report, and I read the hospital report too. Philip had been having dizzy spells and blackouts and they were getting worse. He told the investigator he'd collapsed in his office a few days before and must have been blacked out for almost an hour. He was experiencing an irregular heartbeat and his blood pressure was all over the place. It had been happening for months, but he'd been delaying having the operation that could help him because he didn't want to take time out from the job. He was having a health crisis, but he told no one, because he knew if he did he'd have to step down and hand over control of the investigations. He wanted to keep doing the job, even if it killed him; even if it took him from his own family. But him not taking due care killed that little girl, as well as nearly

265

killing him.' Lizzie exhales hard. 'It wasn't ill health that ended his career. He was forced to retire because of the lies. The Internal Affairs report recommended disciplinary action and dismissal due to wilful disregard of protocol and lying by omission constituting a deliberate cover-up – leading to a complete breakdown of trust and confidence in his integrity. It was only because of his high profile in the media and exemplary record until then that they allowed him to retire with honour. It was more than he deserved. He lied to everyone, even me. And when I asked him – before the heart attack and afterwards about why he'd had to retire – he lied and he kept on lying. I asked him yesterday and he didn't say anything about the health problems he'd had. I had to break into his filing box to discover the truth. I just don't understand why he'd keep the lie going for ten years. And if he's lying about this, it makes me wonder if there are other things he's lied to me about.' She looks at Moira, trying to see if she understands. 'We've been married a really long time, but now I feel like I don't know him at all.'

Moira looks baffled. Like she's trying to work it all out. 'I don't understand why he didn't tell you. Maybe he was in denial. It must have been—'

A series of beeps from near the cooker stops Moira mid-sentence. They both look over towards the noise. The mobile phone Moira dug up from the trail is vibrating against the countertop. The screen lit up.

Lizzie wants to hear what Moira was going to say, but she can't ignore the phone. If it's working again this could be important to the case.

She hurries to the phone and reads what's on the screen. Feels the nausea recede as adrenaline floods her body. Turning back to Moira she signals for her to come over. Her voice is urgent. 'Quick, you have to see this.'

266

45

RICK

Rick glances across at Philip. He's sitting in the passenger seat of the jeep, hands on his lap, staring straight ahead and not talking. That's odd. Philip likes to talk. He's always jawing on about what they should do and say, not that Rick listens to half of it, but still, it's all kinds of strange that he's quiet on the ride out to Clint's place.

'You want some music?' Rick asks, gesturing towards the radio.

Philip shrugs. Says nothing.

Rick puts the radio on anyways. Wants something to break the silence. An old tune, 'Two Princes', from back in the day comes on. Rick starts to hum along.

Philip tuts loudly. Rick glances over at him. Philip doesn't look at him but there's a muscle pulsing in his jaw and the man's fists are clenched so tight that his knuckles are turning white.

Rick stops humming, but leaves the radio on. Something's up with Philip, for sure. The guy's got a short fuse – they've all seen that over the past couple of days – but how he's looking today is different; like he's stressed but also deflated. And the atmosphere back at the house, with Philip and Lizzie, that was kind of weird.

Eager to get the journey over with, Rick steps on the gas a little harder and wonders what the hell is going on.

Clint Weston lives on Still Water Boulevard in a two-storey two-bed with mustard-coloured stucco and a wraparound porch and double garage. There are no cars on the driveway, so Rick pulls the jeep off the street and parks up in front of the garage doors. He glances over at Philip. 'Here we go.'

'Okay,' says Philip, unbuckling his seat belt.

Rick raises an eyebrow but supposes one word is better than none. Climbing out of the jeep they walk around the front. Rick raps on the door, then takes a step back and waits.

'You think there's a reason Clint didn't give you his log yet?' asks Philip.

Rick turns towards him. Shakes his head. 'Nope. I just figured he'd not had time is all.'

Philip frowns. Says nothing.

'You think different?' says Rick.

Philip opens his mouth to answer, but stops. There's a click as the lock is disengaged. A moment later the front door opens.

Clint's wife, Janice, stands in the doorway. 'Rick. Philip. It's nice to see you. Can I help you boys somehow?'

'Hey, Janice,' says Rick, smiling. 'Is Clint around?'

'Sure, he's in his workshop out back, just like usual.' Janice pulls the door open wider and beckons them inside. 'Come on through.'

Janice leads them through the house and out through sliding doors to the backyard. Across the stretch of neatly kept lawn there's a large wooden shed. 'He's in there. Things are real busy at the moment – we've got so many orders he can hardly keep up with them.'

Thanking Janice, Rick heads across the yard to the shed.

Philip follows. 'Do you know what Clint makes in there?'

'Nope,' says Rick. 'He's never told me.'

'Me neither,' says Philip. His irritation is clear in his voice.

Rick sighs inwardly. Philip is such a control freak, and nosey with it. There's no reason Clint should have told any of them about his hobby, and to be pissed with the man for not telling him seems real out of shape to Rick. He hopes Philip doesn't let that set the tone for their chat. He knows the man can let his emotions get the better of him – just like he'd done at Betty Graften's house. When you're talking to folks – suspects or witnesses – it's better to be even-tempered, and keep a poker face fixed in place to mask whatever you're feeling. You get more from them that way. No one responds well to judgement.

As he stops outside the workshop and knocks on the painted green door, Rick turns back to Philip. 'Well, I guess we're about to find out.'

'Yeah?' On the other side of the door, Clint's voice sounds a little muffled. 'It's open.'

Rick pushes the door ajar and steps over the threshold. He stops a couple of feet inside, taking in the sight. He's sure never seen a thing like it. Inside, the shed looks like Santa's grotto on the night before Christmas. In the half of the shed closest to him there's shelving and cabinets housing hundreds of figurines and carvings – reindeer, turtle doves, three kings, shepherds, nativity figures, Santas, family scenes, snow-covered houses, angels and more.

On the countertop closest to Rick, fifty snowmen of various heights are lined up beside a large cardboard packing box. Painted white and coated in silver glitter, each snowman has little stick arms, big eyes, a tiny carrot nose and a smile that stretches almost the whole way from one side of its face to the other. Rick lets out a long whistle. 'That's a whole lot of snowmen.'

Clint laughs. The part of the shed he's standing in is kitted out with workbenches. There are tools lining the walls, and a big Anglepoise lamp. He's holding a half-painted angel and a paintbrush. 'What can I tell you? Folks just love snowmen. That model there is my most popular seller. I can hardly make them fast enough, especially this time of year.'

'So this is what you do?' says Philip.

Clint grins. 'I love making this stuff. We got ourselves an online shop – Janice runs all that. I make the pieces, and she ships them out. Been doing it a couple of years now and it pays for all our cruises. Beats living on a pension.'

'Did you do this as a trade before?' asks Rick.

'Hell no,' says Clint, laughing. 'I was an accountant. Hated it, of course, but it gave us a nice home and helped put the kids through college, so I can't complain. I always did love Christmas, so when I retired I decided it was time to embrace that passion.'

Rick smiles. It's strange how some people spend their whole lives doing something they tolerate just to be able to buy a bigger house, a fancier lifestyle, and pay the bills to support it. He's never understood that. Law enforcement is a tough gig, and not the best paid, but for some it's a calling. It was that way for him. He couldn't have imagined doing anything else. 'I'm glad.'

'We're here to talk about your patrol logs,' says Philip. His face is expressionless, and there's no hint of friendliness in his voice.

Jeez, thinks Rick. *The man's even blunter than usual today.* He tries to soften Philip's words with a smile. Keeps his own tone real amiable. 'We're checking in with all the patrollers who had eyes on the areas burglarised or where the murder victim was seen.'

Clint scratches his grey-flecked stubble with the paint-splattered hand that's holding the paintbrush. 'You think the two are connected?'

Rick nods. 'Could be.'

'Do you have your logs for the last month?' Philip's tone is unfriendly and accusatory. 'You didn't hand them over yet.'

'Didn't I? I'm sorry about that. Must have clean skipped my mind what with all these orders and—'

'A dead woman skipped your mind?' Philip's eyebrows are raised. His mouth pursed into a thin line.

Clint's cheeks and neck flush. 'It's . . . I . . .'

'If we could get a look-see at the logs we'd appreciate it,' says Rick, shooting Philip a warning look to back up. The man needs to stop treating every citizen like a suspect. It's all kinds of disrespectful.

Philip looks away, but not fast enough to stop Rick seeing the anger in his eyes. Rick wonders what the hell has gotten into him; he's even worse than he was at Betty Graften's house.

'The logs are in the house. It's no problem to get them,' says Clint, recovering his composure. He puts the half-painted angel down on the workbench and the paintbrush into a pot of white spirit, then gestures towards the door. 'I'll go get them now.'

They follow Clint back across the yard to his house. The reports are sitting on the sideboard in the hallway. He hands them to Rick. 'Here you go.'

'Appreciate it.' Rick remembers back to the get-together at the Roadhouse. 'At the patrol meeting a few days ago you said you saw a station wagon with a Bulls sticker parked at the head of the Wild Ridge Trail?'

'That's right. Seen it a couple of times, but I didn't see any folks around. It was empty both times.' Clint gestures to the reports in Rick's hand. 'It's all noted down in there – times, descriptions and all that jazz.'

Clint keeps looking at the logs. There's intensity to his stare, and a rigidity in his posture that wasn't there before in the workshop. There's something he's not telling them, Rick's sure of it. 'Anything else you think we should know?'

'Look here, I haven't forgotten that poor young woman.' Clint looks from Rick to Philip. 'Whatever you might think. It's just a bit complicated.'

Philip stays silent.

'Did you see something?' asks Rick.

'Maybe,' says Clint. 'But I don't want to get no one into trouble.'

Rick nods, hoping to encourage Clint to keep talking. 'Okay . . .'

'But, well, there's been a few occasions, real late at night, that I've seen a person in the distance, crossing the border between my patch – quadrant three – into quadrant two. I never got a close look at them, and always saw them from behind, but I'm thinking it could have been the poor woman who was killed at Manatee.'

Philip steps closer to Clint. 'What makes you think that?'

'There's a couple of reasons. Firstly, the person I saw kinda looked like a woman. They were wearing pants, sure, but the shape of them, you know what I mean, looked female. Then there was the hair. You said the woman who died had long black hair, well so did this person. They had black hair that came almost to their waist.'

'You record this in your log?' asks Philip.

'Of course,' says Clint. 'It was just a few times, and it was real late. After midnight, sometimes way after.'

'And you didn't remember this or think to tell us back in the patrol meeting?' Philip's tone is disapproving.

Rick wishes Philip could get a grip on himself. 'Clint, look, what he means is how come this didn't come to mind straight away?'

Clint looks embarrassed. Sighs. 'So look, I wasn't one hundred per cent sure and I wanted to check my reports first. Also, I didn't want to make another patroller look bad or some such. If they said they'd only seen the woman the once, then who was I to—'

'What are you talking about?'

'If the woman I saw was the woman who was murdered at Manatee, then she walked right through patrol quadrant two a

272

whole bunch of times. I know the cameras around that area are unreliable, but the patroller had to have seen her.'

'You check the logs for quadrant two?' asks Rick.

Philip looks grim-faced. 'Double-checked them this morning.'

'And?'

'There's one mention of the murder victim – on that night a few weeks back that they spoke about at the meeting. No other mentions.'

Rick looks from Philip to Clint and then down at the logs in his hand. If what Clint is telling them is true, the murder victim walked through patrol quadrant two on at least two more occasions, but there's no record of that in the patrol logs. That's not good.

It looks like one of the patrollers is lying.

46

MOIRA

It has to be the victim's phone – that much is clear from the picture of her and a young guy on the home screen with 'Kristen hearts Mikey' above it. There's no passcode or biometrics enabled so Lizzie taps the messages icon and they read the messages as fast as they can. The new ones are from a saved contact – Mikey – the Graften kid, Moira assumes. All the recent ones are variations of 'where are you?'. First they're jokey in tone, then angry, and later worried. But it's the chain of messages with an unlabelled mobile number that are more interesting, and more important.

Lizzie scrolls to the top of the message trail. The most recent messages are dated the day Kristen Altman died.

Kristen had written:

I need more
$10k at least

And the answer came back:

I don't have that

Find it

I can't give you any more
I told you already

Whatever

    I'll tell the cops

Don't

    But I can't keep paying

Give me $10k
Then we're done

    $10k and it's over?

Yeah

    Where/when?

Usual place
Manatee Park by the lap pool
1am

    Ok
    After this no more
    I mean it

Moira feels the adrenaline building inside her. She looks at Lizzie. Her eyes are bright. The upset of a few minutes ago gone. They're close to the truth and they both know it. The person Kristen was messaging – blackmailing – could be her killer.

'Should we call the number?' says Lizzie.

Moira shakes her head. 'Not yet. Let's see some more.'

Taking the phone from Lizzie, Moira scrolls up through the trail of messages. She finds the first contact between Kristen and the unlabelled number. The first message was sent by Kristen a few weeks ago:

I saw what you did

> Who is this?

I saw you.

> Who is this?
> How did you get my number?

I have proof

> Proof of what?

You're a thief

> What??

I have proof
Give me $2k
Or I'll tell the cops

> No

This change your mind?

Beneath the message is a photo. The image is grainy, obviously taken at night, but it's clear enough. It shows a man climbing over a high wall. He's coming from inside a backyard towards the street, the picture capturing him in the moment he swings his legs over the top. There's a large, heavy-looking carryall over his shoulder and he's dressed in dark colours including gloves. But his balaclava has got pushed up and you can clearly make out his face.

Lizzie gasps. 'That's Donald Ettwood.'

Moira turns to Lizzie. 'You know him?'

'He's a member of the community watch. Moved here about six months ago. Keeps himself to himself really – not one for sports and socials – but Philip seemed to think he was okay.'

Moira looks at the man in the picture again. He's medium build, looks fairly tall – he could be the man she saw up on the Wild Ridge Trail, and at the CCTV office. And even if it's not the same guy, the photo is evidence that he's the burglar, or at least, if there were more than one person involved, that he took part in the burglaries. The message trail shows Kristen sent the picture and was extorting money from Donald, and they'd arranged to meet at the pool in Manatee Park on the night she died. Money is one of the oldest murder motives in the book. It all adds up to making Donald Ettwood prime suspect for her murder. 'We need to—'

'When Kristen first messaged Donald he didn't seem to know her,' says Lizzie, taking the phone from Moira and scrolling up to the start of the message trail again. 'So how did she know the man she took a picture of was Donald? And then how did she get his number?'

'Who knows?' says Moira, turning towards the door. This isn't the time for analysing the finer details. They've got a strong lead, and he could be a flight risk. 'Come on, we've got to find Donald fast.'

277

47

MOIRA

Lizzie drives. Moira calls Rick. She wills him to answer, but after four rings it goes to voicemail. After the beep she leaves a message. 'It's Donald Ettwood – he's the burglar and the victim knew it. She had proof and was blackmailing him. They'd arranged to meet at the pool the night she died. Me and Lizzie are heading to Donald's place now.'

'We should call the cops,' says Lizzie, taking a right into Donald's street.

'There's no time,' says Moira. She's scanning the road up ahead. Looking for Donald's place to come into view. 'What number is he?'

'Forty-two.' Lizzie accelerates harder. 'Should be coming up on our right any moment.'

Moira sees the number on the mailbox up ahead. She sees a truck – an old Chevy – is parked nose out in his driveway. The truck's windows are open and there's a load of things in the flatbed – packing boxes of computer equipment, a gaming chair and a huge widescreen TV. There's a suitcase on the paving beside the truck, and the front door is open – more packing boxes are stacked up just inside the hallway.

'He's running,' says Moira, undoing her seat belt and grabbing for the door handle. 'We've got to stop him.'

Lizzie slows the car and peers towards the house. 'Let me pull over before you—'

'There he is. That's the man in the photo.' Moira feels adrenaline fire in her belly.

'That's Donald,' confirms Lizzie.

He's coming out of the house, carrying a stack of boxes. They're piled high, and so partially obscuring his view of the street. Moira knows she needs to act now, before he sees them and gets spooked.

'Stop now,' she says to Lizzie, yanking hard on the door release.

Lizzie stamps on the brake. The tyres squeal as the car skids to a stop. Moira leaps out. As she does so she sees another vehicle approaching along the street. It's Rick's jeep. She looks back at Donald.

He sees her. There's a moment as their eyes meet where it seems like they're both frozen. She knows those eyes. Remembers them looking down at her from the wall as he whacked her with the hard drive. Donald Ettwood is the man she saw on the Wild Ridge Trail, and at the CCTV office; he attacked Hank and he attacked her. And she can tell from the look on his face that he recognises her. Bastard.

Moira breaks into a run. Donald drops the boxes and starts moving. He cuts left, away from her and the road, and loops out across the neighbour's lawn.

'Call the cops!' Moira yells at Lizzie. Back on the road she sees Rick's already out of the jeep and running her way. She sprints after Donald. Can't wait for Rick. Donald can't get away from her – not again.

Moira pumps her arms and legs hard, trying to ignore the pain in her ankle. They race across the neighbour's lawn and out on to the street. Donald ducks down a side street and she follows. Damn, he's fast. She can't keep pace. With every stride he's getting further away.

He weaves between a few parked cars and disappears down an alleyway between a couple of three-storey apartment buildings. As she reaches the corner into the alleyway she feels the asphalt shift beneath her foot, tipping her bad ankle over. Pain shoots through her leg, but she grits her teeth and pushes herself faster.

She's limping now. Still running, but not so fast. Up ahead Donald's put more ground between them. She curses under her breath and tries to lengthen her stride, but her ankle isn't helping.

Then, up ahead, Donald stops. Moira sprints towards him. The distance between them is closing – fifty yards, forty. Now twenty. That's when she realises why he's not running any more – the alleyway is a dead end.

Behind the line of big industrial-sized skips for the apartment block's rubbish and recycling is a high wire fence. It must be ten or twelve feet high at least, and it looks flimsy – not easy to climb.

'Stay back!' yells Donald. He shifts his gaze from Moira to something behind her. 'Both of you.'

Moira turns and sees Rick approaching directly behind her. It feels good to have backup.

Rick slows down as he reaches Moira, but keeps walking towards Donald.

'No, no!' yells Donald. There's fear on his face. He looks around, searching for a way out. But he's trapped. The only way out is up and over the wire fence, but Moira and Rick will be on him before he's free and clear, he has to realise that. In that moment the game is up, and all three of them know it.

Then Donald changes the rules.

'I said stay the hell back,' he yells, fumbling with something around the back of his jeans. 'I won't warn you again, man.'

'Take it easy, Donald,' shouts Rick. He sounds every inch the DEA agent, but he's missing two things – a badge and a gun. 'Keep your hands where we can see them.'

Moira realises what's about to happen. 'Move back!' she shouts to Rick.

But he doesn't listen. Keeps his eyes focused on Donald, and keeps stepping forward, narrowing the distance between them. 'Let's talk, Donald. Tell me what's going on.'

Moira tenses. Adrenaline spikes her blood. 'Rick, don't . . .'

It happens fast. Donald pulls a little revolver with a pearl handle from the waistband of his jeans and swings the gun up, aiming it at Rick. Rick doesn't hesitate. He launches himself at Donald. The gunshot echoes in the alleyway. Rick and Donald hit the asphalt. There's blood. There's a lot of blood.

Moira doesn't move. She can't. It's happening again. *Shit*.

Her hands fly to her chest. Her breath is coming in gasps. It feels like there's a vice around her chest squeezing the air from her. In her mind's eye the alleyway in front of her morphs into the apartment in London and she's hearing the aftershock of a different gunshot.

She sees McCord standing in front of her; an unregistered, non-police issue weapon in his hand. Their colleague, Jennifer, is lying in a fast-spreading pool of blood, her eyes open and unseeing. Porter and the goons have disappeared. There's noise from outside the apartment – an armed response team are on their way up. Moira doesn't move. 'Why?' she yells at McCord. 'What the hell have you done?'

He's backing away. Saying nothing.

She's charging after him.

They're on the balcony. The lights of London stretch out for miles beneath them. The wind howls and swirls around them. The rain is hammering down.

She yells at McCord again. 'Why?'

He says something, but she can't hear it. He's shaking his head. Saying more, but the wind takes most of the sound. '. . . never . . . don't trust . . . I can't . . .'

Then McCord is gone. He lurches sideways, and takes a dive over the balcony railing. Disappears from sight.

They're twenty-four storeys up. There's no surviving that fall.

The panic embraces her like a cloak. Holds her captive in its grip. Crushing the breath from her. She hears the armed response team enter the apartment. She's gasping for breath but no air comes. Her vision swims. Her knees buckle. She's falling then. Hits the porcelain tiles of the balcony hard. Still can't breathe. Can't breathe.

Stop.

Moira digs her fingernails into her palms. Blinks the memory away. She can't let it take her. She has to stay present; help Rick and catch Donald. She focuses on her breath. Tries the quick tricks the doc taught her. Forces herself to believe it will work.

It has to work.

She can't let Donald get away. Not this time.

Her breathing improves. Her vision clears.

Ahead of her in the alleyway, Rick's lying on his back, groaning. There's blood staining his T-shirt down one side and he's pressing his hands against the wound. Donald is scrambling up. The gun isn't in his hand any more – he must have dropped it in the fall. Moira rushes towards Rick.

'I'm okay,' says Rick, grimacing. 'Don't lose him.'

Donald's at the bins now, pushing his way around them to get to the fence. Moira sprints after him. 'Stop, Donald. It's over.'

He glances back towards her but keeps going. Moira pushes herself faster. Sees he's going to climb on to the end bin as a way to get up the fence. She can't let that happen.

Scooting around the end of the bins, Moira slams into Donald shoulder first. She's smaller than him, and lighter, but her momentum and her shoulder connecting hard with his ribs throws him off balance. They land on the ground. Donald seems dazed, and Moira uses that against him. Pushes him on to his stomach and pulls his arms up high behind his back.

'Stay down,' she yells. 'Don't move.'

Donald tries to fight her off, but with his arms pinned high he flounders like a landed fish. She presses her knee into his back for added leverage. Grips his wrists with all the strength she has left and hopes to hell that the cops arrive soon.

48

RICK

'Use these,' Rick says, wincing as he hands the laces from his boots to Moira. 'They'll hold him for a bit.'

She takes them, and gets to work lacing Donald's wrists together in a set of make-do cuffs.

Rick feels light-headed now. Bends his knees and sits on to the asphalt. Swallows to stop the sick feeling getting worse. Pressing against the wound in his side helps. He figures it's likely a through-and-through. There's a lot of blood, but it could be worse. He's had a few worse for sure, back in the day.

'Can I get up?' asks Donald. 'This is real uncomfortable.'

Moira looks at Rick, and he shakes his head. She gives a small smile and he knows she agrees. Donald robbed his neighbours and killed a young woman; he deserves all the discomfort he gets.

'Not till the cops arrive,' says Moira.

Donald looks at Rick. 'You asked me what was going on.'

'Yep,' says Rick. He tries not to grimace or let the pain weaken his voice.

Moira presses her knee harder into Donald's back. 'Tell us why you killed her, Donald.'

'I didn't mean to, man.' Donald's voice has a whine to it now. 'It just happened and didn't . . .'

'Tell us how,' Moira says. Her tone is granite hard. She shoves him in the back again. 'Tell us what you did.'

'She found out about the burglaries. One time I was making my escape and she was right there, on the other side of the backyard wall. She took my picture, man.'

It doesn't make sense, thinks Rick. There wasn't a burglary the night Kristen Altman was killed. There hadn't been one for a few days. 'So you killed her?'

'No, not then, this is like a month back. I ran and I hoped she'd let it go. But she didn't. She recognised me – she'd seen me playing blackjack over at the Flying Mustang Casino.' He shakes his head. His voice turns bitter. 'That goddamn casino, it's the cause of this whole damn thing. If I hadn't gone and played the tables, or if I'd quit when I was ahead, none of this would have happened.'

'You lost big?' asks Rick. Pressing his side harder to try and stop the pain.

'Yeah, and then some.' He looks up at Rick. 'I was going to lose the house, man. I had to do something drastic.'

'So you robbed your neighbours?' Moira's disgust is clear in her voice.

'I was desperate. Coming here was meant to be a fresh start. It was a downgrade, sure, but it was the best I could do after the trouble in Vegas,' whines Donald. 'I didn't realise there was a casino here. But once I'd found it I couldn't stay away and . . . well, I ran out of money. Needed a way to get more, and I thought I'd figured it out, but then that bitch, Kristen, sees me and it gets a whole lot worse. She was blackmailing me. She took five grand off me the first time. Then she wanted ten more. I told her I didn't have it.' He looks at Rick, his eyes pleading. 'And I really didn't have it, man. I had to take some of the valuables I took from the houses to make up the amount – five thousand in cash, and another five from a clock, some medals and jewellery. I just wanted it to be over, man,

285

and she said if I gave her the ten we'd be done. But when I handed the stuff over, she said she'd changed her mind and I should pay her a monthly fee – two thousand dollars every month.'

Donald exhales hard. Moira's glaring at him. Rick says nothing, waiting for him to continue. He's gotten the sense that Donald needs to tell them what happened. He figures if he stays quiet he'll carry on the story.

Donald hangs his head. 'I couldn't pay it, man. I still owed the casino, and I was in big danger of losing my house and getting chucked out of this place because I was in arrears on the amenity and community fees. She'd promised the ten grand was the last. She'd damn well promised.'

'So you killed her?' Moira asks.

'I . . . I shoved the money at her and it unbalanced her – the rucksack was heavy with the valuables inside. When I saw her stagger backwards I acted on instinct. I grabbed the little gun she always held when we met, and pointed it at her. I told her the ten thousand had to be the end of it. I told her and she . . . she just laughed. So I . . .' Donald looks down at the asphalt. Swallows hard. Then turns and looks back at Moira. 'I was real mad then. I yelled at her and fired the goddamn gun. Didn't even aim properly.'

Rick hears sirens in the distance. They haven't got long. 'What happened next?'

'She kind of staggered a bit and then fell into the pool. I could tell I'd hit her – there was blood on her chest and she was making a weird noise, kind of gurgling and gasping. I tried to get the ruck-sack off her, but she'd fallen too far back into the pool. I couldn't reach her or the bag. She was splashing around, trying to keep her head above water, and she let go of the bag and the damn thing sunk.'

'Did you leave then?' asks Moira.

'No.' Donald's voice breaks as he says it. 'I stuck around for a bit. Kristen was in a bad way, but the cash had gotten loose from the bag and it floated up to the surface. I can't swim, so I lay on my belly and scooped up as many dollars as I could.'

Moira narrows her gaze. 'You did that while she was in the pool dying?'

'I needed the money, man,' Donald snaps back. He's silent then.

Moira shakes her head.

Rick clenches his jaw against the pain.

The sirens are getting louder.

49

PHILIP

The scene in the alleyway is buzzing. Four cop cars are parked across the entrance, lights still on, and there's an ambulance due any minute. Uniforms are swarming around and plain-clothes detectives are barking orders, trying to take control. Philip smiles to himself as he takes another big breath in, trying to steady his heart rate after the chase. It's almost like old times. And he's right in the thick of it.

He'd been slower than Moira and Rick on the chase, of course, as they pursued the suspect. But then he's older, so that's to be expected, and Lizzie had been only just in front of him. They'd arrived in time to see the suspect wrestled to the ground by Moira, and hear the confession of how and why he'd killed that poor girl. He'd been able to hear it, even though he'd been wheezing a bit as he tried to get his breathing back under control and was feeling rather light-headed.

They've done it – solved the case – and Philip's proud of that. But the fact that the killer had walked among them – been one of them – within the Ocean Mist community is a problem. He's already planning a complaint to the Resident Selection Board calling out the inadequacies of their vetting process. Donald Ettwood should never have been allowed to buy a home here on The

Homestead. It's not good enough, and Philip intends to make that absolutely clear.

He's moved back, away from the action around Donald Ettwood, to be near Moira, Rick and Lizzie on the pavement. They had to step aside as the local cops arrived, guns drawn and full of bravado and swagger. Philip gives a rueful shake of his head; bit late arriving in a blaze of glory after the real work has finished. Still, let them have the paperwork – he isn't complaining – but he's not going far either. He's an important witness – they'll have to interview him.

Philip turns to Lizzie, Moira and Rick. None of them are looking at him, which he's glad for because his heart has been racing and he was worried he'd pushed things too far on the run. Cautiously he takes his hand from his chest and inhales hard. There's no pain. Relief floods through him. Seems like he'll be okay.

He can't say the same for Rick. He's not looking good. One side of his shirt is soaked in blood. His jaw is clenched, and he looks pale beneath his tan. Moira's full focus is on Rick, her hands pressing the makeshift pad made from a length of her top against his wound, keeping the pressure on. Blood has seeped through the material on to Moira's hands, staining her fingers crimson.

Philip moves closer to them. 'How's he doing? Can I do something to help?'

Moira doesn't turn to look at him. 'He needs a medic. Any sign of the ambulance?'

'Not yet,' says Lizzie, peering down the alleyway to the main street. 'I called as soon as I saw Rick was hurt. Said we needed one urgently.'

Philip had heard Lizzie on the call. She'd called 911 a second time to ask for an ambulance. 'They must be on their way.'

'We need them fast,' says Moira.

There's worry in Moira's tone, fear even. It surprises Philip; Moira always seems so assured and in control, sometimes too in control – like she's the one in charge. Until now that's irritated him, but now he's concerned. Rick's a tough bloke – he keeps himself fit, and has all those muscles – he'll be fine, won't he? He has to be. He's one of them – one of the good guys. As he thinks it, Philip knows that doesn't make a jot of difference – bad things happen to good people; he knows that from bitter experience.

He looks down at Rick grimacing against the pain, and Moira still applying the pressure. Lizzie's walked off, away towards the main street, presumably so she can direct the ambulance crew when they arrive. There's nothing for him to do.

Philip looks away towards the cops. Usually in this situation he'd be in charge; getting things done. Instead, in amongst the uniforms, Detective Golding is directing the movement of Donald Ettwood from his current position sprawled on the ground to standing. Philip can hear Golding's voice, shouting instructions as the uniforms haul Donald to his feet. Donald's saying something Philip can't hear, so he takes a few steps closer. He still can't hear, but the next moment Golding gives Donald a shove and tells him to shut up, then reads him his rights.

Philip listens, interested in the differences between the UK and US wording, but before Golding is finished Philip's distracted by Lizzie. Down at the end of the alleyway, she's jumping up and down and waving towards the main street. Next moment an ambulance appears at the end of the alleyway, blue lights flashing. A couple of paramedics jump out and Philip sees Lizzie talking to them, and pointing towards Rick.

'The ambulance is here,' Philip says to Moira.

Moira glances round. Her cheeks are flushed. Her hair is stuck against her damp forehead. Moira turns back to Rick. 'The medics are here. A couple more minutes and they'll be with us.'

Philip watches the ambulance crew unload a gurney from the back and jog towards them. He starts waving. 'Don't worry, I'll make sure they know we're here.'

Moira doesn't respond. She keeps pressing on Rick's wound and talking to him, telling him he'll be okay. Philip hopes it's true. Rick's face is looking more ashen than even just a few minutes ago and his skin has a strange waxy look. His eyes are closed now, and his breathing looks shallow and rapid. Philip waves harder at the ambulance crew, and wishes they'd hurry up.

They watch as the paramedics load the gurney carrying Rick into the ambulance. Moira turns to Philip. 'Rick might need surgery. I'm going to the hospital.' She glances over at the cops who are putting Donald Ettwood into a marked police car. 'Tell them I'll give a full statement later.'

'Of course. Good idea,' says Philip. 'I'll handle Golding.'

'Thanks,' says Moira.

Philip watches her climb into the back of the ambulance and take a seat on the jump seat beside Rick's gurney. The ambulance crew slam the doors shut and run round to the cab. A few moments later, the lights and siren fire up and the ambulance speeds away.

He turns to Lizzie. 'Let's hope he's okay.'

Lizzie says nothing.

'Good work calling the ambulance,' says Philip. 'And the cops.'

'Yes.' Lizzie doesn't look at him.

Philip's not sure what to say to make it better. She's obviously still cross with him and wants him to talk about what happened back when he retired. She doesn't understand he can't do that. He doesn't want to relive what happened: doesn't want to admit that he couldn't face telling her that his health was failing and he wasn't fit to do the job any more – that he'd been so scared that without his rank and status she'd think less of him. And that since he had the heart attack it feels like she does think less of him; that she feels he's not the man he once was. That she doesn't even want to share his bed.

He blows out hard. There's no point raking it all up. The past is the past – you can't change it – all you can do is move on and try not to repeat your mistakes. 'Lizzie, look, I'm . . .'

She turns away from him, so now he's looking at her back. He wants to reach out to her and tell her he's sorry, but he doesn't because he knows that'll lead to more questions. So he says nothing. Not knowing what to do or say next.

He's almost relieved when he sees Detective Golding and another suit striding towards them.

Golding points at Philip and then Lizzie. 'We're going to need y'all to give a statement.'

'Of course,' says Philip.

Golding looks at Lizzie. 'This is Detective Johnstone, he's ready to take your statement now, ma'am.'

'No problem,' says Lizzie. 'Do you want to do it here?'

'If you'd come this way, ma'am,' says the younger detective.

Philip watches Lizzie walk back along the alley towards the police-liveried trailer that arrived a few minutes after the ambulance and seems to be serving as a mobile incident room. It's just him and Golding now. 'So are you taking my statement?'

Detective Golding's expression is grim. 'I warned you to stay away from this case, Sweetman, yet here we are again.'

'And here I was thinking you'd thank us for catching you a killer,' says Philip.

Looking away, Detective Golding curses under his breath. A long moment passes before he turns back and meets Philip's gaze.

'You just gotta be glad I didn't arrest the whole bunch of you for getting in the way of an active investigation.'

'It worked to your advantage, didn't it? The not arresting us bit. You've got an arrest and a slam-dunk confession.' Philip raises his eyebrows and smiles. 'That is, we got it for you.'

Golding scowls and they stare at each other for a moment. Philip holds the man's eye contact easily. He's in the right on this.

Eventually Golding shakes his head. 'Okay, so here's the thing, we're going to need a statement from you about how all this came about. For the record.' His eye contact gets more intense. 'I'd appreciate it if you didn't mention any of the, erm, joking about between us, while you're on tape.'

Philip can see Golding's uncomfortable, but he's not letting him off the hook that easy. He frowns, pretending to be confused. 'What joking?'

'The thing where you don't stay away from the case and I tell you I know stuff and will make it known.'

'Ah, yes, yes. That.' Philip holds Golding's gaze. The detective is practically squirming. 'Well, it rather depends on whether you're going to be threatening me again.'

Golding's cheeks colour red. He clears his throat. 'I'd say it's a negative to that.'

Philip keeps his tone even. Stays cool. 'Then I'll make sure our "joking" doesn't come up on tape.'

'Good,' says Golding, gesturing over to the mobile incident room. 'Then let's get this done.'

He stays composed, but inwardly Philip wants to punch the air in triumph. Barely twenty-four hours ago the detective was threatening him to stay away from the case. Now he's asking for help and putting him on record. Plus with the 'joking' reference he's got something on the detective, and they both know it. The dynamic between them has changed; now Philip has control.

He glances towards Detective Johnstone and Lizzie. They've reached the mobile incident room and as the detective opens the door for her, Lizzie looks back towards Philip and gives him a smile. Hope blossoms inside him. Smiling, that's a good sign; hopefully she's not cross with him any more. He looks back at Golding and grins. 'Of course, Detective, I'd be very happy to help.'

50

MOIRA

It's the second time today she's been in a hospital room. Unlike Hank who looked dwarfed by the large hospital bed, Rick looks like a giant in a child-sized bunk. He grimaces as he shifts himself a little more upright, taking care not to dislodge the IV line in his hand and the heart-rate monitor attached to his index finger.

'You okay?' says Moira.

'I'm fine,' says Rick. 'It's just a flesh wound.'

Moira smiles. 'Playing the tough guy, huh?'

Rick gives a shake of his head. 'You're the tough one. You took down the suspect. Got him cuffed with those laces. What you did, it was quite something.'

She looks away from Rick and stares at the heart-rate monitor. Its regular beeping and green spiking line is kind of comforting, but she feels far from comforted. 'It wasn't enough.'

'Moira, you doing okay?' Rick sounds worried.

She looks back at him. He's looking concerned. For a moment she says nothing, hoping he'll fill the silence and change the subject, but he doesn't. He keeps on looking at her. Waiting.

Moira exhales slowly. 'Look, I know we got him, but you're hurt and I . . . It's just that, for a minute there, I couldn't do anything. I froze.'

Rick turns a little more towards her, wincing from the movement. 'You want to talk about it?'

The thought makes her feel worse. 'No.'

He raises an eyebrow. 'You sure about that?'

The truth is she does want to talk about it – she needs to run through the play moment by moment; debrief what happened and dissect what went wrong. But she shouldn't be revealing any more of herself to this man. She can't get close. Moira meets his gaze. Knows she's about to make a mistake. 'Maybe.'

'So what happened?'

'I get these panic attacks. That's why I retired early.' She figures that's enough information; it's not like she can tell him the whole truth, but a partial view – perhaps that's okay. 'The first time it happened was in the aftermath of a raid that'd gone bad. We'd been tracking this criminal gang for months, trying to work out the chain of command to identify the real big player at the top. Finally, we'd got the kingpin's name – Bobbie Porter – and their penthouse address. We couldn't get much else – believed the name was an alias – so we planned the approach and made our move.'

Rick stays silent. Keeps his eyes on hers.

Moira continues. 'So the subject's apartment was the penthouse on the twenty-fourth floor of a fancy riverside apartment building. We go in gently – McCord takes the lead as he's got an invite to meet the guy. It's a business meet set-up, using an established alias of McCord's, and he takes me and another of the team, Jennifer Riley, in with him as his associates while the other two main team members – Pang and Kress – hang back with armed response. We needed to get something solid to connect Porter to the gang. On the surface the meet started okay, but Porter wasn't what we'd expected and things felt off to me. I had a bad feeling. But I knew the armed response team was standing by on the floor below if things went south.'

'And they did?'

'Yeah. Big time.' She closes her eyes for a moment, remembering. 'I've been over what happened thousands of times, but I still don't really understand it. There was a moment where McCord and Porter's conversation had stalled and the heavies at the door were looking like they were going to eject us from the apartment. I couldn't let that happen, so I pushed the issue – asked Porter to let us in on a specific shipment we knew the gang had coming in. Made out we had the money to finance more like it.'

'And how'd they react?'

Moira shakes her head. 'That's the thing. They hardly reacted at all. Just sat there, looking as if they were considering the idea. But, when I replayed the events in my mind I realised I'd missed something in the moment. There was something else in play.'

Rick leans closer. Eager for her to continue.

'There was this look between McCord and Porter. It was so subtle I missed its significance when we were sitting there on the white sofas, but Porter blinked and McCord gave the tiniest nod, and a couple of seconds later everything went to shit.'

'They were communicating?'

'Porter was giving an instruction. Then they got up and made to leave the room.' She pauses. Takes a breath. 'That's when McCord pulled a gun. He shouldn't have been carrying it – he wasn't firearms certified. At first I thought he was going to threaten Porter, then, as we all leapt to our feet, he turned away from Porter and shot Jennifer.' Moira flinches, seeing it in her mind's eye. 'He just shot her, no hesitation. He'd been working with her for eighteen months. They were friends. It just didn't . . .'

'And Porter?'

'Gone. Shooting Jennifer had been a diversion, and it worked. Porter used it to move fast. The penthouse had a safe room and escape route that weren't on the building plans we had. They got free and clear, and they're still out there.'

'So McCord shot his own colleague to let the criminal get away.'

'It seemed that way.' Moira exhales hard. 'I tried to stem the bleeding, but the bullet hit an artery, there was no hope. McCord ran to the balcony. He knew armed response would be arriving any moment, and maybe he thought he could get away somehow, but . . .' Her hands begin to tremble.

Rick reaches out and touches her arm.

'I had so many questions, but mainly I wanted to know why he did it. But I didn't get the chance. McCord took a dive off the balcony. It was twenty-four storeys up.' Moira remembers the words he'd muttered on the balcony – something to do with not trusting – and the way he had looked in that last moment before he jumped. It was as if he wanted to tell her something but felt he couldn't. She clenches her fists. Stops her hands trembling. He should have told her. She needed to know. Moira looks back at Rick. 'He was dead the minute he hit the pavement. Jennifer bled out on the white sofa in the penthouse. Half my team was dead in less than three minutes, start to finish.' She looks down. Clasps her fingers together and squeezes. 'Then a smoke grenade went off and the fire alarm started blaring out. The armed response team stormed in and it was chaos. My eyes were burning. My hands were covered in Jennifer's blood from trying to stop her bleeding.' Moira looks down at her hands, remembering the blood. Then meets Rick's gaze again. 'That's when I had the first panic attack.'

Rick lets out a long whistle. 'That's heavy. You get any help afterwards?'

She looks away. 'I saw the doc for a while. Tried to carry on, thinking I'd get past it and be able to get back on the street again. Didn't happen though. Panic attacks kept coming. I knew I'd be a liability, and I couldn't risk putting colleagues in danger. I already had enough blood on my hands so . . .'

'Hey, look at me.'

She raises her gaze to meet Rick's.

He's looking at her all intense. 'What McCord did, that isn't on you.'

'It is. I put him on the team. I took Jennifer up there.'

'No, he'd been turned, and he was forced to choose a side. That was his choice.'

'He chose the wrong one.'

'For sure,' says Rick. 'And it was him that chose it, not you.'

'My whole career I tried not to have favourites, but there's always some people you connect with more than the rest. McCord was one of those people for me. He was a young guy, like a son I guess, and I was like his mentor. We worked together for four years. He was smart and talented. Quick to learn.'

'You trusted him.' It's not a question; Rick's stating the fact.

'But I shouldn't have.' Moira looks down at her hands. 'It made me blind. I should have seen what was going on with McCord – that he'd been turned. If I had, our colleague, Jennifer, would still be alive.'

'You can't know everything.'

Moira glares at him. 'I was their DCI, it was my job to know everything.'

'What I mean is, you're only human.' Rick's tone is calm, amiable. 'If this McCord guy was as smart as you're saying, he could have hidden his true alliances from you. You're a good person, and you were a great cop.'

Moira softens her expression. 'How do you know that?'

'I just do. We've worked together these past few days, and I've seen how you operate. The blood of your colleague isn't on your hands, it's on McCord's and whoever in that gang that turned him.'

'It doesn't feel that way.'

'I know,' says Rick.

Moira thinks she sees a flicker of pain behind his eyes. She wonders if he had something similar happen to him during his career and he's speaking from experience. 'I just wish I knew why he did it.'

'Would that make it any better?' Rick's gaze is still intense, but she can see that he's starting to get sleepy. The drugs must finally be starting to kick in.

'I don't know.' Moira thinks about it. Jennifer would still be dead. Porter would still be in the wind. She'd still have had to give up her career. 'I guess not really, but at least I'd know for sure if it was my fault, if I should have seen it coming, if there was—'

'Like I said, it wasn't your fault.' Rick takes Moira's hand and gives it a squeeze. 'We make our own choices, and we alone are responsible for them.'

She looks down at his big, tanned hand over her small one. The warmth of his fingers against hers is comforting and his words are reassuring. She just wishes she could believe them.

The noise of the door opening makes her flinch. The moment's broken and she slides her hand out from beneath Rick's as she turns. In the doorway is Detective Golding. It seems a lifetime since she first saw him three days ago at the poolside crime scene in Manatee Park.

'We need to take your statement, Miss Flynn.'

She knew this would happen, and there's no sense putting it off. 'Okay, but can we do it somewhere here at the hospital? I don't want to go far from Rick.'

'You're a witness, not a suspect.' Detective Golding smiles, although to Moira it looks more like a grimace. 'So given the circumstances here is fine.'

300

Moira looks at Rick. His eyes are closed now, the painkiller in the IV pump finally getting to work. Standing up, she touches her fingers to his forearm and says, 'I'll be back soon.'

Rick's eyelids flicker, and he smiles as he murmurs something she can't make out.

Moira leaves her fingertips resting against his arm a moment longer, then turns and follows the detective out into the corridor. She tries not to let how much it wrenches to leave Rick bother her. When she moved here she knew if she was to have a chance of staying under the radar she needed to keep a low profile, not form deep friendships or lots of social connections. She can't afford to get emotionally attached. The danger is too great.

Pushing her worries to the back of her mind, she closes the door to Rick's room behind her. She looks at the detective. 'Okay, let's do this.'

51

MOIRA

One week later

The waiter uncorks the second bottle of champagne with a flourish and all four of them clap. It's supposed to be a celebration, after all. They solved the case and the real murderer – Donald Ettwood – has been charged and is being kept in jail awaiting trial, while young Mikey Graften has been released and all charges dropped. From the table on the veranda at the fancy Quayside Square Gardens restaurant, with its beautiful ocean-themed table settings, twinkling candles and the view of the sun setting over the water, everything seems perfect. On the surface.

'This bottle is from the gentlemen over at the corner table,' says the waiter as he starts to refill their glasses. 'To thank you for making them feel safe again.'

Moira looks across the veranda to the corner table. Two men in Hawaiian shirts, both with greying ginger hair, raise their glasses towards them.

Rick waves. 'It's the twins – Mark and Jack.' He raises his voice a little louder. 'Thanks, guys.'

Moira smiles. She knows this picture-perfect moment is an illusion, but for now she's happy to play along. She waits for the waiter to fill their glasses, then stands and raises hers. 'To justice.'

Philip and Lizzie stand and raise their glasses too. Rick raises his glass, but stays sitting.

'To justice,' they chorus.

As they sit back down, Rick raises his glass again and says, 'And to good friends.'

They toast again, and as Moira takes a sip of her champagne she tries not to think about the added dangers her newfound friends could cause her, and that she could cause them.

As Rick and Philip chat about the meal, Moira turns to Lizzie. 'How are things?'

Lizzie shakes her head and leans closer to Moira. 'It's as if he thinks if he says nothing about it I'll forget.'

'And how do you feel about that?'

Lizzie exhales hard. 'How can I forget? We need to talk about it, but every time I try to start the conversation he walks away.' She sighs. 'I just don't understand it. I don't think he'll ever tell me the truth.'

Moira takes a quick glance at Philip. He looks younger than his seventy-one years and has no deep worry lines or bloodshot eyes. There's no sign of guilt or stress. Moira doesn't understand either. 'So what are you going to do?'

Lizzie shrugs. 'I don't know yet. I just—'

'Hey Moira, I bet you'd have loved to have seen Golding's face when he read that piece in the *Lake County News* about us,' says Philip, setting his champagne back on the table and picking up his buttered roll. 'All that talk of us seniors uncovering the killer before the police – I bet he blew his top.'

Moira nods. 'No doubt.'

'That wasn't why we did it though, was it?' Lizzie says. There's a smile on her face as she looks at Philip, but it looks brittle rather than warm, and Moira can see the tension in her friend's body

303

language. Until Lizzie gets some kind of resolution, she doubts that will change.

'Yes, yes, very true,' says Philip, stuffing the roll into his mouth. 'It was about justice.'

Moira smiles at Lizzie. 'I bet the management here at The Homestead went crazy too. They might have got the media to report Donald as having been from a different state and just staying here at Ocean Mist, but those of us living here know that's not the real truth. There's a rising swell of frustration on the community Facebook page about them only allowing positive news stories designed to keep up a perfect image of The Homestead. They're not going to be able to keep a lid on it very much longer.'

'For sure,' says Rick, wincing as he straightens himself up. 'And that's no bad thing.'

'Amen to that,' says Moira, taking another sip of champagne. She gazes out past the boats bobbing in the marina, and across the water. She might have handed in her warrant card, but she's not ready to stop investigating yet; these past couple of weeks have taught her that. Besides the neat lawns, pickleball tournaments and line-dancing parties there's something lurking in The Homestead that's a lot less wholesome. 'You know, I've been thinking a lot about how the management seem to be able to control the way the media report incidents here. And I get they could pay the local outlets, or there's some quid pro quo thing going on. But I wonder if it goes further than that.'

'Further?' says Philip. 'Like the cops?'

'Maybe,' says Moira.

'You know, my guy – Hawk – said his source in the homicide department implied something odd was going on,' says Rick. 'Could be there's someone dirty there.'

'You think they're getting paid off?' says Lizzie.

Philip's nodding. 'That'd be one reason for Golding to be so keen on burying the case.'

'And why he hated us getting involved,' says Rick.

Moira shakes her head. Lowering her voice, she says, 'It's one thing to manipulate the media, but if they're paying off cops, I can't let that go.'

'Then don't,' says Rick. 'Let's make that our next investigation.'

Moira tilts her head. 'Our *next* investigation?'

'For sure.' Rick looks at each of them around the table. 'I don't think any of us want this to be a one-time thing, do we?'

'I'm ready for more,' says Philip, immediately. 'Certainly beats the activities and clubs on offer around here.'

Lizzie's eyes are bright and shining, and she looks happier than she's been all evening. 'Another case to investigate? That would be fun.'

'So what do you say?' says Rick. 'We'll have ourselves our own exclusive club, just the four of us.'

'The Retired Detectives Club,' says Lizzie, with a smile.

'Cheers to that,' says Philip.

Moira stays silent for a moment. She thinks about how it's felt to have a purpose – to do something she's good at, and make a difference. It felt good to solve the case and bring Donald Ettwood to face justice for Kristen Altman's death. And she can't just walk away from this group now, she has to maintain contact – keeping them close is the best way to prevent them getting suspicious of her – and what better way than working on an investigation together? So she smiles, and raises her glass to them again. 'Okay, I'm in.'

Lizzie and Philip leave after dinner. They did a good job of trying to hide it, but the tension is still obvious between them. Moira and

Rick opt for a walk along the water before heading home. Moira keeps her pace slow to allow Rick to easily keep up. He's moving better now than a couple of days ago, and that he's out of hospital is definitely a win, but she can see he's still in pain from the way he's standing.

'Quit looking at me like I'm knocking on death's door,' he says, but there's a smile on his face.

'I'm just . . .' She shakes her head. 'Sorry, I know you're a tough guy, but you took a bullet, you need to take things easy.'

'I'm pretty sure you've told me that already.'

'I can't help it if I care.' She walks on a few steps before realising Rick's not beside her. Turning, she retraces her steps until she's standing in front of him.

He's frowning. 'How are you, really?'

Moira's breath catches in her throat. Her heart rate accelerates. 'What?'

Rick's expression softens. 'I asked you how you are, Moira. I know you're good at putting on a tough exterior, but after what we talked about at the hospital I wanted to check how you're doing. You were so cut up about what happened. How are you now?'

She exhales. Relief floods through her. It's okay; she'd misheard. He'd asked *how* she is really, not *who* she is really. Taking a step closer to him, she breathes in his zesty aftershave and looks up to meet his gaze.

He smiles at her. 'You know I'm here for you, right? You can tell me anything.'

Moira looks at him, this kind and thoughtful man mountain, and wishes that she could tell him the whole truth of who she really is. In some ways it would be a relief to share the secret. But she knows she can't, not right now; it would be too dangerous for both of them. However far you travel, you can never truly hide from your past. And however much good you try to do, you never get

306

a real second chance. So you have to do what you can with what you've got, and try to limit the damage going forward.

So she swallows back the full, unedited truth and forces a smile. Reaching out she gives Rick's hand a squeeze. 'I'm doing much better, thanks.'

He squeezes her hand back, and just for a moment she allows herself to imagine what things would be like if her real name was Moira Flynn and she didn't have to hide her biggest secrets. As she looks into Rick's kind eyes, she wishes she really could start over with the blank slate that the police doc used to talk about.

Letting go of Rick's hand, she turns away towards the water. The smile dies on her lips. Because for her, no matter how hard she tries, she'll never be able to truly escape from the past. What the police doc said was just psychobabble bullshit.

There never will be a *tabula rasa*.

FREE *CONFESSIONS* BOX SET

Join Steph Broadribb's Readers' Club and get a free box set of short stories: 'The Empty Chair', 'Burning Dust' and 'The Lookout Game'.

You'll also receive occasional news updates and be entered into exclusive giveaways. It's all totally free and you can opt out at any time.

Join here: https://stephbroadribb.com/ and click on Join My Readers' Club.

ACKNOWLEDGMENTS

I had the idea for this book after going on a house-hunting excursion with my stepmom – Donna – in Florida. Recently widowed, she was considering the idea of moving to a large retirement community with all kinds of amenities (golf, swimming pools, etc.) right on her doorstep and a packed calendar of social activities and events on tap. In the end she decided it wasn't a good fit for her, but from the viewings and the conversation about pros and cons (and I guess me thinking about ageing and getting older myself) my creative juices started flowing and the Retired Detectives Club was born. Sadly Donna passed away suddenly in April 2021 so although she knew her house hunt had been the inspiration for this book, she never got to read it. I'd like to think that if she'd had the chance she would have enjoyed it.

The book was still a seed of an idea when I first discussed it with the wonderful Jack Butler, and I'm eternally grateful to him for seeing the potential in it and being excited enough to take me, and the retired detectives, on to the Thomas & Mercer list before the book was even written.

It's been a lot of fun writing this book, especially because the T&M team are so fantastic. Massive thanks to my new editor – the brilliant Hannah Bond – whose fabulous enthusiasm and guidance has helped craft this book from initial to final draft, and develop the world and the look of the Retired Detectives Club. I absolutely love working with you. And a super grateful shout out to my other awesome new editor, Leodora Darlington, for leaping into the breach while Hannah is on leave and expertly guiding this book out into the world. You are a total joy to work with.

Another huge thank you goes to the great Ian Pindar whose enthusiasm, structural editing input and insights have been invaluable in getting this book into the best shape possible. And a big thanks to Sadie Mayne and Gill Harvey for your fabulous work in copy-editing and proofing, and to Dolly Emmerson for skilfully guiding me through the production process.

To the whole T&M team – you are all a dream to work with.

A massive thank you goes to my fantastic agent Oli Munson – a legend and a wise adviser – to whom I owe so much. And to all at A M Heath, for always being fabulous.

As ever, a huge thank you goes to all my family and friends for your encouragement and support (and understanding when I lock myself away writing for hours on end).

And last, but very definitely not least, to all the readers, bloggers, reviewers, fellow crime writers and everyone who has supported me – thank you! You are all wonderful and I couldn't do this writing lark without you.

If you'd like to find out more about me, you can hop over to my website at www.stephbroadribb.com or get in touch via Twitter (@crimethrillgirl) or Facebook (@CrimeThrillerGirl) – it's always great to connect.

And, if it's not too cheeky to ask, if you enjoyed reading my book, I'd really love it if you'd leave a review.

Until next time . . .

Steph x

ABOUT THE AUTHOR

Steph Broadribb was born in Birmingham and grew up in Buckinghamshire. A prolific reader, she adored crime fiction from the moment she first read Sherlock Holmes as a child. She's worked in the UK and the US, has an MA in Creative Writing (Crime Fiction) and trained as a bounty hunter in California.

Her other novels include the Lori Anderson bounty hunter series and the Starke/Bell psychological police-procedural books (writing as Stephanie Marland). Her books have been shortlisted for the eDunnit eBook of the Year Award, the ITW Best First Novel Award, the Dead Good Reader Awards for Fearless Female Character and Most Exceptional Debut, and The *Guardian*'s Not The Booker Prize.

Along with three other female authors, she provides coaching for new crime writers via www.crimefictioncoach.com.

You can find out more about Steph at www.stephbroadribb.com, and get in touch via Facebook (@CrimeThrillerGirl) and Twitter (@crimethrillgirl).

Printed in Great Britain
by Amazon